Mercy's Embrace

Elizabeth Elliot's Story

A Novel in Three Parts

Book 1

SO ROUGH A COURSE

by

Laura L. Hile

Wytherngate Press

2009

2009 Wytherngate Press

Copyright held by the author

All rights reserved under International and Pan-American Copyright
Conventions. Published in the United States by Wytherngate Press.

Cover art by Margaret Coleman and Cory Teale

ISBN-10: 0-9728529-7-2   ISBN-13: 978-0-9728529-7-5
LCCN: 2009939351

The characters of Patrick McGillvary and the butler, Longwell, are creations of Susan
Kaye and used with her permission.

Wytherngate Press website: wytherngatepress.com

The principal text of this book was set in a digitized version of 10 point
Baskerville. Title appears in Edwardian Script.

Printed in the United States of America on acid-free paper.

Hile, Laura L
    So Rough a Course/ Laura L. Hile.
    220p.; 21 cm. Revised ed.
    Series: Mercy's Embrace: Elizabeth Elliot's Story; 1.
    ISBN 13 978-0-9728529-7-5
    1. Regency–England–Fiction. 2. Regency fiction. I.
Austen, Jane, 1775-1817. Persuasion. II. Series:
Mercy's Embrace: Elizabeth Elliot's Story; Book 1.

    813.6   2009939351

Table of Chapters

–&–

This book is dedicated to my dear friends Susan and Pamela who
gave me the courage to write and the vision
to succeed.
I offer my gratitude to readers at *The Derbyshire Writer's Guild* and *The
Republic of Pemberley* for their encouragement and
unflagging support.

–&–

Preface

William Elliot drew a cigar from its case and lit it, thankful for an excuse to escape the drawing room. So, Anne was engaged to the sailor. Engaged! At the concert, her countenance had betrayed nothing—she'd been willing enough to receive his addresses then. Mr Elliot blew a stream of smoke into the night air. He'd been prepared to exert himself for Anne. For her, he would really have given up anything. But tonight, as Sir Walter made the announcement, his plans for the future had fallen to pieces. There had been tenderness in Anne's face when she gazed at Captain Wentworth, a thing he'd not seen before. Mr Elliot's lips grew taut as he flicked ashes onto the pavement. Anne would never be his wife.

Presently the door opened and a couple came into the courtyard; Mr Elliot stepped away from the light.

"My dear sir, did you hear something?" Penelope Clay's musical voice carried clearly in the night air.

A man answered. "Perchance we have surprised a cat, my dear." It was Sir Walter. Mr Elliot retreated into the shadows. He had no wish to converse with his fool of a cousin.

Mrs Clay gave her trilling laugh. "Of course, you are right, sir, as always. What a goose I am! And dear me, how tightly I am holding to your arm! Do you mind?"

"Not at all, my dear Mrs Clay, for this is not my satin coat. I shall protect you from the cat. Shall we continue with our little stroll?"

William Elliot extinguished the cigar by grinding it under his heel. Here was the heart of the problem: Penelope Clay, Elizabeth's companion—a lowborn solicitor's daughter. His future as Sir William, master of the Kellynch estate, stood in peril because of this scheming woman! But if Mrs Clay thought to entrap Sir Walter into marriage, she had another thing coming.

So it must be Elizabeth after all. Mr Elliot had courted Sir Walter's eldest daughter when he first came to Bath, once he saw how it was with Mrs Clay. Sir Walter was thrilled with the idea—and so were the gossips. But that was before Anne arrived in Bath, before he'd been fool enough to lose his heart. How he was to repair his suit with Elizabeth he did not know, for she now held him in contempt.

At one time he'd thought her contempt amusing, but not anymore. Nevertheless, Elizabeth was desperate, a situation very much to his advantage. Mr Elliot knew well the power of desperation–and the lure of rank and privilege. His late wife had been caught by the siren song of the promised title; Elizabeth would be no different. They would marry, Mrs Clay would return to obscurity in Crewkherne, and he would await Sir Walter Elliot's demise.

The couple now stood near the lantern at the door, giving him a clear view of their silhouettes. And then, perhaps because of the stillness of the night air or the echo of the courtyard, Mr Elliot heard Mrs Clay give a delicious giggle. The gap of light between them closed.

Was Sir Walter kissing her?

William Elliot thought he had experienced every emotion possible this night, but he now discovered he was wrong. Nausea was added to the rest.

Having completed their kiss, the pair went indoors while Mr Elliot remained in the shadows. So this was the new game. She'd baited the matrimonial trap, and Sir Walter had fallen into it! And if she produced a male heir? He must get Penelope Clay away from Sir Walter–immediately!

~ 1 ~
Distressing Developments

Elizabeth Elliot bit her lip and looked away; it would never do to laugh! But when Mrs Leighton reached for her teacup, the bare skin beneath her arm swung to and fro like a pendulum! Her gown was just as bad. Why, she looked like a walrus wrapped in muslin!

"Have you no tea, Miss Elliot?" Mrs Leighton signed for the footman to correct the oversight. However, nothing in her manner suggested an apology. Though she smiled, her eyes were hard and bright. She was, Elizabeth realized, more formidable than she appeared.

"Do I have this right, Miss Elliot? Your father has left his estate in Somerset to reside among us? Exactly how long ago was that?"

Elizabeth's stomach tightened into a knot. Was she to be peppered with questions? "My father and I took up residence at the end of September, ma'am," she said.

"And has your father come to Bath for any particular reason?" There was significance in Mrs Leighton's tone.

Elizabeth's chin came up. Gossip was a favourite pastime in Bath. Was her own discomfort meant to provide the morning's entertainment?

The footman approached. With a fluid movement, Elizabeth took the cup and saucer. Not for nothing had she practiced this, hour after hour, all those years ago. The slightest rattle of china would betray nervousness, giving Mrs Leighton an advantage. This was something Elizabeth refused to allow.

"We came to Bath on account of my father's health, ma'am," she said. This was a safe, conventional answer. It was also distinctly untrue.

"Father will never admit to such a thing, of course," Elizabeth continued. "If you ask him, I daresay he will give a very different answer." She accepted a serving of cake, mindful not to shift the position of the silver fork. "Men are very private about their health, are they not? But Father had the oddest symptoms."

"Symptoms?" someone said.

What a very good idea! Old ladies loved hearing about symptoms. Since coming to Bath, Elizabeth had been in the company of enough of them to know! She gazed at Mrs Leighton with what she hoped was a soulful expression. "It was not a sickness we could name," she said. "He had difficulty breathing. At times he was pale and weak. And his heart, Mrs Leighton, his heart!" Elizabeth brought a hand to her breast. "I was so dreadfully frightened."

Mrs Leighton's brows lifted. "Dear me," she said.

Elizabeth bit back a smile. Truth to tell, her father's frightening symptoms appeared only when he was forced to acknowledge the enormity of his debts! "But now that we are come to Bath," she continued, "Father is very much better. So we shall not be returning to our estate in Somerset at all." This was perfectly true. It would be here, in Bath, that Elizabeth would make something of her life. For too many years she'd lived buried in the country.

Mrs Leighton speared a morsel of cake; while she chewed no one said a word. Presently she said, with emphasis, "I did hear that your father has been in financial distress."

Elizabeth fought to keep her countenance. What nerve this woman had! And yet, she also knew there was no evading the enquiry. "My father has had some small degree of difficulty," she admitted. "But then, who has not? These are uncertain times."

"Not for all of us, Miss Elliot," said Mrs Leighton.

To buy time, Elizabeth took a sip of tea. The way to deal with gossip was to admit a small portion of the truth and disguise the rest. But this woman and her friends were connoisseurs of gossip; they would not be easily satisfied. Then it occurred to her that Anne had once answered a similar question quite gracefully and with that air of gentle humility that Anne was so good at wearing. Anne, with her piety and lessons of economy and thrift—was there ever a drearier sister? But perhaps Anne could be of use. Elizabeth settled her cup in its saucer. She would give Anne's answer...with a few amendments of her own.

"Does it not seem to you, ma'am," she said, "that when it comes to financial matters, we women have the upper hand? Oh, the gentlemen are more knowledgeable, certainly, but it is we who are the better managers of money?"

A pleasant clucking among the ladies told Elizabeth she had hit her mark. She folded her hands demurely, as she had seen Anne do, and launched into her version of Anne's answer. "So it was with my mother and father. She was the practical one. When she died, he was lost!" Elizabeth looked at each woman's face in turn. How fortunate that so many of them were widows! "Father," she said, "has been so very lonely."

"Poor Sir Walter," someone murmured.

Elizabeth nearly laughed out loud. How fortunate that her father was so handsome! "I daresay," she continued, "that each of you understands the depths of his despair better than I. As a result, some of his expenditures have not been very wise."

Elizabeth's voice was unsteady now but not because of grief. She dabbed at her eyes with the corner of her napkin. "How true it is," she said soulfully, "that the accumulation of worldly goods can never compensate for the loss of a beloved spouse!"

The ladies gave a collective sigh.

From beneath her lashes, Elizabeth stole another look at Mrs Leighton. The woman's expression had softened. "I did hear that Sir Walter has taken a tenant at your ancestral estate. I must own, I was surprised."

"Yes, ma'am. Our tenant is a distinguished gentleman of the Navy, a Rear-Admiral of the White. It pained my father greatly to leave Kellynch Hall but..."

Elizabeth paused. She feared to say too much, and yet, to have the rapt attention of these ladies, all so well placed in Bath society, was too delicious. "May I be honest with you, for I feel that I am among friends here?" Elizabeth's voice took on a confiding tone. "It was my wish that we leave Kellynch Hall, not his. My father was only growing worse there, and I have always enjoyed Bath. My godmother, Lady Russell, spends the winters here; perhaps you are acquainted?"

"Well!" she continued, "life in Bath agrees with us; Father has become so robust! I was soon convinced that if we were to let the estate to a tenant, he would reduce his debt more quickly. It seemed a sensible thing to do, since we are never to live there again."

Elizabeth leaned forward to deliver her final point. "But it is my hope," she said, speaking clearly so that every one of the ladies could hear, "that perhaps here in Bath, at long last, Father will find the desire of his heart: a loving wife. And so, he will no longer be cast adrift, alone."

The sighs among the ladies were audible.

"A wealthy wife, Miss Elliot?" asked Mrs Leighton.

"Well, yes," Elizabeth admitted, returning the smile. "That would be most convenient, of course! But I would much prefer that he find a woman with something more. That is to say, an intelligent woman of proper connections, who has a loving heart and who knows how to care for him. That would be the very best."

This caused quite a flutter. "But of course," said Mrs Leighton. "My dear Miss Elliot, I believe your tea has grown cold. Allow Henry to refresh your cup."

Elizabeth kept her gaze lowered as she passed the cup; she dared not show her triumph, not yet. But she had done it. She had held her own against the very worst of the Bath gossips—and prevailed! No matter that she had told lies. The events were true, more or less; although, her father had never been ill, and in spite of the nasty things Anne said about Penelope Clay, not once had he expressed an iota of interest in taking another wife!

She glanced at the drawing room door. If only he would return from wherever Mr Leighton had taken him, she could make a graceful exit. And leave she must, for every moment she lingered invited fresh disaster! But the drawing room door remained closed and the women continued to talk.

"*Hail wedded love, mysterious Law...*" A slightly built lady in grey now spoke in quavering, reverent tones. Mrs Morton, Elizabeth seemed to recall. Apparently, she was reciting some poetical text. Was this in reference to Sir Walter? "*True source of human offspring, sole propriety in Paradise, of all things common else!*" Mrs Morton ended with a sigh. "Milton."

Lady Jessup laid down her fork. "I don't see that at all, Fanny," she said. "If Sir Walter wishes to marry, well and good; but there will be no offspring, not at his age. Unless he is snared by that tart of a companion." Lady Jessup looked pointedly to Elizabeth.

Elizabeth caught her breath. What was this? The ladies were looking at her expectantly. Did they expect her to say something about her father and Penelope Clay?

Before she could answer, the drawing room opened. All heads turned, but it was only James Rushworth. He stood there blinking, a flush mounting his doughy cheeks.

"Hallo, Mrs Leighton," he said, making a difficult bow. He turned. "Mama, you told me three o'clock. And here I am, just as I promised, to see you home."

Mrs Rushworth, who was as stout as her son, sighed heavily. "In a moment, dear," she said. She turned to Mrs Leighton. "Beryl, might James have a slice of your delicious cake?"

At the word *cake*, Mr Rushworth brightened.

"But of course." Mrs Leighton gestured to the vacant seat beside Elizabeth. "Miss Elliot, I trust you are acquainted with Mr Rushworth?"

Mr Rushworth's head whipped around; his gasp was audible. "Miss Elliot!" he cried. With care, he lowered himself onto the sofa which creaked unappreciatively.

A generous slice of cake was presented, and Mr Rushworth fell to the business of eating, casting an occasional glace at Elizabeth. She paid no attention this. For her, admiration from younger gentlemen was simply a matter of course.

"Now, about Miss Anne Elliot," said Lady Pembridge, leaning forward. "I simply must hear about this engagement. A patched-up affair, was it?"

"A disappointment for the cousin, to be sure," said someone else.

The mention of Mr Elliot nearly threw Elizabeth off her guard. At all costs she must turn the conversation! "Anne and Captain Wentworth were acquainted years ago," she said. "So when they met again in Bath, why, it was like something out of a fairy tale. My father calls it a touching romance." She did not share her own opinion of Captain Wentworth.

"Such a fine-looking man," said Mrs Leighton. "He has a definite air about him, yes."

Elizabeth became occupied with stirring her tea. Frederick Wentworth was opinionated, self-assured, and brash. He was utterly unworthy to become allied with the Elliot family, even if he was marrying only Anne.

"A bosom friend of Admiral McGillvary's, in fact," said Lady Jessup. "He's hosting a dinner for them. Sparing no expense, apparently."

Elizabeth nearly rolled her eyes. This dinner was nothing out of the ordinary. She'd never met the host, but it made no difference. He was probably a loud, common sort of man with the blustering manners of the lowborn. Her father's tenant, Admiral Croft, was such a man. The guests would be naval officers and their wives–if such men had wives. Elizabeth was determined not to attend.

Still, she knew her duty. "I trust my sister will be happy in the life she's chosen," she said. "However, in times such as these, I would be reluctant to marry a man of the Navy."

"Hear, hear!" It was Mr Rushworth who spoke. "Too many sailors in Bath nowadays," he explained.

The conversation veered to a more general topic; Elizabeth was left with Mr Rushworth. She had no desire to converse with him, but politeness demanded it. "Have you lived long in Bath, Mr Rushworth?" she asked.

He swallowed and blotted his lips with the napkin. "Mama lives here," he said. "After Maria and I were married, she–that is–" Mr Rushworth's cheeks flushed scarlet; he pinched his lips together. Eventually he was able to continue. "After my–marriage–Mama left Sotherton and removed to Bath. I am come for a visit."

Elizabeth had heard the gossip, of course. Mr Rushworth's beautiful young wife left him for another man not a year after the wedding; he was now near the end of a lengthy divorce. Such a thing was beyond Elizabeth's comprehension. Mr Rushworth might be a fool–he certainly looked like one–but he had inherited a large fortune and an extensive estate. Why would any woman abandon such a handsome independence? After ten minutes of laboured conversation, however, Elizabeth had a fair idea. When her father came into the room, she rose immediately.

Mr Rushworth also got to his feet, though not very gracefully. Elizabeth could not help but notice the cascade of cake crumbs…and his crestfallen expression.

~ ~ ~ ~ ~ ~ ~ & ~ ~ ~ ~ ~ ~ ~

Her father remarked on this as soon as they were out of the salon.

"Father, really," she said. "Where do you get these ideas?"

"Ah, but young Rushworth was the picture of disappointment. You have quite broken the lad's heart."

"I expect he simply wanted a second piece of cake."

There was a tall looking glass in the entrance hall; Sir Walter caught sight of his reflection. He turned this way and that. "I do not know," he said. "This waistcoat–"

"It looks very well, Father."

"But the colour! Puce is all the crack, to be sure, but–" He frowned. "I daresay it is a bit too bright for early spring. But the pattern of this neck cloth is very nice. And Roberts achieved a tolerable arrangement for my hair. He had a new man in to cut it yesterday. I feared the worst."

At last Sir Walter took his hat from the Leighton's butler and settled it tenderly on his head. When he was convinced all was in order, he offered his arm to Elizabeth. Together they went out the main door and descended the wide steps to the street.

"A pity about young Rushworth's figure," said Sir Walter, "for the Rushworth name and fortune make him acceptable anywhere."

"Not to mention his soon-to-be granted divorce," said Elizabeth. "Really, Father. He is hardly fit to be a suitor, even if he were the proper age!" To change the subject she said, "Did you examine Mr Leighton's gun collection?"

"I was shown something better: his collection of Chinese antiquities. Quite an assortment of baubles, if one goes in for such things. Mr Leighton is, apparently, an enthusiast." Sir Walter glanced at the fog-shrouded sky. "We should present the Leightons with an invitation to our card party."

"I suppose," said Elizabeth. The card party had been his idea. Although the guest list was hers to assemble, he could never resist making suggestions.

"Sir Henry Farley would be another excellent addition," he said, "but I daresay you have already thought of that."

She had, indeed, thought of that, unfortunately. A man of Sir Henry's consequence could not be ignored, especially since she and her father had ambitions to get on in Bath. Elderly, urbane gentlemen were known to be outrageous flirts. His sallies and winks, though uncomfortable, meant nothing.

"We should send an invitation to our cousin as well."

Elizabeth frowned. "Do you mean Lady Dalrymple?"

"No, no. Mr Elliot is the man I mean."

Elizabeth compressed her lips. If she never saw William Elliot again it would be too soon! Why must her father always bring him up? "We've seen nothing of Mr Elliot since Anne's engagement was announced. I daresay he has left Bath for good."

Sir Walter sighed. "More's the pity. To see you and William Elliot wed and settled at Kellynch Hall was the dearest wish of my heart."

"I thank you, sir, for the reminder!"

"Why, I meant no offence. When Mr Elliot met you for the first time, he was smitten. Definitely smitten."

"That," said Elizabeth, "is ancient history."

"Is it?" Sir Walter applied himself to thinking. "Let me see. You were introduced after your mother passed on; you were just sixteen, were you not?" He counted on gloved fingers. "Why," he said slowly, "that must mean…" He slewed round, his eyes wide. "My dear," he cried, "are you now thirty?"

With difficulty, Elizabeth found her voice. "Not until June!"

"Saints preserve us," he said at last.

Elizabeth trod beside him, the chill air pinching at her face.

"Where, oh, where has the time gone?" he said.

"Where, indeed?" echoed Elizabeth.

At last they turned the corner onto Camden Place. The columned façade that was Camden Crescent appeared through the mist. Sir Walter halted. "The hand of fate is cruel," he said. "Kellynch Hall is nobler than the sum of all of these. Yet, it is let to strangers while we, the rightful inhabitants, must live in a corner."

What new mood was this? Was he sorry to be in Bath? "It's quite an elegant corner, if a corner it is," Elizabeth said, bracingly. "Kellynch Hall is the ideal gentlemen's residence, of course, but you must admit, it is rather remote. And so cold during winter! Do you recall how the dining room chimney smokes? The Crofts pay handsomely to live there. I wish them joy of it!"

Sir Walter looked pained, but he said nothing.

Their butler had the door open immediately. Sir Walter waited while Wilson removed his coat; Elizabeth seized the opening to change the subject. "Father," she said, "are we engaged Thursday evening? I would very much like to attend the assembly."

"The assembly in the upper rooms? Certainly not. We have better things to do with our time."

Elizabeth gave her cloak and hat to Wilson and ascended the stairs, followed by Sir Walter. The foot-boy opened the drawing room door, and they went in.

"I would like to attend just the same," said Elizabeth. "What can be your objection? Everyone attends the assembly, even Lady Dalrymple and Miss Carteret, upon occasion."

"That is exactly my objection," said Sir Walter. "Everyone attends." He wrinkled his nose. "Tradesmen, Elizabeth. Solicitors and military men. I prefer small, select gatherings. We do not attend a public ball."

"But–" Elizabeth hesitated. If she handled this poorly he would become even more stubborn. "My new ball gown," she said, allowing disappointment to creep into her voice. "I long to wear it with the diamonds, as I had it made especially to–"

Sir Walter lifted a hand. "No, no," he said. "Impossible. The diamonds have gone to the jeweler's for cleaning. And speaking of jewellery…" He held out his hand. "Come," he prompted.

"Now?" Elizabeth sighed, dropped her gloves onto the table, and worked at the clasp of her necklace. Lately, he insisted on locking up the jewels the instant she arrived home. "Are you having every piece cleaned, then?" she asked, passing the ruby pendant with its chain. "What is left for me to wear to the concert?"

"What is left? What is left? A fine way to speak to your father!"

With effort Elizabeth kept her temper in check. "I need to know what you have sent for cleaning and what you have not. The rubies are here, but what of the others?"

Sir Walter's cheeks flushed. "You may wear the emerald set," he said, "but not the rubies. And not for the assembly. We do not attend the assembly."

"But Miss Carter–"

"The Honourable Miss Carteret is a sensible young woman who will do as her mother bids," said Sir Walter. "Lady Dalrymple has as much aversion to public spectacles as I."

Elizabeth almost laughed. Of all of his stories, this surely was the worst! "Lady Dalrymple enjoys her position in Bath, Father," she said, "and she takes every opportunity of making a display of herself!" *As do you*, she added silently.

"But not at a public assembly."

"I know assemblies are crowded with inferior persons, and I am quite aware that the atmosphere in the ballroom is wretchedly stifling! I wish to practice my dance steps."

"Then hire a dancing master!"

"But why should I when you subscribe to the assembly?"

"I subscribe to show my public spirit, Elizabeth."

Wilson came into the drawing room, forcing Elizabeth to bite back her reply.

"A person by the name of Cripplegate is in the book room, sir," said Wilson. "He claims to have an appointment."

Sir Walter gave a start. "Already?" He glanced at the clock on the mantelpiece. "Fifteen minutes early, imagine that." He put the jewellery pieces on the table and examined them. "Bracelet," he murmured, "two earrings, pendant. But...how is this? Where is the ring?" He turned to Elizabeth. "A valuable piece, missing! How many times must I tell you that Bath servants are not to be trusted!"

Elizabeth twisted the ring from her finger. "Here it is," she said. "What is the point in having jewels if we must always be locking them up?"

"My dear girl," said Sir Walter, "one can never be too careful." He collected the jewellery and went out. Elizabeth flung over to the window. As usual, her father thought only of himself.

~ ~ ~ ~ ~ ~ ~ & ~ ~ ~ ~ ~ ~ ~

Penelope Clay, who had not been invited to Mrs Leighton's, spent her morning in the back sitting room. As soon as she heard voices, she made her way to the drawing room, bringing with her an enormous bouquet of roses. She could scarcely conceal her triumph; what would the fine Elizabeth say to this? She paused outside the door; the voices within were sharp. Penelope withdrew a pace. Her father had called the Elliot's move to Bath a retrenchment, but Penelope was not taken in. As always, her father must be cautious. Sir Walter and his daughters lived in a style far above anyone else she knew. No doubt Elizabeth had overspent her allowance again.

Sir Walter left the drawing room and, without noticing her, descended to his book room. Penelope watched him go and then slipped inside. Of course, Elizabeth noticed the flowers. She smiled broadly and held out her hands–did she think they had come for her? How delightful to be able to set her straight!

"A gentleman has sent these, Miss Elliot," said Penelope. "To me."

Elizabeth's brows went up. "Indeed? Is there a card?"

"Not a card, but a letter. It is...unsigned." Penelope felt the blood rush to her cheeks. "These are hothouse roses, are they not?" she said.

"They are. So you have an admirer. And what does he say to you?" Elizabeth held out her hand.

Penelope knew it was useless to object. Slowly she drew the folded paper from the bosom of her gown. Elizabeth unfolded the sheet and read:

My dear Penelope,
Shall I compare thee to a summer's day?
Thou art more lovely and more temperate...

"That is a very generous sentiment," said Elizabeth. "How kind to apply it to you. I wonder who sent it."

The note was from Sir Walter, Penelope just knew it. Still, she wished to be certain. "Miss Elliot, I hesitate to ask, but your acquaintance in Bath is now so extensive. Do you recognize the handwriting? It looks familiar, somehow."

Elizabeth gave the page a quick glance. "No, I have never seen it before. Do you know, I am rather hungry. I couldn't eat a thing at Mrs Leighton's. Ring for Wilson, won't you?"

Penelope did as she was bid, smiling as always. Miss Elliot never allowed her to forget that she was only a paid companion. But, the note and the flowers were from Sir Walter all the same. The fine Miss Elliot would sing a different tune when she became mistress of the house!

Sometime later, Sir Walter came in. Immediately, he noticed the flowers. Penelope lowered her head, wishing she did not blush so hotly.

"Elizabeth?" said Sir Walter. "What is this? A gift from young Rushworth already?"

"The flowers are Penelope's, Father. A gentleman sent them."

"For Mrs Clay? Why would a gentleman send flowers to Mrs Clay?"

"Why, because he thinks she is lovely, Father! What other reason is there?"

Sir Walter puffed out his cheeks. "I don't see what one has to do with the other." He found the tray with the post and began sorting through the letters.

"We think she has a secret admirer. How amusing it will be to guess his identity!"

Sir Walter looked up. "It's no one we know, surely. He must be someone she's met in a shop or on the street."

Penelope's heart was hammering. How clever Sir Walter was! How well he disguised his intentions!

Sir Walter held up a square white envelope. "This looks promising!" he said, smiling. He broke the seal, pulled out the card, squinted at it—and felt for a chair. When at last he spoke, Sir Walter's voice was reverent. "My word! Chalfort House!"

Elizabeth put aside her cup and saucer. "Father?"

"It seems," said Sir Walter, "that we have been invited to a house party at Chalfort House, Lord and Lady Claverling's estate in Richmond!" He studied the card more closely. "Gracious, but we've not much time to prepare! We have the shiftless mail service to thank for that!"

Elizabeth and Penelope crowded around his chair. "My new wardrobe ..." said Elizabeth, and she gave her father a nudge. "And all you could do was to complain about the expense. Now what do you say?"

"I have never been to Richmond," offered Penelope. "Shall I like it, sir?"

Sir Walter's smile fell a little. "I believe everyone likes Richmond." He passed the invitation to Elizabeth. "Do you know, perhaps this would be a good time for you to visit your family in Crewkherne, Mrs Clay."

"Visit Crewkherne?" she faltered. "Oh, sir, do you think so?"

"Surely you miss seeing your children, Penelope," said Elizabeth. "After your holiday, you must return so that we may enjoy the remainder of the season together."

Penelope spoke slowly. "Oh. Yes. That would be very well, I suppose."

"You must write to your father straightway," said Sir Walter. "We shall leave for Richmond at the end of the week. You must do the same."

Penelope did not trust herself to speak. If Sir Walter had sent the flowers, why was he now sending her away? He and Elizabeth resumed discussing the party heartlessly, with no regard for her feelings. Indeed, to them she had ceased to exist! She excused herself and fled to her bedchamber.

~ ~ ~ ~ ~ ~ ~ & ~ ~ ~ ~ ~ ~ ~

"Oh dear," said Elizabeth, as the door closed behind Penelope. "That was rather awkward."

"But what was I to do? Mrs Clay's name was not on the invitation! Even Anne was not invited!" Sir Walter took another look at the card. "'Sir Walter Elliot and Miss Elliot,' it says. Of course, this must refer to you, for by Saturday next there will be no other Miss Elliot."

"Father!"

"Why my dear, there is no need to take that tone! So long as you marry, all will be well. Even if you are at your last prayers, this invitation is clearly the hand of Providence! Which reminds me…" He brought out a velvet-covered box. "Here is the emerald set, nicely cleaned." He passed it to Elizabeth. "Open it. I want to see what you think."

Elizabeth did so. There was nothing remarkable about the emeralds. She removed the pendant with its chain, as she lacked a necklace.

"Do you see how the stone sparkles?" said Sir Walter. "Mr Cripplegate is a genius; a master craftsman."

Elizabeth returned the box. "Perhaps you'd prefer to keep the others until I dress for the concert?" She could not resist adding, "Since the Bath servants are such thieves?"

"I no longer have any worries on that score." Sir Walter pocketed the box. "And now, I have a bit of business which needs my attention."

"Business?" said Elizabeth. "You?" Her father never conducted business on his own!

Sir Walter waved aside her questions and went out, humming a snatch of a tune. Elizabeth sank onto the sofa, the emerald pendant in hand. What luck that the emeralds had been cleaned; she would certainly wear them at Chalfort House. Idly, she studied the stone, watching the light play across its rectangular surface. Her father was right, it sparkled beautifully. *Too beautifully, in fact.* Elizabeth sat up. Something about the stone was different, but what?

Dissatisfied, she went to the window for a better look. Large emeralds like this one should display an inner light of vivid green. Emeralds were never transparent; there were inclusions called *jardin*. Today, however, the stone was a darker green, rather like an apothecary bottle, and the *jardin* were nowhere to be seen!

Elizabeth went immediately to the landing. "Wilson!" she called.

The butler came to the base of the stairs. "Is something wrong, miss?"

"Has my–" Speaking was difficult; she began again. "Has my father returned from his errand?"

"No, Miss. Shall I send the boy after him?"

"No. Thank you, Wilson." Elizabeth returned to the drawing room, biting her lips. There was a mistake, she was sure of it. Her eyes must be playing tricks on her. And yet, how could that be? She hunted in the drawer of the escritoire. Her father had a pair of spectacles; where did he keep them?

The book room. He used them in the book room, not here in the drawing room where he would be seen. Elizabeth glanced at the clock. If she worked quickly there would be time.

~ ~ ~ ~ ~ ~ ~ & ~ ~ ~ ~ ~ ~ ~

Penelope did not see the letter at first, for as soon as she entered her bedchamber, she flung herself headlong on the bed. It waited on her dressing table, well sealed, with her name clearly written. The message was short and to the point:

> My Dear P,
> I know you are engaged to attend the concert tonight. Stay behind. Join me for dinner instead. I'll have my carriage waiting near the corner at nine.
> W.E.

Penelope studied the signature. W.E. must refer to William Elliot, but how could that be? She'd heard he'd left Bath days ago. And how had this come? Had he bribed the maid to deliver it? Penelope read the words again and again. Wasn't he the most presuming man! He did not ask her leave; he simply ordered her to dinner. She folded the paper in half. Just because she was in Elizabeth's employ did not mean she was at William Elliot's beck and call!

There was only one thing to be done with this note—burn it. Or else, tear it to shreds. Both would be delightful! But then she thought of something. Out came the secret admirer's note, and...what was this? The handwriting matched exactly. And here was something more—Mr Elliot had written not on plain paper, as before, but on stationery bearing the Elliot crest. Penelope bit a fingernail, thinking. Sir Walter had not sent the flowers, Mr Elliot had. Mr Elliot, Sir Walter's heir.

No one needed to tell her that it was improper to dine alone with him; she knew that. He was a man of the world, as her late husband had been. Such men were dangerous and, yet, so very enticing. And in the end, in spite of everything, she'd become Mrs Clay. Not for nothing was her father a solicitor!

She gazed again at Mr Elliot's letter. Perhaps she ought to risk it?

~ ~ ~ ~ ~ ~ ~ & ~ ~ ~ ~ ~ ~ ~

Heavy net draperies covered the windows of Sir Walter's book room, but there was enough light for Elizabeth's purpose. She slipped into the chair behind his desk and opened the top drawer. There were the spectacles, but there was also something else: a stack of open letters. The one on top was from Mr Shepherd, her father's solicitor. Elizabeth knew better than to read her father's correspondence, but the word *drastic* caught her attention. She glanced at the clock. There was time to read it if she hurried.

Mr Shepherd came right to the point. He was receiving requests for payment from tradesmen in Bath at an alarming rate. He was concerned lest these debts become in excess of the income of the estate (which monies included the rental fee paid by Admiral Croft). Did Sir Walter understand the nature of a retrenchment?

Elizabeth's eyes narrowed. How dared Mr Shepherd write such things! Did they not follow his advice to the letter? "In Bath you may be important at comparatively little expense!" Mr Shepherd had said. Little expense? Hardly! How he had misled them! But there was more: something about quarterly payments and the terms under which Sir Walter's primary creditor had agreed to make over the loan.

Loan? Elizabeth gazed at the letter in amazement. She knew nothing of a loan. She struggled to make out Mr Shepherd's closing paragraph.

> With funds so low at present, it appears that securing the
> two hundred pound payment due on Lady Day could be a
> close-run thing. Therefore, I respectfully advise that you
> exercise whatever means are in your power to raise the
> ready cash payment yourself. I further advise a drastic and
> severe course of action: All extemporaneous spending
> must cease immediately.

Extemporaneous spending? What more was there to give up? They had already sacrificed their customary trip to London, along with gifts to various charities. Elizabeth's allowance was only half of what her father had promised. Grand dinners had become a thing of the past as well; they now hosted insipid card parties with meagre refreshments. What more did Mr Shepherd expect?

The clock chimed the half-hour. Elizabeth hurried to replace the letter. Back in the drawing room she went directly to the windows. Carefully she brought the emerald into focus. She adjusted the spectacles and looked again, scarcely daring to believe what she saw. Inside the stone were bubbles. Her mother's prized emerald was nothing more than green glass.

Elizabeth's heart was hammering. She could be wrong–she must be wrong! She looked again. Sure enough, there were the bubbles– three of them. Elizabeth compressed her lips. Not only was this *paste*, but it was particularly bad *paste*! How and when had the stone been changed?

And then she remembered that the emeralds had gone for cleaning. Her father had been especially pleased with the results. He'd called her attention to the stones, in fact, and to the man who'd done the work.

Cripplegate, the craftsman.
Cripplegate, the genius.

The man whom he called Cripplegate had robbed them!

Elizabeth sat very still, willing herself to think. She must not give in to panic. She must be certain about what had happened, absolutely certain. If she alerted her father and it turned out that nothing was wrong, he would be furious. He'd cut her allowance once already; would he do so again to punish her?

Ideas came swiftly. She must consult an expert. There were jewellery shops on Milsom Street; a simple repair would be reason enough to consult a jeweller. She could say that one of the surrounding diamonds was loose. And she would lead the man to converse about the quality of the emerald. Better yet, she would say that she feared that it was false–a mere bauble–and then wait for the jeweller to contradict her. And he would contradict her. He had to!

Elizabeth's fingers closed over the stone. She would go now, and she would send Penelope away to make a purchase while she went into the shop. With luck, she would be back within the hour; and her father would be no wiser.

But if the stone was false?

Elizabeth had no answer for this. Nor had she any idea how her father would raise the two hundred pound payment for this shocking loan.

~ 2 ~
Better than Wine

The décor at Bendle and Hurlingsford hadn't changed for generations. Here were the same glass-fronted display cases, the same mahogany wainscoting and highly polished floor. Patrick McGillvary tested the carpet with the toe of his boot. This, perhaps, was new.

"Papa, you are not attending!" Cleora gave him a look that was half-reproachful, half-pleading. She lowered her voice to a whisper. "Might I have a necklace like this one? It is grander than any of the others."

McGillvary's lips twitched, but he did not allow himself to smile. "Cleora, my love," he said, "you may choose from any on this tray. You are but fifteen, dearest, not fifty! There will be time for the grand gems when you are older."

She shifted in her chair. "I suppose."

There was disappointment in her voice; he could not allow that. Not on her birthday! McGillvary leaned over the glass display case. "On second thought," he said, "I suppose you could wear that one." He pointed to a crusted creation of citrines and amethysts. "But I'd have to rig you out in a get-up to match. Including one of those feather-trimmed turbans."

"Papa!"

"Like the one Aunt Agnes has with all those dangling spangles? And didn't it have a stuffed bird on it somewhere?"

"Oh, Papa! Of course not!" Cleora dimpled charmingly. "You are such a tease!"

"Shall we have this out for you to try?"

Smiling, Cleora shook her head. She bent over the tray once again.

The jeweller's lamp illumined her features. She was lovely, this daughter of his. Her hair was red, as his had once been. Her cheeks had the delicate blush of a newly opened rose. And she was as unspoiled as she was lovely. For this McGillvary gave credit to his late wife's sister with whom Cleora had lived these last three years. What did he know about raising a daughter? But he could handle special occasions such as this birthday visit.

Her gentle sigh brought him back from his musings. "I cannot decide, Papa! I wish Miss Lytton had been allowed to come. She is so helpful in that way!"

"Ah, but this is your birthday, dearest, not hers. It is fitting that we spend the day together, just ourselves. However, you may choose a small gift for Miss Lytton, if you like."

"Oh yes, Papa! And I shall try to decide for myself this time, truly."

"There you are," he said. "I am sure you will make a fine choice." Cleora was very like her mother, persuadable and indecisive. *But delightfully so*, McGillvary reminded himself. Cleora had Clare McGillvary's innocence and beauty without her fondness for hysterics.

McGillvary shifted in his seat, curbing his desire to yawn. What was the hurry, after all? The only other event they'd planned was tonight's concert. The proprietor hovered at the end of the counter, ever watchful. McGillvary had warned the man not to press Cleora, and so far, he was complying. The doorman, obviously bored, moved from one foot to the other. McGillvary smiled slightly. How well he recalled the tedium of standing watch.

Presently, the man came to attention and, with a flourish, opened the door. McGillvary could not see the woman's face, but he could see the doorman's. McGillvary raised an eyebrow. Very well, he would have a look.

The woman walked directly to the counter and settled into one of the upholstered chairs. Her features he could not see, but no matter. Her fur-trimmed spencer served to accentuate her lovely figure. Her hair was chestnut, twisted into an elegant knot beneath a smart hat. The effect was delightful. Not many women could wear that shade of green, so dear to an Irishman's heart.

"Do you like this one, Papa?"

McGillvary returned his attention to his daughter, and together, they selected the gift for her governess. At his prompting, Cleora reapplied herself to choosing her own gift, and McGillvary's gaze wandered again to the woman in green. She was a young matron, he decided. The proprietor was most attentive. She removed a chain from her neck and presented a pendant. The man's expression told McGillvary that the piece was valuable. She was a person of rank, perhaps?

She turned her head slightly, allowing him to see a little of her profile: a straight nose, high cheekbones, flawless complexion, curling lashes...

The door opened to admit another woman. "I have made my purchase," she said to the woman in green. "Shall I wait for you here?"

She turned and McGillvary caught his breath. *No wonder the footman stared! Even with a frown, she was gorgeous! What might she look like when she smiled? And who was she?* McGillvary studied the carpet, thinking. It was not like him to forget such a face.

The proprietor had his pencil out and was writing on an envelope. "Your name, ma'am?" McGillvary heard him say.

"Miss Elliot," she said, speaking distinctly. "Number 8, Camden Place."

Elliot? McGillvary's brows went up. Elliot was the surname of Wentworth's *fiancée.* He took another look. *Was this the elder sister? Wentworth had had plenty to say about her!*

"I would like to speak to the jeweller as soon as possible," she told the proprietor. "I shall return within the hour."

As she turned to go, McGillvary touched the brim of his hat in salute—and experienced a shock. Miss Elliot's beautiful eyes swept over him without as much as a flicker of acknowledgment. The footman opened the door, and she sailed out. She had completely ignored him.

Ignored? Women, unmarried or otherwise, never ignored him!

"Papa?" Cleora laid her hand on his arm and looked into his face. "What do you think of this one? I love it better than the others. At least, I think I do."

He covered her hand with his own. "It is perfect, my dear," he said. "Pearls always are, as your mother would say." He caught the eye of the proprietor, who came over immediately. "We would like this one, please," he said. He presented his card. "If you will send your bill to the attention of Mr Starkweather, it will be taken care of immediately."

The proprietor made a respectful bow. "Very good, Admiral. I will have this wrapped up for you right away."

"And now," McGillvary addressed his daughter, "shall we continue with our shopping? Then home for a rest, an early dinner, and then–" He paused, smiling.

"–and then the concert," said Cleora, with a happy sigh.

The shine in his daughter's blue eyes made up for Miss Elliot's negligence. Almost.

~ ~ ~ ~ ~ ~ ~ & ~ ~ ~ ~ ~ ~ ~

McGillvary poured himself a glass of Madeira before strolling to the full-length mirror. His dress uniform was of the latest cut; the gold braid and decorations glinted in the soft light. He made a slight adjustment to his neck cloth, grimacing slightly. Even in this light he could see the grey in his moustache. Cleora had been after him to remove it, the minx! So far, he had resisted. A knock sounded on the door. "Come," he called.

It was Jamison, his butler. "Admiral, sir," said he, "a gentleman of the Marines has come. Shall I bring him up?"

McGillvary raised an eyebrow. He knew what this meant. Time and again, Whitehall had proven that 'business before pleasure' was no idle slogan. "No, I'll be down directly, Jamison," he replied. "Put him in the blue salon; I'll see him there. And Jamison…don't forget to feed him."

After the orders were presented and signed over, McGillvary headed for the library. Two footmen were waiting in the hallway when he got there. McGillvary unlocked the door, and they went in before him to light the candles. When they left the room, he locked the door behind them.

"Orders, orders," he muttered, seating himself behind the massive mahogany desk. The wineglass he set beside the blotter. "'Every man must do his duty,'" he murmured, breaking the seals. God only knew what it would be this time.

The orders were intentionally vague–typical for Admiral Blankenship. McGillvary could be summoned for any variety of tasks. He might find himself sitting on a promotion board or attending tedious meetings about officers' pensions–or worse, dancing attendance at some social function. This was precisely why McGillvary had not brought Cleora to live with him. The war might be dying away, but the monster of bureaucracy that was Whitehall was as robust as ever. All the more reason to retire, he reminded himself. July would not come soon enough to suit him.

By the time his man Pym knocked at the library door, the orders were stowed in the vault. McGillvary exited the room and relocked the door while issuing orders of his own. "Pym, I shall be travelling to Whitehall tomorrow, immediately after Wentworth's dinner. If I know Blankenship, I'll be making the society rounds. Cleora and her governess will return to Richmond on Thursday as planned." He then checked his timepiece. "We leave for the concert within the quarter-hour. Any questions?"

Before Pym had finished the requisite "No, Admiral. Very good, Admiral," Patrick McGillvary was halfway down the corridor on his way to share the news with his daughter.

~ ~ ~ ~ ~ ~ ~ & ~ ~ ~ ~ ~ ~ ~

"You mean to say that all of it is in Italian?" Sir Cameron Greene looked up from the concert bill. "Really, Paddy," he grumbled. "I had no idea you meant to drag me to such high-brow nonsense!"

"Careful, Cam," murmured McGillvary. "Cleora has been studying Italian; the concert is her choice. Her birthday treat."

"A waste of my time is what this is," said Sir Cameron, "your charming daughter aside. I can't abide the language or the company." He gestured to the crowded Octagon Room. "Look around, Paddy. There's nothing but old women here."

McGillvary's smile widened. "Cam, dear," he said, "the pot cannot be calling the kettle black. According to Cleora, you and I are old."

"Must you remind me? Whatever the issue, I haven't a taste for withered crones!"

"You're so pessimistic, my dear! Not all of them are so. Where's your sporting spirit?"

With more good-natured grumbling, Sir Cameron resumed his study of the concert bill. "Ah," he said at last, lowering his voice for McGillvary's ears only, "look here, Paddy. The singer for the first act is Lily Stile. She's a fetching bit of jolly fun! Met her at Labcock's dinner a fortnight ago. Good dancer, too."

McGillvary studied his friend's expression. "I'm afraid you're out, Cam, if you were hoping for more. From what I hear, Farley's already taken her under his, er…wing."

Sir Cameron gave a snort. "Another?" said he. "So close to home, too. That wife of his ain't dead yet." He shook his head. "Dashed risky, if you ask me. Used to cart 'em off to Venice, or wherever that curst villa of his is. Or kept 'em in the Metropolis. Never here."

"There's no fool like an old fool, they say."

"There you go again, spouting on about age! What is it with you tonight? Besides," Sir Cameron added, "Sir Henry's my idea of old! About the age of that chit Lily's grandpapa, eh?"

But McGillvary never replied. "Well, well," he murmured. "What have we here?"

"How's that?"

"Wentworth's soon-to-be in-laws, just there." McGillvary nodded in the direction of the door. "His *fiancée's* father, Sir Walter. There's no mistaking him. And I believe the other is the sister." It was the woman from the jewellery shop.

Sir Cameron raised his brows. "Easy on the eyes, those two. The girl in particular."

McGillvary watched as Sir Walter and Miss Elliot found seats in the row ahead. Handkerchief in hand, Sir Walter examined the seat of his chair. "Coxcomb," Sir Cameron murmured. "Looks to be high in the instep."

McGillvary cocked an eyebrow. "My dear, you don't know the half."

Miss Elliot opened her concert bill while McGillvary studied the graceful curve of her neck and shoulders. She was even more beautiful than he'd first supposed. If Wentworth were to be believed, she was a termagant. McGillvary leaned back in his chair as he considered this. Frederick Wentworth's opinion was not to be lightly regarded. On the other hand, who made Wentworth an expert on women? He'd lived the life of a monk! And his *fiancée* was a timid little thing–lovely, but spiritless. Very like Clare, in fact.

"Surprise! Surprise!" A man's voice broke into McGillvary's reverie. He turned to see James Rushworth come bounding down the aisle.

"Hallo! I have surprised you, Miss Elliot! I have made you jump!" Mr Rushworth made an energetic bow.

McGillvary nearly laughed out loud, for Miss Elliot's face was a picture of dismay. "I-I understood there were no available tickets, Mr Rushworth," he heard her say.

"Ah, but I have managed without one!" he said. "One of Mama's friends knew just what to do. A contribution to the Society for Arts, or some such place, and here I am!" He pointed to the empty chair beside her. "May I join you?" Before she could answer, Rushworth plumped himself down on the too-narrow chair.

McGillvary's eyebrows climbed higher. Rushworth's failed marriage had taught him nothing about women, apparently. Miss Elliot visibly recoiled in his presence, but did he notice?

Sir Cameron had finished with his examination of the ladies. "No one here holds a torch to the sister," he said, "but then, what can one expect in Bath?"

McGillvary shrugged. "Such is my fate if Blankenship and company will leave me alone."

"You'll remain in Bath for the entire spring?"

"My dear, I haven't any choice. The trustees have made an unbelievable tangle. The only way to set it straight is to oversee the work myself."

"You sound like a curst tradesman minding his shop."

McGillvary kept his eyes on Miss Elliot. "Tell me. Do you entrust Malvern entirely to the care of your steward? Do you never peer over his shoulder? Nor check his ledgers?"

"Of course I do! But an ancestral estate is different. As well you know."

"Is it? Not to my mind. I watch over Madderly and Kinclaven as carefully as my other properties. When my watch is up, I intend to leave the family coffers brimming."

"Your brother will appreciate your generosity, I'm sure."

"I was referring to the fortune Cleora will inherit! Ronan," McGillvary said, "may go to...er, Hades!"

Sir Cameron made a face. "Don't tidy your speech on my account!"

McGillvary nodded to Cleora's empty seat. "One must make the attempt, from time to time. I'm off to Richmond next week, so I need the practice."

"Richmond? You don't attend Lady Claverling's curst rout?"

"Certainly, I do."

"Well, if that don't beat all! How'd she manage to bullock you into it?"

"Actually, Cam, I volunteered."

"You wish to go?"

"By order of Whitehall, no less. I had a hand in arranging the guest list; her ladyship owes me a favour."

"What does that signify?" complained Sir Cameron. "She and My Lord Dull-Dog will fill the place to bursting with jubilarian gossipmongers, if I know anything about it."

"That's part of the charm. One never knows whom one may meet in the crush."

McGillvary's daughter and the governess returned to their seats, ending their private conversation. Cleora laid a hand on his arm. "Papa, look!" she whispered. "They're lighting the candles for the musicians!"

Presently, the members of the ensemble entered and took their seats. They began to tune their instruments. The audience grew quiet as footmen extinguished the candles along the walls.

McGillvary leaned in. "Happy?" he asked, smiling.

"Oh, Papa!" Cleora whispered back.

A flutter of polite applause accompanied the soloist, Miss Stile, as she walked to her place. The conductor opened his score and raised his hands expectantly. The musicians readied their instruments, and the music began. As it swelled to a crescendo, Miss Stile gave a toss of her head. Then she began to sing.

~ ~ ~ ~ ~ ~ ~ & ~ ~ ~ ~ ~ ~ ~

Penelope Clay descended to the entrance hall, wrapped in her cloak. Carefully, she drew back the bolt of the main door and slipped out into the night. There, at the far end of Camden Place, stood a chaise-and-four. She drew nearer and by lamplight made out the Elliot crest emblazoned on the door. Its significance was not lost on her. An attendant opened the door and with meticulous care assisted her to enter.

The interior of the chaise was empty. Penelope sank back against the cushioned seat and drew the fur lap robe close. This was certainly more elegant than anything Sir Walter had ever used. Indeed, when he came to Bath, Sir Walter had given up his carriage. His heir was a man of taste, sophistication, and substance. She had done well in accepting his invitation. Penelope Clay's lips curved into a smile. She had done very well, indeed.

~ ~ ~ ~ ~ ~ ~ & ~ ~ ~ ~ ~ ~ ~

By the Interval, McGillvary had heard enough of Miss Stile's wide vibrato. As she took her final bow, he glanced at Miss Elliot.

She appeared to be holding her own. Still, it was amusing to see Rushworth, so obviously her junior, bent on pursuit. As soon as the lights came up, she sent him away to procure a cup of tea. At least McGillvary thought this was the case, because Rushworth bounded off like a puppy fetching a stick. As soon as he was out of sight, Miss Elliot rose. McGillvary saw her hesitate and look to her father, but he was conversing with another. She did not disturb him but made her way into the aisle.

McGillvary glanced to Cleora and Miss Lytton, then, again, to Miss Elliot's retreating form. "I'll meet you in the tea room," he said to Sir Cameron and rose to follow.

The doorway was blocked by the crowd. McGillvary could sense Miss Elliot's impatience. Fortunately, Rushworth was nowhere to be seen. She made her way into the vestibule and escaped through a side door.

McGillvary waited a moment before he did likewise. Noiselessly, he closed the door behind him. He found himself in a dimly lit service corridor. His smile grew wider; the setting was perfect. Miss Elliot did not appear to have noticed his presence. She walked to the very end of the corridor, where a candle burned in a wall sconce. There, she bent and examined her shoes. "Blast!" he heard her say.

McGillvary bit his lip to keep from laughing. The woman was an original!

Along the wall was a bench on which Miss Elliot sat down. Straightway, she began tugging at something on one of her shoes. But the bangle, or whatever it was, held stubbornly. She pulled harder, but it would not budge. "Blast!" said Miss Elliot again.

Grinning, McGillvary dug in a pocket. "Pardon me," he said, stepping forward. "Perhaps this might be useful?" He held out his silver clasp knife.

Miss Elliot gave a huff of annoyance but did not look up. "Thank you, Mr Rushworth, it would," she said.

Rushworth? Swallowing laughter, McGillvary opened the knife and solemnly presented the handle. She took it from him without looking at his face. "I have lost the ornament from one of my shoes," she explained. "Which is rather a disaster, for I had them especially designed. So now I must remove the other." She paused to sigh. "It has been the most wretched day."

McGillvary murmured sympathetically.

The knife's blade was sharp; with a single swipe it cut the bangle from her shoe. Miss Elliot examined the knife. "How clever you are

31

to carry one of these," she said. "When I have need of a weapon, I must rely on whatever is at hand."

McGillvary was surprised into a laugh. "When you have need of a weapon?" he said.

She closed the knife. "Indeed, yes," she said. "Suitors can be incredibly irksome, Mr Rushworth. You have no idea."

"Then keep the knife, please," said McGillvary. "It would be my pleasure to know that when irksome suitors present themselves, you are armed for battle."

At that, Miss Elliot looked up. A flush appeared on her throat and cheeks. "Why," she said, "you are not Mr Rushworth!"

~ ~ ~ ~ ~ ~ ~ & ~ ~ ~ ~ ~ ~ ~

William Elliot opened a second bottle and filled both the glasses. The deep red of the wine was pleasing in the candlelight. So, too, had been the conversation; Penelope had not been so well entertained for a very long time. William Elliot did not hesitate to speak openly of the Baronet. This was so unlike his usual, careful self that Penelope did not know what to think. Indeed, she could scarcely believe what he was now saying:

"...for Sir Walter not only insulted you, but me, as well. Wondering why you should have an admirer, indeed! Good lord! A man would be an idiot if he did not admire you, my dear!"

The wine loosened her reserve enough for her to say, "I thought you admired Miss Anne above all others."

His smile was disarming. "Anne is a dear girl, but my affection arose from a desire to rescue her from a life of poverty."

Penelope raised her glass. "How noble," she said.

"Yes, it was; wasn't it?" A slight smile crossed his face. "But you must not think I am cast down, my dear. Fate intervened and kept me from a disastrous mistake. I have lately learned unhappy news about the Baronet. Once I knew the truth, I lost interest in assisting my cousins."

Penelope was caught by this remark; she knew she dared not enquire about the particulars–yet.

"And once Anne became engaged, what could I do?" Mr Elliot leaned forward. "Not for anything would I wed Elizabeth!"

Penelope had to smile. "You are not a true philanthropist, then?"

"A desire to assist a woman of one's family is one thing. Self-immolation is quite another. Marriage to Elizabeth would be a continual cat fight!"

What delicious talk this was! "But you must admit," she said, "Elizabeth is very beautiful".

"Beautiful and opinionated. One must agree with her upon every point—or be annihilated!" His voice softened. "I don't see how you have borne it, my dear. But then, I am forgetting; you must work for your living. You have no choice but to bear with the whims and tempers of a fashionable woman." He put down his wine glass. "By the bye, has Sir Walter been prompt in paying your salary?"

"My salary?" she faltered. "Why, I..."

"I have learned from a reliable source that Sir Walter is in serious difficulty, more so than he suspects. I suggest you approach him at the earliest opportunity."

"Oh, but, I..." Penelope swallowed. The truth was, she did not wish to remind Sir Walter of her inferior status by asking! But she could hardly explain this to Mr Elliot! "The Baronet and Elizabeth have been quite generous. They have given me gifts and—"

"Elizabeth's cast-offs, do you mean?" he interrupted. "I do not call such things gifts." His voice grew quiet. "Sir Walter Elliot is ruined. Surely, you have seen the signs."

Penelope did not know what to say. William Elliot had the most compassionate eyes. Why had she never noticed this before?

"It is as I have told you from the beginning, dear Penelope," he said softly. "Yours was an admirable attempt, but it would never have worked. Sir Walter cannot love anyone but himself. Even if you could convince him to wed, what would you have? Only the title. Your husband would be a foolish old man. In addition, there is no longer any provision for a widow's pension in his will. As the man's heir, I am in a position to know this." He spoke even more slowly now. "Upon his demise," he said, "you would be left penni-less, as well as homeless.

Penelope groped for her wine glass and took a bracing swallow. "You would call Sir Walter's financial situation desperate, then?"

"Absolutely and completely. Your father is his man of business, is he not? I suggest you apply to him for the facts. Nevertheless," he continued, "I do pity the Baronet. He is nearly a comic figure in Bath now. All pretend respect while they laugh at him behind his back, poor old fellow." William Elliot held out a silver serving dish. "Have a sweetmeat, my dear."

~ ~ ~ ~ ~ ~ ~ & ~ ~ ~ ~ ~ ~ ~

Miss Elliot had amber-coloured eyes, he realized. In the half-light of the corridor the effect was lovely. "We've not met formally, I realize," said McGillvary, extending a hand to assist her to rise. "Will you permit an introduction? Patrick McGill–"

He was interrupted by a gusty sneeze. Both turned. At the far end of the corridor stood Sir Walter Elliot. He lowered his handkerchief. "Elizabeth!" he said hoarsely. "The second act is about to begin! Come at once!"

"I..." said Miss Elliot. She removed her gloved hand from McGillvary's and took a step back.

"Do hurry, Elizabeth!" urged Sir Walter. "Sir Henry wishes to speak with you."

Miss Elliot raised her eyes to McGillvary's. "My father..." she said. She smiled slightly and returned the knife. "Thank you."

Sir Walter's voice carried the length of the corridor. "It is not like you to run off," he scolded, taking hold of her arm. "What will Sir Henry think? And to find you here, of all places! Who is that man?" The door closed, and Miss Elliot's reply was lost.

Patrick McGillvary remained where he was. "Elizabeth," he said aloud. It was quite the perfect name for her. And she was a wit! Who would have guessed? And the father? He felt his smile harden. Such a look from him!

But McGillvary's annoyance was short-lived. He had learned well the value of patience and timing as far as manoeuvres were concerned. Here was a chase, indeed, in the form of the beautiful Elizabeth. As luck would have it, Wentworth's dinner was set for tomorrow. Sir Walter would be made to regret his slight. As for the man's daughter, he must convince Wentworth to seat Elizabeth at his end of the table.

~ ~ ~ ~ ~ ~ ~ & ~ ~ ~ ~ ~ ~ ~

Mr Elliot reached across to place his hand on Penelope's. "I wish to part as friends," he said. "Unfortunately, I must return to the Metropolis shortly."

Penelope swallowed her surprise. "You are...leaving us, sir?"

"I have business that can no longer be delayed." Mr Elliot rotated the stem of his wineglass. "Did I mention that I have lately purchased a house in Town? As you know, I shall be officially out of mourning in June."

Penelope did not know what to make of this news. She must tread carefully. "We shall see you at Miss Anne's wedding, surely?"

"Unfortunately, no. You and I must bid one another *adieu* to-night." He fell silent. "I wish Anne well," he said presently. "She will make a good wife. Dull, but good. One must always admire Anne's goodness."

"Yes, of course."

"But to be honest, Penelope, I prefer a different sort of woman—a woman who enjoys amusing conversation and entertainments—in short, the fashionable world of Society." He lifted his wineglass. Over the rim of it, his eyes met hers. "Tell me," he said, "when do Sir Walter and Elizabeth make their pilgrimage to Town? Perhaps you and I may meet in some ballroom or other."

"They travel only so far as Richmond this year."

"Oh? And you do not care for this arrangement?"

"They have been invited to join a select house party." Speaking became more difficult. "At that time," she managed to say, "I am to make a visit to my family in the country." Penelope took a deep breath. "I suppose it will not be so very bad for a week or two. And, it will be lovely to see my ch–"

She caught herself in time. So far she'd avoided mentioning her two children. Mr Elliot knew nothing about them, of this she was certain.

"It will be lovely to see my *church*," she amended. "We have the loveliest church in Crewkherne. But, enough of me. Tell me more about your fine house in London."

He shrugged. "There is not much to tell: bare walls and empty rooms; all needing paint and paper, carpets and furniture, an efficient staff. As well as that intangible something which makes a house into a home. It is the latter which presents the greatest difficulty. It lacks a woman's touch."

"Oh." Penelope did not know what to say, so she took another sip of wine.

~ ~ ~ ~ ~ ~ ~ & ~ ~ ~ ~ ~ ~ ~

Elizabeth was half-pulled, half-pushed into the vestibule. She hardly knew where to look. That her father should find her in such a situation was worse than anything! *Who was that man in the corridor?*

He kept a firm grip on her arm as they manoeuvred through the crowd. "Of all the things!" he said into her ear. "What am I to say to Sir Henry? That I found you in a closet flirting with a sailor?"

"I was not in a closet!" she whispered back, "and I never flirt!" *And was the man a sailor?* Apart from the smile and the moustache– and a strong, well-shaped hand–she'd noticed very little about him.

"Perhaps you should consider flirting a little!" said Sir Walter. "With the proper sort of gentleman, of course. That is the trouble with you, Elizabeth. You never exert yourself in the proper direction! How many eligible suitors have I brought to your notice, yet you refuse to take the hint?"

Eligible suitors? Men her grandfather's age were hardly eligible suitors! That was the only type of man she'd met since coming to Bath! Was she so old, so at her last prayers, that she must welcome the attentions of worn-out men of fashion? "I cannot imagine why you bring up Sir Henry," she said. "He is hardly a suitor! He has a wife!"

"An invalid wife," he corrected. "The end could come at any time! She is not at all well!" Sir Walter hesitated, held up a hand, and sneezed. He went hunting in his pockets for a handkerchief.

"Neither, it appears, are you!" said Elizabeth.

Sir Walter ignored this remark. "We must think ahead, my dear. We must be far seeing. Do you expect a titled husband to simply fall into your lap?"

Sir Walter sneezed again, which was very well because it saved Elizabeth from answering. "And why didn't you wear the emeralds tonight?" he said, sniffing. "You look so well in them."

Elizabeth went rigid. "I think you know the answer to that."

"Ah, the *paste*. As I said before, it is unsafe to wear valuable gems in public. Everyone wears *paste* nowadays."

"I am not everyone!" said Elizabeth. "I do not wear *paste*! I would like the original stones replaced, if you please."

Sir Walter's gaze shifted. "Isn't that your Mr Rushworth? Why, I believe he is coming this way."

"I sent him for tea...and he is not *my* Mr Rushworth!"

Mr Rushworth carried two teacups, though not very nimbly. "I don't know how you take your tea," he confessed, flushing a little, "so I brought it both ways: with milk alone and with milk and sugar."

"Elizabeth prefers her tea with lemon," said Sir Walter, "and so do I. Come along, daughter, we have friends waiting." He took hold of Elizabeth's elbow and plunged into the throng.

Mr Rushworth was left to make his way through the crowded vestibule. It was not until he reached the Octagon Room that he appeared to realize what Sir Walter had said. Off he went to fetch more tea and Elizabeth had the grace to feel sorry for him.

Before long, Sir Henry Farley came over. "Miss Elliot," he said, bowing over her hand. "You look...divine." He brought her gloved fingers to his lips. "The Intaglio necklace—perfection! But then," he added, twinkling, "should I expect any less from the most beautiful woman in Bath?"

Elizabeth drew her hand away. Sir Henry would be gallant, but his compliments made her feel uncomfortable. His thin-lipped smile reminded her of a cat's.

Sir Walter gave another mighty sneeze.

Sir Henry turned. "My dear Sir Walter," he said, "are you unwell?"

Sir Walter quickly lowered his handkerchief. "Certainly not," he said. "We Elliots are never ill!" But he broke out in a spasm of coughing. Heads turned as Sir Walter continued to cough. He and Elizabeth did not remain for the second act.

~ ~ ~ ~ ~ ~ ~ & ~ ~ ~ ~ ~ ~ ~

It was almost midnight when William Elliot's carriage turned the corner onto Camden Place. Penelope peered out of the window. "Leave me at the corner, sir. Please."

Mr Elliot scowled as he pulled the check string. "It is not as if you have committed a crime by joining me for dinner!"

Then it was time to say good-bye. Penelope stood on the dark street, her hands clasped in his. She struggled for the proper words. "Farewell, Mr Elliot," she said at last.

He smiled. "Such formality!"

"Farewell, *William,* then, if you prefer." Penelope could feel the colour rise to her cheeks. "Please, do visit us when you are next in Bath."

"You remain with my cousins, then? In spite of everything?"

Penelope thrust the uncertain future aside. "Of course, sir," she said.

"Your loyalty is touching, my dear. Forgive me for misjudging you." He leaned forward and gently kissed her cheek. "Good-bye."

She gave his hands a parting squeeze and quickly turned away. This farewell cost more than she expected; she did not wish him to see her tears. With a brisk stride, she walked toward Sir Walter's house. As she neared, her steps slowed. Every window of the house was dark. *But...why weren't the lamps lit? Had Sir Walter and Elizabeth already returned?* Penelope approached the door and reached for the knob. The door was locked!

~ ~ ~ ~ ~ ~ ~ & ~ ~ ~ ~ ~ ~ ~

This was the moment for which William Elliot had been waiting. Escape without detection was simple; it was the return that posed the challenge! Mrs Clay was now clearly in distress; even at this distance he could see it. Yes, it was the perfect conclusion to a profitable evening.

Then, he sat back against the squabs, thinking. It was too bad, really, for Penelope Clay was an engaging companion. And so delicious to look at in that daring crimson gown! He'd planned to leave her standing on the street, an object of disgrace. He knew that eventually she would be forced to seek entry at the service door, and her precious secrecy would be destroyed. Through the servants, the gossip would spread like wildfire and compel Sir Walter to dismiss her from his service. Thus would Penelope Clay's threat to his inheritance end.

But a new, more provocative course of action now presented itself. A slow smile spread over William Elliot's face. Why had he never thought of this before? Quickly, he lowered the window and ordered the driver to pull forward. He did not wait for the carriage to come to a stop before he opened the door. Swiftly, he moved to Penelope's side and laid a gentle hand on her shoulder. Through the fabric of her cloak, he could feel the tremors of her distress.

"Penelope!" he whispered. "Dearest, what is wrong?"

She turned toward him with tears in her eyes.

"No, no. Do not speak, dear one," he said. "Not here on the street." He held out his hand. "Come," he whispered, enfolding her hand in both of his. "There is no need to fret. Indeed, what is a locked door to us? Was I not saying that my house lacks a woman's touch?" He lowered his voice to a whisper. "Come away with me, instead."

~3~
Saltash Luck

Elizabeth did not discover Penelope's absence until late the following morning. After looking everywhere, she summoned Wilson to Penelope's bedchamber.

"Mrs Clay is out, miss," he said, unhelpfully.

Elizabeth bridled at the smug pucker of the man's lips. "So I see," she said. "At what time was her tray sent up?"

"To my knowledge, Mrs Clay did not request a breakfast tray, miss." Wilson put up his chin. "According to Elise, her bed was not slept in."

"Surely you are mistaken! Elise speaks with a heavy accent; perhaps you misunderstood?"

Wilson stood at rigid attention. "Very good, miss," he said.

"However," continued Elizabeth, warming to her subject, "if you suspected something was amiss, why was Father not informed?"

"That is a question for Roberts, miss. The Baronet has been in a delicate state all morning; I was not about to disturb his peace because of a nasty Frenchwoman's suspicion."

Elizabeth put her hands on her hips. "What about my peace? Did it not occur to you that I would wish to know?"

Elizabeth rang for Elise, but she was no more helpful. "That one," said she, with a sniff. She shuffled to Mrs Clay's wardrobe and opened it. "You see, *mademoiselle?*" she said, pointing to Mrs Clay's gowns. "The red, gone. The best shoes, gone." Her eyes crinkled into slits. "And the trinkets?"

Elizabeth opened the dressing table. Inside were hairpins and a discarded handkerchief. The jet necklace, a gift at Christmas, was not there. "Father must have put Mrs Clay's jewellery in the vault," said Elizabeth. "Yes, for I recall her asking him. And very sweet he was about it, for she owns nothing of value."

Elise sniffed again and pulled open another drawer. There were Penelope's smallclothes, neatly folded. "You see? She goes out for the evening. She does not come home."

"An emergency?" suggested Elizabeth. "Perhaps one of her children became ill. Yes, and her father sent for her in the night! Crewkherne is not so very far."

She looked past Elise to Wilson. "Were there callers yesterday evening?"

"There was no one, miss."

"Into the night she go, yes," said Elise. "But not to her father, *mademoiselle*. She does not go to her father in the red gown."

Elizabeth pushed the drawer closed.

But Elise was not finished. She gave Elizabeth a sidelong look. "Always looking at the men, she was."

Elizabeth found her voice. "Now see here," she cried, "Mrs Clay is my friend. I'll thank you not to speak in that snubbing way."

"Miss Anne, she knows. She sees."

"Upon my word, Elise! Penelope would never run off with a man. It isn't as if she is pretty. Who would have her?"

"A woman not pretty has charms, *mademoiselle*. She has plans, that one. Big plans."

Elizabeth folded her arms across her chest. "If Penelope had plans, she would have told me. She tells me all her secrets, every one!"

Elise shrugged. "How she can lie."

"There is a reasonable explanation for this," insisted Elizabeth, "And until I find a letter telling me so, I refuse to believe that Penelope has left me."

Elise bowed her head. "As you wish, *mademoiselle*."

"This room is to be kept ready for her return." She turned to Wilson. "And a place set for Mrs Clay at every meal. Is that understood?"

Elise laid a work-worn hand on Elizabeth's shoulder. "No letter will you find, *cherie*," she said. "A great danger you have avoid."

~ ~ ~ ~ ~ ~ ~ & ~ ~ ~ ~ ~ ~ ~

When Elizabeth shared the news with her father, he waved it aside. He was, as Wilson had said, in a delicate state. "It's my nose, isn't it?" he said, peering into the hand mirror. "It seems to me that it is swollen, just here, on the left side!" He raised anxious eyes to

Elizabeth's face; she noticed that they were bloodshot. "You must go down alone this morning," he said. "I cannot receive callers in this state." He gave a ferocious sneeze.

"Perhaps you ought to cancel your plans for this evening as well," said Elizabeth.

"Our plans, you mean. Nonsense! The dinner is being held in Anne's honour. If I do not attend, what does that say about Anne's engagement? A scandal is something we can ill afford!"

"Along with everything else," muttered Elizabeth, going out.

She had no choice but to descend to the drawing room, for this was their morning at home. Naturally, Anne did not join her. Anne had been so occupied with plans for the wedding and with the purchase of the bride clothes that she was living entirely at Lady Russell's. Elizabeth had not seen her for days. There was only one caller–the Reverend Alston, who would not stay–and one letter for Elizabeth. It was from Miss Caroline Bingley.

This was hardly a treat. Elizabeth had met Miss Bingley in London, thrown together as they were by similarity of age and circumstance. Somehow, Miss Bingley had learned that Elizabeth was to be a guest at Chalfort House; supposedly, she longed to see her. Elizabeth was not taken in. From beginning to end the letter was nothing but sweetly worded boasts and snubs.

> Perhaps I may visit you this autumn, my dear Eliza, when the Hursts go into to the country. I long to see what entertainments Bath has to offer.

Entertainments? Compared to London, Bath had nothing to offer! How very like Caroline Bingley to rub it in!

And so the morning wore into afternoon. Elizabeth watched the window for the carriage that would return Penelope from her errand. None arrived. She worked out a little speech with a nice combination of accusation and forgiveness, but Penelope never came to hear it. Shadows lengthened; the afternoon post was delivered, but there was no word from Penelope. Up and down the stairs went the footboy, catering to Sir Walter's requests. Presently, two footmen came in to light the candles against the gathering gloom. Elizabeth abandoned her post at the drawing room windows. She could, at least, assemble a packing list for Chalfort House. Even so, it was a silent, solitary task. How she missed Penelope Clay's nonsensical chatter!

At last the long day ended, and all Elizabeth's hopes ended with it. By morning there would be nothing Elizabeth could do to explain away Penelope's absence. Elise was right; Penelope was gone for good.

At six-thirty, resplendent in his evening finery, Sir Walter came into the drawing room to wait for Lady Russell's carriage. His cold was much improved. His eyes were inclined to water, but otherwise he appeared to be fine. He did not press Elizabeth to join him. She was in no state to attend a dinner; one look in the mirror had told her that. But to spend the evening alone in her bedchamber was unbearable. She established herself in the wingchair by the fire with a lap blanket and a stack of fashion periodicals. The house grew quiet. A half-burned chunk of coal fell apart with a dry whisper

So silent was the house that she fell asleep. At least, she thought that was the case, for her limbs felt stiff and sore. Someone was climbing the stairs. Presently she heard the footsteps returning. It couldn't be a servant, for none of their Bath servants moved so quickly. It was too early for her father's return. Perhaps...

"Penelope?" called Elizabeth. There was a long silence.

Then the drawing room door opened. Elizabeth came halfway out of the chair. "Penelope," she cried, "where on earth have you been?"

But it was not Penelope. It was Anne. "Hello, Elizabeth," she said softly. "Are you awake?"

"Oh," said Elizabeth. "It's you."

Anne was dressed for dinner, but an ugly woollen travelling cloak covered her beautiful gown. Elizabeth was hardly surprised. Cold weather was to be endured, not accommodated—but did Anne care? As always, Anne must do exactly as she wished, without regard to fashion.

"Elizabeth," she said, "I have come to bid you farewell." A dimple quivered in Anne's cheek.

Elizabeth pretended not to notice this. She smoothed a fold in the blanket. "Good bye, then," she said. "I suppose I shan't see you until Wednesday next; although, it would be helpful if Lady Russell could bring you on Tuesday. We ought to go over the details for the wedding breakfast. Not that Lady Russell will wish to do so, of course, but it would be helpful."

Anne's calm deserted her. "Oh, Elizabeth," she cried, smiling. "Something has happened to change all that. Frederick has received orders. There is just time to be married if we leave tonight."

"Leave?" Elizabeth raised herself on her elbow. "So, if you are leaving for Lady Russell's..."

"But I'm not!" Anne hesitated, studying her in that careful way Elizabeth hated. But her eyes were dancing. "Frederick and I are going to be married," she announced.

"Yes," said Elizabeth, "at your wedding on Wednesday next."

"No," said Anne, "we are leaving now, tonight. We will be wed in a few days, if we are lucky. I came to collect a few things. Frederick is waiting downstairs." She made an impatient movement.

It was then that Elizabeth noticed the valise at Anne's feet. Was Anne...eloping? Elizabeth sat up in amazement. "Frederick," she said, "may take himself to Hades!"

"Elizabeth!"

"It won't answer, Anne! Your wedding date is set! The announcement has been sent to all the papers!" Her eyes narrowed. "Does Father know?"

"Of course, Father knows." Anne's gaze shifted to the clock on the mantel piece. "And within the hour, so will the dinner guests. Admiral McGillvary thought it best to wait until we were gone before he made the announcement."

"Admiral Whoever-He-Is should mind his own business! You take yourselves back to that dinner and retract the announcement!"

Anne's smile vanished. "Elizabeth," she said, "Frederick and I are not asking for your permission."

"You will not run off to be married in London! It simply isn't done!"

"But we are not running off to London! The instant Frederick sets foot in London he must report to Whitehall!" Anne lifted her chin. "No, we shall be married in Gretna."

Elizabeth gave a strangled cry.

"I know what you're thinking," said Anne hastily, "but you are wrong! We are not eloping! Father is aware of our plans. As a matter of fact, Father will be standing beside the Admiral when he makes the announcement. So will Lady Russell and Admiral and Mrs Croft."

"But the Wedding Breakfast! What about the Wedding Breakfast? A patched-together affair from start to finish—and now we must cancel it?"

"I am sorry, Elizabeth, truly. It cannot be helped."

"God only knows what Lady Russell will think. She paid for the whole thing!"

Anne's smile slipped a bit. "I trust Lady Russell will find it in her heart to understand."

Elizabeth's heart was beating very fast now. "Anne," she said, fighting rising panic, "you cannot do this. You do not understand the consequences. No, how could you? You've always lived apart from the world. You've never cared about anyone's opinion but your own! Think of us! Father and I shall never live it down!"

Anne drew herself up, speaking with a curtness that surprised her. "I am sorry," she said. "I am afraid you must." There was a tiny pause; Anne's voice became wistful. "Wish me joy, Elizabeth," she said.

Elizabeth found it hard to continue. She choked and said, "You'll live to regret this, Anne. Do not come crying to me when your life is in a shambles!"

Anne took a step toward Elizabeth's chair. "I am sorry you are feeling so poorly. You would have enjoyed the dinner. Even Father was—"

From below came the sound of a man's voice. He called Anne's name.

She spun round. "It's Frederick! I've tarried too long! Farewell!"

And then Anne was gone. Elizabeth could hear her footsteps running down the stairs. Seconds later came the slam of the door and, in another moment, the clatter of horses and the rumble of wheels on cobbles. Elizabeth dropped her head in her hands.

Sir Walter returned within the hour, but he did not come into the drawing room. Elizabeth ran out to the landing and called after him, but he continued on his way. She heard his bedchamber door close with a slam.

The stillness of the house was maddening and served only to magnify Elizabeth's misery. Penelope was gone for good and in a truly disgraceful way. Now Anne had run off to Gretna to be married out of hand—the gossips would have plenty to say about that!

Elizabeth pressed a hand to her temple. She knew exactly how it would be. Tomorrow a stream of inquisitive callers would come, and who must receive them? Not her father! And then there was the cancelled wedding. A note of explanation must be written to each of the guests. As Anne's godmother, Lady Russell ought to help with this chore, but she was probably so angry that Elizabeth would have to do everything herself!

And then there was the business about the missing gemstones and the payment mentioned in Mr Shepherd's letter. How could even half that amount be raised? Elizabeth drew the blanket to her chin. Her misery was complete.

~ ~ ~ ~ ~ ~ ~ & ~ ~ ~ ~ ~ ~ ~

Sir Walter's illness worsened in the night. The following morning he did not come down to breakfast but remained in bed, complaining of a variety of ills: his throat was sore, he had difficulty swallowing, his ears ached. When Elizabeth ventured to open the draperies, he complained that the light hurt his eyes. Eventually she tired of trying to amuse him and made for the drawing room. There was work to be done. The most important guest to notify was their cousin, the Dowager Vicountess Dalrymple. And then there was Mary.

Elizabeth rolled her eyes at the thought of her sister. Mary's letter must be sent first, before the others, and by express. If only she could manage to inform her through a more reliable means! It would be very like Mary to pretend she hadn't received word and come to Bath anyway. Life without a companion might be dull, but a fortnight's visit from Mary would be intolerable!

~ ~ ~ ~ ~ ~ ~ & ~ ~ ~ ~ ~ ~ ~

Elizabeth's letter reached Uppercross Cottage on the following morning, owing to excellent connections. Once Mary digested its contents, she fairly flew out of the door. "Charles!" she called. There was no response. Charles had not taken out his gun or the dogs; where could he be? Mary skirted the house and made her way up the gravel path.

Although the weather had been dry for days, the path was muddy in places. Mary grimaced as she picked her way along it. Now that she thought on it, she knew exactly where to find her husband—with that wretched beast of Captain Wentworth's!

Mary pushed open the heavy door to the horse barn, wincing at the dirt and the horse smells. She squinted into the dimness. There! Someone was humming a tune. Sure enough, she could just make out Charles's blond head above the wall of the last box. He was brushing a horse.

Mary rushed forward, waving the letter. "An express has come from Bath with such news!" she cried.

Charles straightened. "How's that?" he said.

"You'll never imagine!" said Mary. "Captain Wentworth had received orders, or some such thing. He and Anne have gone off to be married, Charles! My sister, married! Even before Henrietta!"

"Is that so?" Charles resumed brushing the horse. "Good for them."

Mary wrinkled her nose. "You like this news?"

"Well, sure. No reason to wait."

It was then that Mary got a good look at her husband. "Good gracious, Charles. You are simply covered with the hairs from that horse! Isn't brushing it supposed to be Coney's job?"

"It is; but I don't mind. I like animals."

"So you say, but I do not believe it seeing how you enjoy killing them so much."

Charles ran a hand along Belle's flank. "You don't understand the first thing about the sport of hunting or the peaceful quiet of the woodland if you think that."

"Quiet? With that gun of yours and all those dogs?"

"At least the dogs don't talk," muttered Charles. He bent to examine the brush.

Mary did not catch his remark, but she saw the expression that went with it. "As if this letter was not bad enough, I find you out here doing farm chores! At this rate, I shouldn't wonder that you will be raking dung from the floor or washing and polishing the gig! Coney will have nothing to do at all, thanks to you!"

"Raking dung? Washing the...? Belle is a creature, Mary. She must come to know me—to trust me—before I can work with her. My time here is far from wasted."

Mary inclined her head. "A true gentleman," she said, "has a man to care for his horses."

"A groom, yes, who must be housed and fed and given a wage."

"A wage." Mary gave an unhappy huff. Why must everything be so expensive? "If only we had a larger income!"

"Well," said Charles, "since the wedding's off, we won't have the expense and trouble of travelling to Bath."

Mary blinked. She had not thought of this. "Not travel to Bath?" she cried. "But my new gown ..."

"Wear it next week for Henrietta's wedding. Weren't you complaining that it wouldn't be finished on time?"

"But ...but ..." Mary's face puckered. "But I wish to go to Bath! It is most unfair of Captain Wentworth to get himself ordered away! And what if he is sent to some foreign place?"

"I imagine Anne will do as Mrs Croft did and accompany him."

"To some heathenish place like the Indies? Never!"

Charles shrugged. "I don't see why not."

"It is bad enough that Anne is marrying a man of the Navy. So ignoble!"

"Then it must be for Elizabeth to marry a duke, so that you must bow and scrape to her."

"Bless me, no! Elizabeth will never marry; who would have her? Although I suppose it is very well that Anne will not marry a man of distinction. For when you are become the squire..."

"...my father will be in his grave. I thank you for the reminder."

"Good gracious, Charles, I did not mean it that way!"

Charles laid down the brush. "Do you know, Mary, you think too much of precedence and rank."

"And what is wrong with that? You cannot know the degradation I suffer."

"Oh, I think I do, for you are forever telling me of it."

For once, Mary had the sense to be silent, but she continued to fuss and fret about the spoiled trip to Bath for the remainder of the week.

~ ~ ~ ~ ~ ~ ~ & ~ ~ ~ ~ ~ ~ ~

Elizabeth's week was no better. Sir Walter's condition continued to worsen. He did not attend church on Sunday, even though he had been invited to join Lady Dalrymple and Miss Carteret in their pew. On Tuesday, he instructed Elizabeth to cancel their card party. As news of his illness spread, the number of callers dwindled. The post piled up on his desk, unopened.

By Thursday, Elizabeth's growing anxiety came to a head. So far her father had refused to consult a physician, but was this wise? Should she take matters into her own hands? Elizabeth knew nothing of illnesses or physicians. Sickness was Anne's province.

She brought out her social ledger and paged through it. There were several she could ask about this. The most proper person to advise her would be Lady Russell, but Elizabeth discarded this idea immediately. Besides, it would be a shame to throw away a prime opportunity to flatter one of her father's influential friends. Lady

Dalrymple was the most obvious choice, but she was about to depart for London. Wealthy, old Mrs Rushworth would answer nicely as well, but she, too, was gone from Bath. That left the woman's good friend, Mrs Leighton. So Elizabeth wrote out a prettily worded request, sealed it up with a wafer, and rang for Wilson.

Presently, the sound of the doorbell and Wilson's voice caught her attention; someone had come to call. Elizabeth put aside the fashion periodical and smoothed her gown, but Wilson did not come in. Instead, she heard someone climbing the stairs in Wilson's wake. Apparently the caller was being taken up to the bedchambers! Had her father sent for a doctor after all?

Elizabeth slipped out of the drawing room and looked up at the landing above. She heard voices and shortly after a distant bell sounded to summon a servant. Seeing the footman ascend the stairs gave her an idea. She arranged to have her own message sent: Would her father's caller be pleased to grant Miss Elliot an interview at the conclusion of his business? Then Elizabeth sat down to wait.

Presently, she heard footsteps descending. Elizabeth jumped to her feet and returned to the landing. When the man came into view, she almost laughed. His ancient black frockcoat reached nearly to his knees. The man paused in his descent and looked her over. Elizabeth's mouth fell open. The man was staring at her breasts!

"Very nice," he said, nodding. "Carnelian is often orange. I prefer blood red."

Elizabeth covered the carnelian beads she wore with her hand. The man's pale eyes, alert beneath bushy brows, made her squirm.

He moistened his lips. "Carnelian is not difficult to replicate," he said. "Fortunately for you, perhaps?" With a touch of his hat he resumed his descent, leaving Elizabeth to stare after him. Was this Mr Cripplegate?

She went immediately to the drawing room windows. Below, in the street waited a hired hack. She watched as the driver's boy jumped down to open the door. Before he entered, Mr Cripplegate turned and looked up at the house. He rubbed his chin, as if thinking and through the glass his eyes met Elizabeth's. Mr Cripplegate's lips twisted into a smirk.

Elizabeth lifted her chin and returned the stare. So, which of their jewels would be missing this time? Her mind raced to catalogue the pieces not yet replaced with *paste*: the Stevenson diamonds, her mother's pearls, and–

Elizabeth's heart stood still. Surely her father would not touch the estate jewellery! She left the windows and headed for the door. This time he would answer her questions!

Elizabeth entered her father's bedchamber hard upon her knock and went straight to his enormous bed. "Hello, Father," she said, drawing forward a chair.

His eyes remained closed, but she noticed straightway that his breathing was more laboured. Elizabeth was not taken in. He was hiding, just as he had at Kellynch when things were so bad. "Who was that man who was with you just now?" she said, keeping her voice pleasant. "Is he a physician?"

Sir Walter opened his eyes. "He is my banker, dear."

"Indeed?" said Elizabeth. She handed him a glass of water and watched him take a swallow. "I find it odd that a banker would visit your bedchamber."

He returned the glass. "We need funds, daughter, for our journey to Richmond."

Elizabeth's brows arched higher. "Are things so bad that you must do business from your sickbed?"

"This isn't a sickbed. I have simply caught the cold."

"I cannot like your banker," she said. "He is so shabby and disagreeable. His name is Cripplegate, is it not?"

Sir Walter plucked at the fringe of the blanket. "One cannot be particular about the appearance of businessmen," he said. "He is an expert in the area of finance."

"Finance?" she said. "I thought you said he was an expert in jewellery. He remarked on my carnelian beads."

Sir Walter hitched himself higher on the pillow. "And I am not at all surprised, for they are uncommonly ugly."

"Might I enquire which jewels remain for me to take to Chalfont House?"

Sir Walter was convulsed by a fit of coughing. "All of them, of course! Take whatever you like!"

"I would like to wear my garnets, if you please," she said lightly. "But no, how stupid of me! They've gone missing, haven't they? Along with several other pieces."

"Stolen, more like!" said Sir Walter, around a wheeze. "Stolen by sneaking, thieving servants!" Another wracking cough assaulted him. "I have always suspected that Frenchwoman, Elise. I should have sent her packing years ago."

"Father," cried Elizabeth, "how could you!"

He fidgeted with the bedclothes. "Yes," he said, watching her, "I should have dismissed Elise. The snake! And when I am well enough–"

Wilson opened the door just then, so Elizabeth's cutting reply went unsaid.

"Your pardon, sir," said Wilson, coming to the bed, "but this has just arrived. I had to sign for it."

Sir Walter lifted the letter from the silver tray and glanced at the sender's address. "Good heavens," he said, wrinkling his nose, "you disturb my peace for this?" He cast the letter aside.

"Will there be an answer, sir?"

"No, Wilson. That will be all." As the door closed, Sir Walter motioned to Elizabeth. "Throw it into the fire."

"But Father," she said, "you haven't opened–"

"I said, throw it into the fire."

Elizabeth took up the letter. "If this is a tradesman's bill, shouldn't it be sent to Mr Shepherd?"

"I know what it is: a piece of high-handed insolence!"

She glanced at the letter and then at her father. "But–"

"Kindly do as you are bid!"

Elizabeth obeyed, but slowly. The letter curled as it burned.

Sir Walter's breathing became laboured again; his face was ashen. "You may leave me now," he said.

Elizabeth slowly descended to the drawing room. There was nothing to be done but wait for Mrs Leighton's reply, and who knew how long that would take? Presently there came the encouraging sound of a carriage pulling up before the house. In a moment, Elizabeth was at the window. Her smile faded when she saw Lady Russell emerge.

She *would* come today. Indeed, her godmother's visits were becoming more and more frequent. Elizabeth had assured her that her father had merely caught the cold, but would she listen? True to her nature, Lady Russell must pry; and so these visits of mercy must be graciously endured.

No sooner had Elizabeth withdrawn from the window than her ladyship swept into the drawing room. She waved Wilson aside. "Elizabeth," she said without preamble, "how is he?"

"Well enough, or so he claims. Good morning, Lady Russell. Would you care to sit down?" Elizabeth suppressed a smile of triumph; it was not often she caught her stuffy godmother in a breach of manners.

But her shaft missed its mark, for Lady Russell simply brushed the remark aside. "He is not well enough to come down from his bedchamber, I see. Why is that?" Fixing her gaze on Elizabeth she added, "I hope he does not insist upon taking that ridiculous trip to Chalfort House."

"It is his expressed intention to do so, ma'am."

"Or is it yours? He must not sacrifice his health to gratify your vanity, Elizabeth."

Elizabeth bristled. "He was well enough to receive a man of business, ma'am."

Lady Russell considered this. "A good sign," she said. "Yes, a very good sign. Nevertheless, he should consult a physician. Have you spoken to him about this?"

Elizabeth explained about the letter to Mrs Leighton. This did not sit well with Lady Russell.

"I take it that your answer is no," she interrupted. "Therefore, I shall see to it myself!" She wheeled and left the room.

"But–", said Elizabeth, following.

"If he was well enough to see a man of business," said Lady Russell, ascending the stairs, "he is well enough to see me. Wilson," she said over her shoulder, "I am going up to see Sir Walter. You may announce me."

In the end, there was nothing for it but to send the foot-boy to fetch Lady Russell's own physician. Sir Walter's objections were entirely overruled, thanks to her ladyship's high-handed manner.

"My dear Sir Walter," said Lady Russell later, as she brought Mr Hargrave to his bedside, "it is crucial to nip these trifling ailments in the bud, for at our age we must take care! Lingering illnesses can so easily rob one of vitality and good looks!"

Sir Walter's eyes grew large. He submitted to his examination without complaint.

Mr Hargrave's report was anything but encouraging. Sir Walter was in no immediate danger, but he must observe a month's rest with no outings of any kind. Elizabeth knew her father would comply, thanks to Lady Russell's waspish comment about losing his looks!

Dinner that night was a melancholy affair. Elizabeth rotated the stem of her wine glass, watching the light from the candelabrum play along the surface of the cut crystal. Such a wondrous invitation, and she must give it up on account of a trifling cold!

She tossed her napkin onto the table and pushed back the chair. Her father *would* choose this week to become ill! And there was choice involved, of that she was certain. His might be feeling poorly, but he wasn't as ill as he claimed. He was hiding. Those dreadful letters she'd seen, the business with Mr Cripplegate, and the letter he'd burned today all confirmed it. But would he disregard Mr Hargrave's advice about the need to rest?

It was so miserably unfair, for Lady Claverling's parties drew all of London to Richmond—a perfect opportunity to mingle with the *ton*. If he chose to remain in Bath, *she* would be the one to pay the price! Not even Lady Russell could stand in his stead, for she had not been invited. Besides, Elizabeth would rather die than go to Chalfort House with Lady Russell.

The drawing room was empty, as usual. Elizabeth signed the foot-boy to build up the fire and then dismissed him. It was to be another solitary evening. Elizabeth took up the newspaper, then cast it aside, prey to uneasiness. How could her father be so heartless? Had he forgotten her situation? Did he understand nothing of what the coming birthday would mean?

But it had been this way for some time. Season after season, Elizabeth had smilingly attended dinners and balls and card parties on his arm—all for nothing! Oh, there had been suitors, but her father had always found a flaw. His standards were impossible!

Elizabeth took a turn about the drawing room. The longer she paced, the angrier she became. "Father shall go to Richmond, recovered or no! He owes it to me!" She spoke aloud—why not? There was no one to hear.

But she knew that this could never be. One did not cart an ill person to a house party, any more than one could show up alone and unattended.

Alone and unattended—just as she was this evening. Elizabeth wheeled and came back to the fireplace. She was not a child. Must she wait upon her father's convenience for everything she did? Would it be such a crime to travel to Richmond without him? How delicious it would be to be free and independent with no more catering to his idiotic whims!

Because there was nothing else to do, Elizabeth allowed her misery free rein. Surprisingly, it was ideas, not tears, which came rapidly. She could travel with Elise, claiming that her father had planned to meet her at Chalfort House. Since most of the guests would be strangers, who would guess the truth? And when Sir Walter never showed up, why, what could she do?

A letter! She would send a letter, as if from her father, informing her of his sudden illness and instructing her to wait for a coach to fetch her home. It would be so wonderfully simple!

Now, what to do with him while she was away? Her father's friends would think her an inhuman monster if she left him alone. What a shame that Anne was not in Bath. It would be the most natural thing in the world to leave their ill father in her care. And then it occurred to her: Anne was not Sir Walter's *only* daughter.

Elizabeth struck her hands together. Mary! Mary could jolly well come to Bath and play nursemaid! Yes, it was high time Mary did her share as dutiful daughter! And was she not an excellent nurse? To hear Mary talk, one would think she single-handedly brought Louisa Musgrove back from the dead!

Elizabeth's heart was hammering; she could scarcely breathe as thoughts crowded her mind. There would be trouble at the end of it, but did this matter? Her father would be desperate to escape the gossip. He would send a post-chaise to bring her home, and no one would be the wiser. And if by that time she had formed an eligible alliance…

Elizabeth pressed her palms together, and then realized that her eyes were closed. A smile swept across her face. Why was she praying? Elizabeth hadn't prayed in years, and she was not about to begin now. After all, one could hardly pray for a lie! But this daring plan was simply too perfect. Indeed, she could not get it out of her mind! She walked restlessly about the drawing room.

All at once, she made her choice and flung herself into the chair before the escritoire. To reach Mary in time, the letter would need to be sent tonight by express. And once her plan was set into motion, there would be no drawing back. Elizabeth noted that her hands did not tremble as she pulled forward a sheet of stationery. She took up the pen and dipped it into the inkpot.

"No, my dear Mary," she said, as she waited for the pen to mend. "For too long you have paraded your precedence over me. Now, it is time to pay!"

~4~
It's Always Something

Friday morning found Charles Musgrove's gig bowling along toward Crewkherne. The tranquil beauty of the rolling patchwork fields, crisscrossed as they were by tree-dotted hedgerows and small woods, were a wonder to behold. "Here now, Benwick, that's very nice," he said, as his soon-to-be brother-in-law navigated a bend in the road. "And you said you were a bad driver."

"It requires no special skill to drive a horse as well trained as this," said Captain Benwick, narrowly avoiding the ditch. "Wentworth once told me I'm nothing but a whipster, which I perceive is not a compliment."

"A whipster! That's very bad of him. Wentworth's a capital fellow and all, but lord, he's one to talk! He's been at sea all his life; what does he know?"

"Whereas you have lived with horses all of yours."

Charles stretched a leg. "Well, to be sure. Was thrown into the saddle when I was Little Walter's age. Eh, half a moment, Benwick," he said, catching sight of a farmer's dwelling. "There's Jonas Elkins. Must have a word with the old fellow, you know."

He took the reins from Benwick and drew up in front of the house.

"You'll make an excellent squire, Musgrove," said Benwick later, after Charles had climbed back into the gig. "And this is fine country." He gave him a sidelong glance. "How much of this belongs to your family, by-the-bye?"

Charles shrugged. "All of it, I suppose."

"All of it," Benwick repeated. "Do you mean everything I can see, all this land? And none of it entailed away?"

"Of course not."

"Why, Musgrove," said Benwick, a slow smile playing at the corners of his mouth, "you are a wealthy man."

"Not according to my wife. Mary claims I am unable to support her in the manner she deserves. While the curst truth is–" Charles made a futile gesture. "The curst truth is, all Mary can see is the money, or rather the lack of it. She sees no value in the land. It's nonsensical, but–"

Charles attempted to shrug it off, but the presence of a sympathetic listener proved to be too much. "Burn it, the way she carries on about Henrietta marrying Charles Hayter, as though my sister were making the worst mistake of her life! She refuses to see that once he inherits Winthrop, Hayter will be very well off. Two hundred and fifty acres, besides the farm near Taunton. Some of the best land in the country. And she counts that as nothing!"

Benwick was smiling. "The truth is, Musgrove, you are far and away Sir Walter Elliot's superior. Or, at least, your children will be, when it comes time to inherit."

Charles gave a snort. "The Great Man leaves behind only his exalted name...and his curst pile of debts."

"Those pass to the cousin, I believe, along with the dignities of the estate."

Charles laughed. "He is well-served, then! I wish him joy of them, for they are considerable!"

The two drove for a mile or so before Charles recalled the purpose of their drive. "Here," he said, passing the reins back to Benwick, "you're neglecting your lesson." The horse dropped to a walk.

"You have not asked what I will teach you in return."

Charles looked at him. "Some obscure poetical quotation, no doubt."

"No, I had something quite different in mind. Something more to your taste." Benwick gave him an appraising look. "Actually you could begin now, as the wearing of it takes some getting used to."

"The wearing of it? The wearing of what?"

"We'll need to use a corner in one of the barns, if it's not inconvenient," Benwick continued. "Also, do you happen to have any mallows lying about? And some sort of animal, such as a hog, that we can bring in afterward to clean up the mess?"

"A hog!" cried Charles. "You're going to teach me how to ride a hog?"

"How to butcher one, more like," said Benwick. "Here." He returned the reins and reached behind the seat. "This sort of lesson can be rather untidy, as one must have something to hack up. Hence, the mallows. I thought some animal could eat the remains of–"

"My word!" Charles cried, as Benwick brought out a narrow canvas-wrapped bundle. The clank of metal against metal left no doubt as to the contents.

"I wore one while travelling, you know," said Benwick. "And I brought along my spare for you to use. While the sun shines, we ride and shoot–and I shoot rather worse than I drive, by the bye. And when it rains, we get in a little practice with the swords. Pull up, and I'll show you how to fasten the belt."

"Sword-fighting!" Charles could hardly contain his delight. "My dear Benwick! Anything you like, anything at all! Shooting, riding, you name it! I am entirely at your disposal! Let Mary and Louisa go to Mother's plaguey luncheon! We shall fight with swords in the barn!"

"And afterward," Charles continued, once the sword belt was in place, "I'll break open a cask of scrumpy. Er, that's hard cider, you know. Made from our own apples. A Musgrove specialty."

"Just so long as it is after the lesson, not before. Now then," said Benwick, taking up the reins once again, "what is it I say to Belle? Walk on?"

"Walk on? I should say not! I've a lesson waiting!" Charles reached behind. "In cases like these," he announced, "one uses this!" And without bothering to give Captain Benwick fair warning, Charles cracked the whip above Belle's head. She lunged forward and galloped full-tilt down the rutted country road.

But when Charles and Captain Benwick drove into the yard, they found a saddled horse in front of the cottage. At the door stood the rider and Mary, who was signing for a letter. "There you are, Charles," she called. "Be a dear and pay this man."

Before Charles could reach her, she had the packet open. "It's from Elizabeth," she said, squinting at the paper. It took Mary a few moments to digest the contents. Then she began to shriek.

~ ~ ~ ~ ~ ~ ~ & ~ ~ ~ ~ ~ ~ ~

The two men huddled over the letter. "Well?" demanded Mary. "What's to stop us from leaving now?"

Charles did not trust himself to speak. Mary noticed this; her face crumpled. "Charles Musgrove," she wailed, dabbing at her eyes with a handkerchief, "you are the greatest beast in nature!"

Charles felt himself weaken; he mustn't lose his resolve! In his hand was Elizabeth's summons, and a pretty position it had put him in! With his sister's wedding tomorrow and his wife accusing him of being a monster, he knew himself to be cursed on every hand!

Out of the corner of his eye, he saw Louisa touch Benwick's arm, but he could not catch her whispered comment. He did, however, hear Benwick's reply: "That will be for Musgrove to decide."

And then Benwick waited, looking at him in a solemn, expectant way that unnerved him. Clearly, the man was expecting him to take charge of the situation. But how?

Charles returned to studying the letter. There was something about it that wasn't quite right, but what? For the life of him, he couldn't make it out.

Mary, meanwhile, continued to sob. "He's dying! My father's dying! I just know he is!" she howled from behind her handkerchief.

Louisa placed a hand on Mary's shoulder. "Elizabeth does not say his condition is hopeless, or even serious."

Charles threw Louisa a grateful look. "I'm curst if I know what Elizabeth means," he said.

"You know how Elizabeth is," said Mary. "She must always be gracious and condescending and frightfully snubbing, no matter what the circumstance!"

"Yes, but in a moment of crisis, one tends to forget one's affectations." Captain Benwick was looking over Charles' shoulder now. "When my parents became ill," he said, "and when it was clear that they would not recover, the message was very unlike this."

"What does that signify?" said Mary. "I wish to go to Bath! Why are we delaying?" She threw off Louisa's hand. "I'm not over-reacting, Louisa! My father is dying! And he is asking for *me*!"

"He isn't dying, Mary. And we are not going to Bath." Charles braced himself for the onslaught he knew would come. He thrust out his chin, as if to ward off Mary's wrath. "Tomorrow is Henrietta's wedding day," he said, more firmly. "I will not slight my sister to gratify a whim of your father's!"

"A whim?" Mary sputtered. "How can you!"

Charles stood his ground. "You are a Musgrove, Mary. Your place is here with your sister Henrietta. It was so when Louisa was injured at Lyme, and it is so now." He paused to draw a breath. "We will leave for Bath on Monday morning. Though how I'm to arrange transportation with the hullabaloo of the wedding..."

"I am willing to take her to Bath, Charles," said Benwick. "If we leave at first light tomorrow, I should be able to return before midnight. You may join her in Bath when you are able."

Mary's head came up. "Yes!" she cried. "That's it! I shall travel with Captain Benwick!"

"But…" said Louisa. "Won't that be dangerous? To travel by night?"

"Nonsense! We shall travel during the day," said Mary. "Oh, I suppose you mean Captain Benwick's trip home. I daresay he'll be fine. Who would rob him? Now that I think on it," she added, "since we're taking the coach, there will be room for several trunks!"

Louisa and Benwick exchanged a look, and Charles realized that he was no better off than when he began.

~ ~ ~ ~ ~ ~ ~ & ~ ~ ~ ~ ~ ~ ~

On Saturday morning, Elizabeth was up at first light from both necessity and the state of her nerves. Everything depended upon how she handled her father. She could not order a travelling coach, but he could—indeed, he already had—and what could be easier than to arrange a change of destination? Nevertheless, it was a tricky bit of business. Elizabeth's conscience was already smarting under the lies she must tell.

They weren't lies exactly, she reasoned, as she went over the plan. Her most pressing worry was whether she could keep the various stories straight. She would simply be visiting a friend. Surely there was nothing wrong with that.

From her pocket came Miss Bingley's letter. Elizabeth had to smile at her own ingenuity. What could be better than to hear from a friend at an opportune time? Instructing Elise to wait, she collected her things and left her bedchamber.

It so happened that she reached the landing just as the foot-boy came up from the kitchen with Sir Walter's breakfast tray. She took it from him. She would deliver it herself and inform him of her departure. She went along the corridor and rapped on his door. Fortunately, he was awake. Ignoring his protests, she proceeded to unload the breakfast things. Placing his teacup on a small table beside the bed, she brought the pot and filled it.

"There is something I've been meaning to discuss with you, Father." She took up her own cup and settled into the nearby chair. "Are you feeling well enough for conversation this morning?"

"Well enough? Of course I am well enough." He gave her a scowling look. "If I appear unwell, it is because I am unused to being accosted at this ungodly hour!"

"Ah, but I am compelled by necessity. I have been invited to visit a friend of mine, Miss Caroline Bingley. You remember Caroline Bingley, do you not?"

"Bingley?" Sir Walter puffed out his cheeks. "I do not recall any Bingley." He took a cautious sip of tea.

"We have met the Bingleys during our visits to London. Caroline's sister is married to Mr Hurst. Surely you remember Mr Hurst?"

"Bingley? Hurst?" Sir Walter brought out his handkerchief. "Bah! Mushrooms, all of them! *Parvenu*! Pigs in clover!"

Elizabeth set her cup in its saucer and waited.

"Guttersnipes!" he continued gleefully, beating the bedclothes with one hand. "Upstarts! Vulgarians!"

"Miss Bingley's brother has taken an estate in Hertfordshire," Elizabeth said. "Or is it Derbyshire? Bah, it makes no difference; I am not going to that place. Miss Bingley lives in Grosvenor Square." She paused to allow the effect of this prestigious address to sink in.

Sir Walter's brows went up. "Good gracious, Elizabeth, you cannot mean that frightful, over-dressed creature! A jeweller parading his wares could hardly be worse!"

Elizabeth had to smile at this home assessment. "Dear Caroline does tend to over-do a little."

"And she is hideously ill-favoured, besides!"

"And who taught me the advantages of being seen with such a woman? For by comparison..."

"Yes, well...enough of that," he said.

"Caroline's invitation came last week. Surely you remember me mentioning it." She had done no such thing, of course. Let him think he was losing his memory! "And," she continued, "because we have already arranged–and paid for–the travelling coach, I think it best that I make use of it today."

Sir Walter lowered his cup. "Make use of what today?"

"The coach. To visit Caroline Bingley in Grosvenor Square."

"Ah, but I sent word yesterday evening," he said. "The coach will not come."

Elizabeth had intercepted the message before it went out. "I do not know about that," she said. "But the coach is here now, and I intend to make use of it."

"Do you mean alone?" Sir Walter's face grew red. "Nonsense!"

"Now, Father..." Elizabeth laid a hand on his arm. "Remember what the physician said."

"Don't you 'Now, Father' me, miss!" he said, drawing back. "I am not a child to be coddled! Or hoaxed!"

Elizabeth met his scowl evenly. "Nor am I." She lifted her teacup and said serenely, "Richmond is not so far; Miss Bingley and I will attend my Lady Claverling's rout-party on Tuesday night. All of London will come, of course. They always do. Except for you and I, who have never before been invited."

Sir Walter's complexion paled; he now looked every bit the invalid.

"I understand Lord Burnham will be there," continued Elizabeth. "He lost his wife last winter, poor dear. Perhaps by now he is wishful to find another?" She set down her cup and saucer.

"Not alone!" said Sir Walter. "Elizabeth, you shall not travel to London alone!"

"Of course not. I shall have Elise and old John with me. And did you not engage a reputable coach for us?"

"It will not do!"

Elizabeth rose from the chair. "I am very much afraid it will have to do, Father. Mary will arrive by..." She hesitated. When would her sister arrive? Would she even come at all? It could not be helped. "Mary will arrive by tomorrow night to look after you."

"Mary?" he cried. "What do I want with Mary?"

"You were enquiring about her just the other day, don't you recall? I wrote and invited her to come. She will keep you well entertained with all the news of Uppercross, I am sure. And I shall return from Caroline's within the week."

"Elizabeth! You may not go!"

"I have no choice, Father," she said, "and neither do you." Her voice became sharp. "Before the spring is gone I shall have another birthday. I've not much time to find a husband. And my new clothing, which was such an extravagance," her voice now shook, "will be outdated by summer's end. I cannot wait for another opportunity like this one."

"Opportunity?" he cried. "You call this an opportunity?"

"I am leaving now," said Elizabeth, "so I must bid you *adieu.* Give my love to Mary."

Sir Walter set the bell pealing for Roberts; Elizabeth nearly collided with him in the corridor.

"Father's in a temper, Roberts. Best not to mind what he says. Come, Elise," she called, and ran down the two flights of stairs to the waiting coach.

~ ~ ~ ~ ~ ~ ~ & ~ ~ ~ ~ ~ ~ ~

Some hours after sunrise, the Musgrove's travelling coach rolled into the yard of an inn—which one Captain Benwick neither knew nor cared. His limbs were stiff from sitting so long. His head ached as well. Companionable conversation was one thing, but Mary Musgrove exceeded all bounds! Her tongue had been running on wheels since they had left Uppercross nearly four hours ago. She did not address the young maid who travelled with her. No, she must converse with him! The inn was a busy place. Coaches rolled in and out, baggage cluttered the entrance, and servants bustled about. The innkeeper came onto the porch to greet them and Mary Musgrove began talking all over again.

Benwick supposed it was the result of nerves; surely she was anxious about her father. But it occurred to him that she was more excited than worried. Why else had she brought two trunks filled with clothes, including, according to Louisa, her favourite ball gown?

Captain Benwick sighed heavily. He'd seen how much help Mary had been while Louisa was convalescing. She'd even indulged in a little sea bathing—in November! This trip to Bath would be more of the same. After all, hovering over a sick bed needn't occupy every hour of the day. One could pace anxiously before the door, hold whispered consultation with the doctor, and then nip off for a bit of dancing in the evening hours and be home in time for a bedside breakfast with the sufferer!

Fortunately, Captain Benwick would immediately return to Uppercross to fetch Charles Musgrove. His wife obviously needed watching.

~ ~ ~ ~ ~ ~ ~ & ~ ~ ~ ~ ~ ~ ~

It cost Elizabeth something to travel in a hired coach without a crest emblazoned on the door to distinguish it above the others, but she had risen to the occasion. Last night she had rummaged through the storage room upstairs; the results of her hunt rested snugly in the large basket on her lap. She knew that eventually the coach would stop to change horses; then she would have a part to play. A ruffled cap, left at Camden Place by Mary, was brought out first. Mary always wore her caps well back on her head, so as not to hide her curls, but Elizabeth pulled it firmly down. This cap did not have ear covers and a tie-string, like old Mrs Musgrove's, which was a pity. Still, Elizabeth pushed every one of her auburn curls beneath it. When she put on an old hat of Anne's, the most beautiful woman in Bath disappeared.

A pair of ancient black gloves came next. She removed the fingertips with scissors, taking care to make the cuts jagged. She arranged a fringed dresser scarf about her shoulders to hide the elegant neckline of her dark gown. The last item pleased Elizabeth the most: her father's spectacles. With these positioned on the bridge of her nose, Elizabeth could travel through every provincial town in the kingdom and change horses at every wretched coaching inn. No one would pay the least attention to a poor old maid. She had even thought to bring her mother's little Testament to place beside her plate while she took her meals.

Elise watched the masquerade with narrowed eyes. Naturally, Elise would disapprove; she disapproved of everything Elizabeth did. Always, she must compare Elizabeth to her mother. But, Elizabeth reasoned, her mother had been rich. She had married after her first season. What did she know of trouble?

The coach slowed its pace. Elizabeth let down the window to better see the buildings. The name *Standen Arms* was written on the inn. She checked the map and smiled. She was making excellent time. Richmond would be gained by nightfall. At that time, she would throw off her disguise and enter Lord and Lady Claverling's house with her travelling dress well hidden beneath a stylish evening cloak.

For the first time, Elizabeth dared to indulge in hope. It was within her grasp! There was nothing that could stop her now!

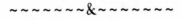

The Thames was crossed, the phaeton gathered speed, and soon the bustle of London was left behind. Its lone occupant cast a fleeting glance at the river before turning back to the papers in his hand. The breeze ruffled his hair, but he paid it no mind. This was a glorious day for a drive, yet today his coachman held the reins, not he. There was business to be done.

This day and every other! Admiral McGillvary searched through the stack for a referenced page, muttering an oath. He could appre-

ciate Cockburn's talent on the quarterdeck, but must he come to
Town this particular week? It was as bad as being the man's lackey,
the way he was at the beck and call of the Admiralty Office. His
summons to Whitehall was a case in point. Official business had
occupied only a fraction of his time. McGillvary was as fond of
society as any man, but spending night after night in card and supper
rooms doing the polite to men who were the dullest bores in Christ-
endom was too much! And now he was bound to Richmond to do
more of the same. Yet, he could hardly complain, since the invitation had been of his own contriving.

At length, he returned the pages to the cloth packet, tied it firmly
closed, and thrust the whole into the leather satchel at his feet. Curse
Whitehall and its deadlines! Within the hour he would be at his
destination, and he intended to enjoy himself. He stretched a leg and
took in the beauties of the spring afternoon. Enormous trees hung
over a section of the road, their overarching branches casting patterns over the road. The air was very warm for the time of year–
almost Mediterranean. *Quite perfect for a moonlit stroll through my Lady
Claverling's famous gardens.*

This style of thinking was more to McGillvary's taste; the lines
about his mouth relaxed into a smile. The love of the chase had
always captivated him. Indeed, now that Napoleon's Navy had been
disabled, there was not much to fire the imagination...save the
elusive Miss Elliot.

Yes, the lovely Elizabeth was a prize worth pursuing. Even her
name was intriguing. No, he had not forgotten her beautiful eyes--
they were amber, were they not?–and her witty, almost caustic
replies. Delightful! She had not known who he was, and she had not
cared! Tonight, he knew, they would meet at last, for he had been
privy to my Lady Claverling's guest list. What a delight to see her
name written there!

McGillvary gave himself over to speculation. Should Lady
Claverling make the introduction, or should he seek out someone
else? Should he request her as his dinner partner, or should they
meet within the figure of the dance? And should he wear the uniform? Very well did McGillvary know its drawing power with
women. He suffered a check here, for Miss Elliot had not been
impressed at the concert, nor had she attended the dinner he'd given
for Wentworth.

She might be made to regret that, he thought, smiling a little. Yes,
she deserved to be punished.

And so it was that the glorious sunlight, the sparkling river, and even the commotion at the Admiralty Office were all forgotten as Patrick McGillvary lost himself in laying plans for what promised to be a most fascinating and diverting game of chase.

~ ~ ~ ~ ~ ~ ~ & ~ ~ ~ ~ ~ ~ ~

Mary arrived at Camden Place shortly before sundown. It was vexing, after so much trouble, to be deprived of her role as comforter and companion. Sir Walter was sleeping soundly and was not to be disturbed. At least, that was what Wilson said. His man Roberts was even less helpful. He could not recall Sir Walter asking for his youngest daughter, and at no time had he been delirious with fever. However, Roberts was pleased to tell her that Sir Walter had made improvement today. Just this morning, he left his bedchamber for the first time in nearly a week.

Roberts knew nothing about Elizabeth's whereabouts, but Wilson did. Miss Elliot had gone to London in the company of Elise and John. When she planned to return, he could not say.

So, Mary was left in the drawing room with nothing to do but watch the occasional carriage pass by. Soon, however, things began to look up. Wilson came in to say that a Mr Savoy was here, sent by Mrs Leighton of Torridon House. Wilson pronounced Mrs Leighton's name with careful emphasis, Mary noted. Furthermore, Mr Savoy's calling card was rather nice. It was ornamented with an edging of gilt. She agreed to see him.

The sandy-haired man who came in was certainly unlike any medical practitioner Mary had ever met. For one thing, he was dressed in extremely good taste, not at all like the sombre Mr Robinson at home. Furthermore, his manners were just what they should be, a nice blend of competence and deference. He came forward and made a polite little bow.

"Good evening, Mr Savoy," said Mary, in her grandest manner. "I am Mrs Musgrove, Sir Walter's daughter. Won't you please sit down?"

Naturally, he asked the sort of questions physicians ask but in a charming way. Mary hastened to correct him with quite a friendly smile. "My father is never ill, Mr Savoy."

Mr Savoy returned the smile. "I beg your pardon. Mrs Leighton was under the impression that he came to Bath for reasons of health.

The healing waters of our nurturing font draw many illustrious persons."

"I am certain that they do," said Mary, "but it is not so with Father. He removed to Bath as a means of retrenchment. Although," she added, "it was most unnecessary. He's been in fine spirits ever since he arrived."

"Retrenchment?" Mr Savoy leaned forward. "Has your father financial worries, then?"

"Good gracious, no! Those troubles are a thing of the past. My father," she added impressively, "is quite well-to-do."

"But has he had signs of anxiousness, Mrs Musgrove? Pains of the stomach? Tremblings and fits of nervousness? Sleepless nights?"

"Father? Goodness, I suppose he must have suffered some of those things, although no one has told me. My father has the Elliot constitution."

"And how does your father do this evening? Will it be permissible for me to see him?"

Here Mary hesitated. Her father wouldn't like it, but she could hardly offend a man sent by the august Mrs Leighton. She decided to risk it. "I'll take you up directly," she said, rising from her chair, "but I should warn you, he will be grouchy. I daresay you won't mind that."

"No, indeed, Mrs Musgrove. I never mind that."

~ ~ ~ ~ ~ ~ ~ & ~ ~ ~ ~ ~ ~ ~

As the Wentworth's hired chaise entered Bath, the street lamps were being lit. This, then, was the end of their adventure. The journey to Bath had taken hours longer than Captain Wentworth had planned; he must leave for London almost immediately. Anne sat very close beside him, holding his hand in both of hers. Every moment with him was precious.

The nearer they came to Gay Street, the more serious he became. He spoke of many things, as if he were on one of his ships and she was his second-in-command. "As soon as you feel up to it, you must take possession of the house," he told her.

"As soon as I am—Frederick!" Anne smiled up at him. "I am not such a poor creature!"

"You've only to send a note round and McGillvary—or his man of business—will come with the keys. I've already signed the lease.

The servants are to remain. If anything about the house isn't to your liking, Anne, you must speak up. McGillvary will set things right."

"I liked the house very well when we went through it," she said, nestling her head against his shoulder.

"Ah, but the faults of a place don't appear until after the ink is dry on the lease!"

Anne gave his hand a squeeze. "I shall be fine, Frederick. In any case, I might wait to settle in until after you return. I'm sure I'll be very comfortable with your sister and Admiral Croft."

He shrugged. "If you fall out, there's always your father's...or Lady Russell's." She threw him a swift look. His eyes were dancing.

"I have no intention of falling out...with anyone!"

"Not even with Elizabeth?"

"Especially not with Elizabeth! I suppose I shall have to call at Father's eventually..."

"Oh, surely not," he said. "We'll send round a bottle of wine at Christmastime and..."

Anne had to laugh; what notions he had! "It's facing Lady Russell that will cause the most difficulty," she confessed. "Our departure spoiled so many of her plans, but that could not be helped. And besides, I do not care!"

"That's the spirit!"

The coach turned a corner, and Captain Wentworth peered out of the window. "And here we are," he said. "Gay Street."

"Oh, Frederick," said Anne. How she wished he hadn't been ordered to London. Why he felt the need to remain in the Navy made no sense to her, but it was a wife's part to be supportive of her husband's endeavours. She might as well begin now. "I will miss you," she said softly. "You have no idea how much."

~ ~ ~ ~ ~ ~ ~ & ~ ~ ~ ~ ~ ~ ~

"Now then, Sir Walter, how have we been feeling lately?" Mr Savoy came to Sir Walter's bedside and placed the branch of candles on the table. "Might I say, your daughter is a charming woman."

"That is debatable."

"She is most concerned about your recovery."

"I do not see why she should be." Sir Walter eyes followed Mr Savoy's movements. "Have you daughters?" he said. "Mine are the veriest plague! Ungrateful, demanding, scheming vixens, all of them!"

Mr Savoy placed a hand on Sir Walter's brow. "It is in the nature of women to coddle and cosset us," he said.

"And to plague us to death."

"And that, too," said Mr Savoy. "As for myself, since you ask, I have found daughters to be extremely expensive." He paused, his pale eyes intent on Sir Walter's face.

"Hah! Do I not know it."

"The demands for new finery, for society and entertainments," Mr Savoy felt Sir Walter's wrist for a pulse. "Why, there seems to be no end to it. But daughters offer much in return. They are charming and companionable."

"I suppose they can be," grumbled Sir Walter. "But mine...why you would not believe it if I told you! If only Hargrave had not confined me to this bed–"

"Matthias Hargrave? Has he advised a stringent convalescence?"

"Oh, you would not believe the strictures he has imposed! No society whatsoever–for an entire month! Not so much as a single card party." Sir Walter pursed up his lips before adding, "He insists that I have a complete rest. It is cruel, too cruel!"

"Indeed, I quite agree."

"You do?" Sir Walter's eyes popped open. "And my youngest daughter, whom you have met already, has come to Bath to make certain I am kept confined!"

"A prisoner of your daughters and of your physician." Mr Savoy shook his head. "Sir Walter, that is criminal. You deserve better, sir."

"Eh?" Sir Walter sat up straighter.

Mr Savoy cast his eyes to the ceiling. "How can you be free to regain your health under such philistine conditions?"

"How indeed? That is exactly what I have been asking myself."

Mr Savoy drew nearer. "But you need not be a prisoner, good sir. You are not ill, not truly. You simply need care, very special care, while you regain your robustness." Mr Savoy brought a hand to his chest. "Your spirit needs to be free to soar. When that happens, your body will likewise follow. You will be restored to complete and vigorous health."

"Indeed, Mr Savoy," said Sir Walter, "you have no idea how shabbily I have been treated by my family."

"Then I suggest that you take matters into your own hands. You need not remain here against your will. You are the master of your fate." Mr Savoy smiled more broadly. "There are alternatives..."

~5~
Sundown's Shadows

The sun's last rays glittered on the Thames, tinting the clouds pink against a sky of gray. The hired coach came past the gates and ascended the gentle rise on which Chalfort House was situated. Elizabeth gazed at the fine Stuart mansion with its rows of tall, many-paned windows, now lit against the gloom.

The coach rumbled to a halt, and the main door of the house opened. Light spilled onto the pavement, and servants emerged to offer assistance. Elizabeth gathered her courage and alighted. She felt now very small and meek and very much alone. Elise and old John were taken away to the servant's entrance. Elizabeth followed the butler through a vast entrance hall and into a nearby sitting room, where she was instructed to wait.

He did not immediately return. Elizabeth stood alone, shivering, though a cheerful fire crackled on the hearth. A pair of damask-covered sofas invited her to sit, but Elizabeth remained where she was; not even for a moment did she dare let down her guard. She studied her reflection in the mirror over the mantelpiece. Her dark gown was presentable, and Elise had tidied her hair. Why then did she feel as if she was standing in her under dress, alone and vulnerable?

Again she went over the speech she'd prepared. But it was no good—surely her ruse wouldn't deceive a child! And yet, what else could she do?

Brisk footsteps sounded in the entrance hall. Shortly after, Elizabeth could make out a woman's voice and the butler's reply. And then she heard words. "I'll see her myself."

Elizabeth assumed a contemplative pose.

"Miss Elly?" A slender white-haired woman in evening attire came into the room. "That is your name, is it not? Robbins was unsure." The woman's voice was decidedly musical. "I am Lady Claverling."

Elizabeth's heart hammered against her ribs. Lady Claverling was more beautiful–and more self-assured–than she expected. There was nothing of the grandmother about this woman. Her white evening gown was cut in the latest mode; a Grecian scarf hung carelessly at her elbows. Her magnificent pearl and cameo necklace was beyond compare.

"My Lady Claverling, good evening." Elizabeth made her curtsey and found her voice. "I am Miss Elliot."

"Miss ... Elliot. My dear, have you been travelling all this day? From your home in–?"

"I have come from Bath, milady."

"Is that so?" Lady Claverling looked her over. A frown was in her eyes. "Robbins," she called sharply. Immediately the butler came in. "I would like to see Gardiner's list," she said.

Elizabeth gathered her courage. It was time to put her plan into action, but this was more difficult than she'd expected. "I wonder if a message might be conveyed to my father, milady?" she said. "To inform him of my arrival."

Lady Claverling's frown deepened. "Your father?"

"Sir Walter Elliot. He will be relieved to know that I have arrived safely."

There was a pause. "My dear, forgive me," said Lady Claverling. "I'm afraid I do not comprehend your meaning."

"He is not here?"

"Should he be?"

"But–he was to arrive at midday! That is what he said. I–"

Lady Claverling's brows shot upward.

Elizabeth turned away. "I knew this would not work; did I not tell him so?" There was no need to feign anxiety now. Her handker-chief was at the ready, though her eyes were dry. "Is it possible for a man to be sensible when making plans? Indeed, I think it is too much to ask!" Elizabeth raised her eyes to Lady Claverling's face. "And what must you think of me, to arrive with only my maid and an elderly manservant?" This, at least, was an honest question.

Robbins came in with a paper which Lady Claverling took from him. "What did you say your name was? Ah yes, Elliot." She studied the paper for some time. "Robbins," she said slowly, "have someone direct Miss Elliot to her room. And set another place at dinner."

Elizabeth looked at Lady Claverling with some anxiety, her cheeks hot with shame. "Perhaps it will be best if I retire early?" she said impulsively. "My father is not here; it would not be right to trespass upon your hospitality."

Lady Claverling looked surprised. "My dear, such a mishap can happen to anyone. Indeed, considering the ramshackle nature of the plan, it was almost inevitable. You will meet up with him in the morning, no doubt." She smiled slightly. "And you are very right. Men are perfectly impossible."

Elizabeth was left alone to wait. Several people passed through the entrance hall, but no one came in.

"Admiral!" Lady Claverling's voice called. "I am in a bit of a quandary, I fear. I need your sharp wits and keen mind."

Elizabeth did not mean to eavesdrop, but the enormous hall carried Lady Claverling's voice perfectly. "My dear, a young woman has just arrived," Elizabeth heard her say. "For the life of me, I have no idea who she is. She says her name is Elliot, but I recall neither the name nor the face."

Elizabeth's eyes grew wide. She remained very still, scarcely daring to breathe.

"Gardiner has her listed for the White Chintz Room, so she must have received an invitation. Do you know anyone by that name?"

The man said something Elizabeth could not catch. She moved nearer to the doorway to listen.

"She lives in Bath, and she is very lovely. And she is unmarried." Lady Claverling gave a fairy laugh. "If anyone would know her, it would be you."

"If her surname is Elliot," said the man, "then I believe her Christian name is Elizabeth."

"How clever you are! Elizabeth. I must say, I am agreeably surprised in her."

"And is she to be my dinner-partner, O most excellent of hostesses?"

"Not at all. She will dine in her bedchamber. She is fatigued from her journey."

"Fatigued?"

"Yes, and rather anxious. The father, whose name I do not recall, has not yet arrived. Apparently he has concocted an elaborate scheme of travel, with the two of them meeting here."

"That would be Sir Walter Elliot. His absence is no loss, milady."

"Miss Elliot refuses to trespass upon my hospitality; is this not charming?" There was a pause. "Aha! Now we'll solve the mystery. Claverling!" she called. "Do you know a gentleman by the name of Elliot?"

"Elliot Walters?" said a hearty voice. Was it Lord Claverling's? "Friend of Argyll's. Met him at Tattersall's last year. Splendid fellow. Has he arrived?"

"Not yet!" Lady Claverling called back. "Oh dear," she said. "Elliot Walters is not on the list. But Sir Walter Elliot is." There was a pause. "Claverling's new secretary has been such a trial."

Others came into the hall; their echoing voices prevented Elizabeth from hearing any more. Trembling, she sank into a chair. This was worse than anything! Her grand invitation was all a mistake! And Lady Claverling knew it!

The doorbell sounded—a great, clanging noise that made Elizabeth jump. She was cold all over. She'd risked everything to come—for nothing! And what would happen if the guests learned of the mistake? What would be said about her?

Elizabeth heard the front door open. "It's Robbins, isn't it?" A woman's voice carried above the others. "Will you kindly tell Lady Claverling that her cousin Leah has arrived? I am quite exhausted. Might I be shown to my room straightway?" There was a pause. "James my dear, you are perfectly right." The woman spoke again, this time with careful emphasis. "Robbins, kindly inform Lady Claverling that Mrs Leah Rushworth and Mr James Rushworth have arrived."

Elizabeth raised her head. James Rushworth? James "twelve-thousand-a-year" Rushworth? She closed her eyes. She had not come all the way to Richmond to spend time with a man like James Rushworth! Snatches of conversation came to mind: his estate, Sotherton; his fine house on Grosvenor Square; his soon-to-be-unmarried state. The frank interest in his eyes when he looked at her. Elizabeth let out a long breath. Surely there were other eligible gentlemen here! There had to be!

~ ~ ~ ~ ~ ~ ~ & ~ ~ ~ ~ ~ ~ ~

Of all the bedchambers at Chalfort House, the White Chintz Room was obviously the least elegant. It contained a narrow bed with a white coverlet and one matching stuffed chair. Why, it was like the servants' quarters at Kellynch! There was no dressing room, not even a proper dressing table! Over the chest of drawers hung a swing dressing-glass and a sconce. Elizabeth's status as an unknown was brought home with a vengeance.

Elise had been at work unpacking; a blond silk evening gown hung ready on the wardrobe door. Elizabeth studied it dispassionately. Perhaps she should go down to the drawing room after dinner? It was foolish not to—no one would dare to speak openly of the mistake if she were present. Then too, perhaps she could change Lady Claverling's unfavourable opinion? If only she had Penelope Clay's cloying ways!

Elise said nothing, but her dark looks spoke volumes!

Elizabeth went out and wandered the length of the corridor. The household was now at dinner. Sounds drifted up: the chime of silver against fine china, the hum of conversation, and the bustle of the servants on the back stairs.

A door was thrown open and a serving girl carrying a tray came hurrying along. She rapped on Elizabeth's door. Here was dinner! And what a very good thing this was. For in the privacy of her bedchamber, Elizabeth could eat as much as she wished, without regard to leaving polite morsels on the plate.

And then there was nothing to do but to sit in the chair and endure Elise's disapproval. To escape, Elizabeth rummaged in the basket for her social ledger and the London newspapers purchased by John. Her mother's little Testament fell to the floor. Elizabeth picked it up, aware of Elise's critical gaze. Usually she cared nothing about what Elise thought, but tonight was different. Although there was nothing she wanted to read less, Elizabeth kept hold of the little book. With a glance to make certain that Elise was watching, she opened to the place marked by a slip of ribbon. She read the first thing her eyes fixed upon:

A certain man had two sons; and the younger of them said to his father, Father, give me the portion of goods that falleth to me. And he divided unto them his living.

Was this a story about an inheritance? Elizabeth continued reading.

And not many days after that, the younger son gathered all together, and took his journey into a far country, and there wasted his substance with riotous living.

This was troubling, although she could not say why. After all, she had neither asked for her inheritance, nor had she spent it in riotous living! Elizabeth shut the Testament with a snap. But her thoughts would not let loose of the story. She had taken leave of her father, as that son had, and she had journeyed into a far country, alone. She reopened the book. Riotous living? In her real-life version of this tale, the roles were reversed. Her father was the one who engaged in riotous living! She found the place and resumed reading.

And when he had spent all, there arose a mighty famine in that land; and he began to be in want.

Elizabeth nearly laughed aloud. Certainly, he spent it all! Just like her father had!

And he went and joined himself to a citizen of that country; and he sent him into his fields to feed swine. And he would fain have filled his belly with the husks that the swine did eat; and no man gave unto him.

This brought to mind the retrenchment. At least she had not descended so far as this, to be feeding swine! But the word 'swine' brought to mind Mr Rushworth.

And when he came to himself, he said, How many of my father's hired servants have bread enough and to spare, and I perish with hunger! I will arise and go to my father, and will say unto him, Father, I have sinned against heaven, and before thee, and am no more worthy to be called thy son...

Elizabeth stopped reading. Return to her father? For mercy? He would never give it! Treat her as a servant? Her father's servants fared a good deal worse! And besides, she had not sinned against him.

But the parable did not speak of an earthly Father. Elizabeth knew this, too. She shut the Testament and tossed it into the basket. "I have done no wrong," she said aloud. "I have done no wrong."

Elise turned round. She looked directly at Elizabeth.

Elizabeth stood up. "I believe I shall go down after all," she said.

~ ~ ~ ~ ~ ~ ~ & ~ ~ ~ ~ ~ ~ ~

Elizabeth reached the ground floor without discovery. Following directions given by a footman, she turned to the left and found herself in a long, carpeted hallway. As she walked its length, she counted the doors. The third door, the footman said, led to the conservatory.

The door swung open with a tiny squeal; warm air rushed to meet her. Elizabeth hastily stepped inside. Shafts of moonlight shone through the high glass ceiling and splashed onto the floor. Cautiously, she moved among the potted palms and ferns, searching for the outer door. The conservatory was not silent; there were crickets chirping. With trepidation, she crept past a tall cloth-covered cage. Was a noisy, exotic bird within? She glanced at the palms overhead. Lady Claverling *was* the sort of woman who would own a monkey.

She had almost reached the door when the delicate fabric of her gown caught on a thorn. Elizabeth compressed her lips; what else could go wrong? At last she freed herself from the clutches of the vine and found the outer door. It opened onto a wide, flagged portico. It was deserted.

Elizabeth swung her cloak over her shoulders and went out. To her left were the brightly lit windows of the drawing room; the strains of a pianoforte reached her ears. The gentle tune was lovely in such a setting, but Elizabeth knew better than to linger.

She descended the wide stone steps to the lawn. A rose garden was before her, kept in order by a privet hedge. By the light of the moon, she could make out an arched trellis and white stone benches. At midsummer this garden would be lovely. Then again, by midsummer she would have passed her birthday. Sighing, Elizabeth moved on.

On either side of the lawn were trees—massive elms very like the groves of Kellynch. Elizabeth followed the gravel path in the direction of the river. The river was so beautiful, so free...

She gazed searchingly at the sparkling water. The river might be free, but Elizabeth was anything but free. What disappointment this day had brought!

A slight scent caught her attention; was it smoke? She swung around. Sure enough, there was a gentleman—or were there two?—now standing beneath the portico. She had made her escape just in time. At the river's edge was a terrace with a white stone balustrade. She mounted the steps, mindful to keep to the shadows. It was the river that had drawn her here, shining silver in the moonlight. These gardens, this mansion—everything spoke of home. She knew full well that she would never return to Kellynch as mistress.

And her immediate prospects were even worse. She had come to find a husband here—it seemed so simple in the drawing room in Bath. But could it be done? And at the end of it all, how would she face her father?

"I have done no wrong," she whispered urgently, speaking to the river. "I have done no wrong!"

The river took her words and flowed on.

~ ~ ~ ~ ~ ~ ~ & ~ ~ ~ ~ ~ ~ ~

There was music in the drawing room that night. A pair of sisters now sat at the pianoforte performing a duet. The playing was not bad, but the singing! Patrick McGillvary kept his face impassive. He considered himself inured to such performances, but the combination of Mrs Hurst and her sister was more than he could bear.

As there seemed to be no end to it, he resorted to an old ploy. Out of his pocket came his friend, the pipe. He toyed with it as he listened, then he rose from his chair. Very carefully did McGillvary observe the faces of the guests, waiting for an opportunity. At length it came. The song reached a crescendo, and when all eyes were on Miss Bingley, McGillvary slipped from the drawing room and exited the house.

The outer door closed behind him with a muted click, and McGillvary breathed a sigh of relief. Even here the pianoforte could be heard, but at least Miss Bingley's energetic soprano was muted.

He fished in a pocket for his tobacco pouch. A lantern near the door provided the flame, and soon he was blowing a stream of smoke into the star-filled sky. He wandered beneath the colonnaded portico, humming under his breath.

Presently there came a smattering of polite applause. McGillvary paused to tamp the tobacco with his thumb, and then drew on the pipe once again. Wide stone steps and a gravel path beckoned invitingly. The music began again—an encore. That settled it. He descended at once into the shadowy garden.

How McGillvary knew he could not say, but he was not alone here. He stepped into the shadows. Sure enough, a figure emerged from the trees and crossed the terrace. McGillvary drew nearer. It was a woman. She paused to gaze at the river, a white hand on the balustrade.

The fabric of her cloak shone faintly in the silver light and rippled in the breeze. Obviously this was no kitchen maid escaped from the scullery! Who was she, and why had she come? He studied her more closely.

And then she threw back her hood, revealing an enchanting profile. McGillvary had to smile. Apparently Miss Elliot was weary of being shut up in her room. He knocked the ashes from his pipe, straightened his coat, and prepared to step forward.

Just as he was about to speak, the crunch of footfalls caught his attention. McGillvary's eyebrows rose. Was Miss Elliot expecting a visitor?

"Good evening, my dear."

It was a gentleman who spoke. He strolled sedately across the terrace to meet her. Elizabeth did not immediately turn to face him, McGillvary noted. The man's hair shone silver in the moonlight. "Can you have forgotten your old friend so soon, Miss Elliot?" the man said, making a graceful bow.

"Sir Henry," said Elizabeth. "You startled me, sir. Good evening." Her voice was clipped and polite, which pleased McGillvary.

Sir Henry Farley moved to stand beside her. "Lady Claverling told us the news about your father. I must say, I was shocked and grieved to hear it."

There was a pause. "In what way was the news shocking, Sir Henry?"

"Why, that you have left your father behind on the road!"

Elizabeth gasped and McGillvary groaned. Farley was known as a charmer of woman; McGillvary certainly expected better than this!

Sir Henry laughed easily. "I was only jesting, my sweet. May I say how sorry I am to hear about your unfortunate fiasco?"

"You are very kind, sir. It is rather awkward, yes."

"I understand your feelings perfectly." Sir Henry gave a heavy sigh. "I myself have been cast adrift while travelling. It leaves one rather at a loss." There was another pause. "Odd that we should meet like this, you and I..."

McGillvary rolled his eyes.

"Is it?" Elizabeth's dry tone showed no interest.

McGillvary grinned. Farley was too old for this one!

Sir Henry spoke again. "I have missed seeing you about Bath, my sweet. You were absent from Lady Arundel's ball. And from Thursday's assembly, as well." Sir Henry's voice dropped. McGillvary was barely able to catch Sir Henry's last wistful words: "I so much wished for a dance..."

McGillvary nearly groaned aloud. God grant Miss Elliot better judgment than to fall for such obvious palaver!

Elizabeth pulled her cloak more closely about her. "My father has been ill, Sir Henry."

"So I have heard. I trust it isn't catching. And you are left...alone." There was another pause. "I trust I do not interrupt a lover's tryst, Miss Elizabeth?"

This tasteless statement missed its mark. "Good heavens, of course not!" she cried. McGillvary saw her lift her chin. "You must know that at Kellynch I am accustomed to walk about whenever I please."

"Ah, yes." There was another pause. "But, this is not Kellynch, is it?"

"Do you mean I am in danger, sir?"

"Not while I am here to protect you."

McGillvary had heard enough. Protector, indeed! The ground near his feet was littered with debris from the trees. He put his foot on a dry, sturdy limb. *Crack!*

~ ~ ~ ~ ~ ~ ~ & ~ ~ ~ ~ ~ ~ ~

Elizabeth's nerves, which had been strained to the breaking point, suddenly snapped. She bolted across the dark terrace.

"Miss Elliot!" Sir Henry called. "Come back! Miss Elli-ot!"

She could hear Sir Henry's reedy voice, but she paid it no mind and kept running. She made for the safety of the shadows. After running some little way, she flattened herself against the rugged bark of an elm. She fought to control her breathing and strained to listen.

There. Someone was following; someone with long strides such as a man would take. Elizabeth pressed more closely against the tree. Patience would carry the day, although it was unnerving to remain still for so long. Presently the night sounds began to re-establish themselves. She studied the empty terrace. Sir Henry was gone.

But Elizabeth's relief was short-lived. Shame rose to take its place, along with a good measure of fear. She had been discovered, and by Sir Henry, the very last man she expected to find here! Very well did Elizabeth recognize her precarious position. As a leader in Bath society, Sir Henry Farley was a dangerous man. What would come of tonight's exchange?

And that noise in the dark! Some animal had made it; she did not care to speculate which kind! But Elizabeth now realized that she was less afraid of an animal than of Sir Henry's inclination to gossip. For a long while she studied the moonlit lawn and the lighted mansion. She took a few tentative steps away from the tree.

"Hold a moment, Miss Elliot," said a voice. "That fox Farley has not yet returned to the house."

Elizabeth swung round. A man's shadowy form was there, but she could see nothing of his face. He raised an arm and pointed. "There," he said quietly. "Do you see? On the steps?"

Elizabeth knew she should have screamed; she knew she should have run away. Instead, her eyes followed the direction he indicated. Sure enough, someone was mounting the steps to the portico.

Elizabeth turned to find the man perilously near, though still concealed in the shadows. He extended his hand toward her, his palm clearly visible in a patch of moonlight.

"You should have taken this, you know," he said. "You told me once that you need a weapon from time to time. I should have believed you." His smile shone white in the darkness.

It was a silver-handled clasp knife. This was the man from the concert!

Elizabeth flushed in sudden surprise. "Good evening," she said, in a fair imitation of his calm. "I daresay, this must look rather odd to you..."

His smile flashed again. "Farley has never been so thoroughly rejected by one so lovely. I count myself privileged to be a witness."

"Rejected?" Elizabeth repeated. "So that is what he meant with all that talk of being alone." She realized she was trembling. "I would not have had this happen for the world! For Sir Henry will talk and..."

"Oh, you shall come about in jig-time, Miss Elliot," said the man. "I take it you are acquainted with his wife?"

Elizabeth stared at him. She was ruined—and he sounded quite cheerful about it! "Come about?" she said frostily. "I take it this is an example of horrid naval cant?"

"You disapprove of the Navy, Miss Elliot?" He sounded amused. "You will find yourself alone in that opinion."

Elizabeth set her teeth. There was no reason to be polite to a vain, impertinent sailor, no matter how handsome he might be. "Oh, no. I admire the Navy prodigiously," she said. "Such an industrious group of men! Bath is filled with officers who have been—how do you say?—thrown ashore? Low-born, dull-witted, podgy, self-important admirals and captains like my sister's husband, who have nothing better to do than loll about, disfiguring the landscape!"

"Disfiguring the...you don't say." He gave a rich chuckle. "And what should be done with these unfortunate freaks, Miss Elliot?"

"How should I know?" Elizabeth directed her attention to the house; there was now no sign of Sir Henry. "Put them on a ship together," she suggested. "Send them back to sea. Let them..." She paused, thinking. What useful thing might such bumbling men accomplish? "Let them catch fish," she said.

The man made a choking sound.

Elizabeth smiled, for she had made a hit. "That is what gentlemen do at sea, is it not, sir? Catch fish?" She shrugged. "Nothing else comes to mind."

"Officers of the Navy are fighting men, Miss Elliot. We do not...fish." The smile was gone from his voice.

"So I have been told. However..." She purposely did not finish the sentence.

"May I ask who was responsible for the downfall of Napoleon, ma'am?"

He was proud, this lowborn sailor. Unfortunately for him, Elizabeth knew exactly how to depress such pride. "Ah, but could the Navy keep him down?" she said sweetly. "Unfortunately, no."

There was a sharp intake of breath. "You blame us for Napoleon's escape?" the man demanded.

By this time Elizabeth's hood had fallen back; she no longer cared that her face could be clearly seen. The dangerous note in his voice spurred her on. She faced him squarely.

"Elba is an island, sir," she said, speaking as if to a dull-witted child. "A land mass surrounded by water. Of course, the Navy is responsible! Who else should we blame? The dear, valiant men of the...Army?"

"I *beg* your pardon?" he shouted.

Elizabeth smiled, pleased to have discomfited him so thoroughly. "I bid you good evening, sir. Thank you for coming to my aid. although your assistance was entirely unnecessary."

Having fired her parting shot, Elizabeth stalked off across the moonlit lawn. This house party might prove to be a complete disaster, but at least she had the satisfaction of putting one man in his rightful place.

~ ~ ~ ~ ~ ~ ~ & ~ ~ ~ ~ ~ ~ ~

Patrick McGillvary paced the shadow beneath the trees as if it was his quarterdeck. Such insolence! Such disdain! Even in one so beautiful, open ingratitude was intolerable. She deserved to be flogged! And her proposition, to send the Admiralty to fish in the waters off Elba–!

Choice words formed on his lips, words that he could not utter to her, but his imagination led to his undoing. Images rose to fill his mind, courtesy of Elizabeth Elliot: flabby, highly decorated men on the bridge of a ship, working to preserve dignity while holding fishing poles...

McGillvary's lips twitched; despite his pique with her, he laughed. Who knew which podgy officers she had seen about Bath and taken a dislike to as they lolled about disfiguring the landscape? Against his will he began to assemble a list: Birmingham, Croft, Brigden, Glidcrest–

Old Gliddy, now he would fit every one of her scathing descriptions! No, he could not hate Miss Elliot for describing Gliddy so delightfully! And Meldrum, too! Come to think on it, he'd left Meldrum lolling about in the drawing room. He burst out laughing again.

McGillvary strolled across the lawn toward the house, following in Elizabeth's wake. She'd gone in through the conservatory door. Very well, so would he. He caught up with her in the entrance hall, though she did not see him. McGillvary's eyes rested for a long moment on Miss Elliot's graceful form. No, it was a shame to hate one so lovely. What a pity old Farley reached her first. What would she have said if he had been the one to meet her on the moonlit terrace? Something outrageous, no doubt. On the other hand, she might be brought to regret her unfortunate opinions.

At that moment, Miss Elliot drew her shoulders back and lifted her chin. She took a deep breath and held it, as if coming to attention. McGillvary smiled in recognition. Hoisting her colours, she was. Preparing to engage. Was Meldrum still in the drawing room? What would he do when she fired a bow-chaser, accusing him of being a nincompoop in addition to disfiguring the landscape?

A touch on his arm recalled McGillvary to his surroundings. He turned. Lady Claverling smiled up at him.

"I have your promise for Tuesday's ball?" she said, twinkling. "Unless, of course, you are sent sailing away."

"Failing that, you have my word of honour, ma'am. I have your cards for Cockburn and the others; we shall not fail you."

"What a very good thing it would be if you could bring this Elliot Walters," she said. "For there is no sign of the other gentleman."

She lifted her hand from his arm and was about to drift away when an idea struck him. "Milady," he called. "I wonder if I might have your opinion about something. As a woman, that is."

"Indeed?" Lady Claverling looked interested.

"If you were in an awkward situation socially," he said, "and I told you that you would 'come about in jig-time,' what would you think I meant?"

"Dear me," she said slowly. "A jig is a dance, is it not?"

"Actually, it is a cant expression, my lady, meaning right away."

"I see," she said. Of course, she did not see. McGillvary repeated the sentence.

"To come about," she said, frowning. "This signifies something which is about to happen. As in: 'It shall surely come about.'"

"It shall surely–!" McGillvary stared at her. "Not within this context, milady. To 'come about' means to change direction, to make a recovery, to shift to a new tack."

She became even more perplexed. "Tact? This is a situation requiring tact?"

McGillvary gave a shout of laughter. Yes, it had been a situation requiring tact, and he had bungled it! "Do you mean to say, that after she told me she was ruined, I, with the best good will, informed her that yes, it would surely come about? And speedily? Good lord! No wonder she hates me!"

"She?" said Lady Claverling. "My dear, I cannot think what you mean."

"Nor can I," he admitted. Still laughing, he made his bow. "I'd best look in on the others. Birkett and Weathersbee will have sustained heavy damage by now. Billiards, milady," he explained.

"Pooh, billiards," said Lady Claverling, and waved him away.

The click of ivory balls announced a successful shot. Lord Claverling gave a yell and held his cue aloft. "A two-ball cannon!" he crowed. "Let's see you counter that, sir!"

McGillvary stifled a yawn. Birkett was indeed taking a beating. A writing desk stood in a corner, presumably for the writing of promissory notes. Birkett would be doing some of that.

Despite the fascination of the game, McGillvary couldn't shake Elizabeth Elliot from his mind. Even if her anger was justified, her stinging remarks rankled. Why let her off easily? He took a seat at the desk and drew forward a piece of stationery. The letter gave him some trouble, at least at first, but over the course of his career McGillvary had developed a knack for writing apologies that were not exactly that. Presently, he sat back to study his handiwork. Yes, it would serve his purpose nicely. He would see her change her tune.

He folded the page carefully and dropped a flat, silver object inside. The desk drawer held sticks of wax. McGillvary melted it into blobs, and then pressed his signet ring into each seal. He dug in his pocket for a coin and went in search of a footman.

"You are to give this to Robbins and no other," McGillvary told the man. "Tomorrow at breakfast he will deliver it." He brought out the coin. "I shall, of course, make this extra trouble worth your while."

McGillvary returned to the billiard room, smiling to himself. Miss Elliot would change her tune, sure enough.

~6~
Much to Bear

Elizabeth came down to breakfast as late as possible, hoping to avoid Mr Rushworth and his mother. The breakfast room was not quite deserted. She glanced up in time to see Caroline Bingley coming her way, a teacup in each hand. Elizabeth smiled as best she could and directed her eyes elsewhere. The colour of Caroline's gown was painful, especially so early in the day.

"Miss Elliot! How are you, my dear?" Caroline spoke with an affected, throbbing accent. She placed the cups on the table and saluted Elizabeth's cheek with a kiss. "I have not seen you this age!"

This was not the best time to mention the word age, and Elizabeth always hated to be kissed. It cost her a great deal to reply graciously. Unfortunately, Caroline took this for an invitation and slid into the chair beside hers.

"And your gown, why, my dear! It has that certain *je ne sais pas*..."

Je ne sais quoi, Elizabeth corrected silently. Caroline *would* toss off foreign expressions she did not understand.

"And your necklace, my! I've never seen the like!"

Elizabeth's hand travelled to her neck. She wore a pendant of green jade, a gift from her sister. When she mentioned this, Caroline was impressed.

"I had no idea the wife of a simple country squire would have such exquisite taste." Caroline paused, her cup poised in midair. "Your sister is married to a country squire, is she not?"

"My youngest sister, yes." How appalling that Caroline remembered this! If only she would go away! Or at the very least, stop talking so much! She forced herself to say: "My middle sister, Anne, was married very recently to an officer of the Navy."

Caroline set her cup in its saucer. "The Navy!" she cried. "Oh, my dear Eliza, there was such a stir this morning! Such excitement!" She lowered her voice. "A marine brought orders this very morning to one of the guests."

Elizabeth's smile stiffened. How she despised being called Eliza!

Caroline went on talking. "You see," she explained, "there was no servant to mind the main door when the marine came–a gentleman of the Royal Marines, I should say, and so distinguished in his red uniform!" Miss Bingley gave a girlish gurgle.

"Well," she continued, "what do you suppose happened next? One of the household boys answered the door. When he was told that the man must deliver the orders to the Admiral in person and at once, why, the boy brought him here! Right to the breakfast table!" Caroline's smile became cat-like. "I do not believe the Admiral was best pleased by that."

"Nor would I be."

"And oh, Miss Eliza, we are completely desolated! For of all the gentlemen, why must Admiral McGillvary be the one to be ordered away? It is too unkind!" Caroline leaned in. "I sat opposite him at dinner last evening," she confided, "and he was perfectly delightful. So handsome! So charming! I could scarcely keep my part in the conversation with the gentlemen on either side, so amusing were his stories and anecdotes." She lowered her voice further. "He is a widower, you know. Even Lady Calef looks at him with longing eyes, and you know how old she is! Scandalous!"

"Admiral McGillvary, did you say?" said Elizabeth. "McGillvary?"

"Admiral Patrick McGillvary." Caroline gave her a knowing smile. "He is descended from a noble Irish family, which explains his penchant for the lovely moustache. I am told his family's mansion in Bath is most impressive."

Elizabeth worked to digest this. That Lady Calef should look on the sailor from the garden as a potential husband was stunning. There was more.

"Miss Gribble, who has quite set her cap for him as well, tells me he is now head of the family. 'The McGillvary' they call him. Isn't that quaint?"

Elizabeth found her voice: "You are certain about the name? McGillvary?"

"You should know, dear Eliza! Surely you have seen him in Bath?"

"Why, yes, I...we have spoken upon several occasions and..." A sudden thought occurred to her, and she choked. This man was the host of Anne's dinner!

"Really! And what did you find to converse about?"

Elizabeth felt colour flood her cheeks. She lifted her chin. "Politics," she said woodenly. "We discussed politics. Specifically, Napoleon's escape from Elba."

"How clever of you, Eliza!" cried Caroline. "I should never dare to converse about such a thing!"

Elizabeth closed her eyes. Very much did she wish that she hadn't dared to either.

A polite cough caught her attention. She turned to find the butler standing beside her chair with a silver tray. Even without looking Elizabeth knew what it was: her letter, which was supposed to arrive on Monday. Reluctantly, she took it. The shape and weight of it brought a frown. "But this is not–!" The words died on Elizabeth's lips. This was not her letter, yet there was her name.

"Will there be an answer, miss?"

The butler's words made no sense. "An answer?" she repeated. "Yes, I imagine so, but..."

Fortunately, a commotion in the entrance hall required the man's attention. Elizabeth's hands shook as she broke the seals. Something flat and silver slid out and landed in her lap: Admiral McGillvary's silver clasp knife!

And there was more. Something was written on the sheet of paper! After their heated exchange last night, what could he have to say to her?

"Why, what have you there, my dear?"

Elizabeth looked up; Caroline Bingley's gaze was fastened on the letter. Elizabeth whipped the sheet away and pushed back her chair. "Goodness, look at the time. We must hurry!"

Caroline gave her throaty laugh. "Whatever do you mean?"

"It's Sunday morning. Surely Lady Claverling expects us to attend service."

Caroline lowered her teacup. "You cannot be serious. Attend church? But–"

"Pray excuse me," said Elizabeth. On the way out of the breakfast room she nearly collided with Mrs Rushworth. "Might you direct me to the chapel, ma'am?" Elizabeth said. "I do not wish to be late for service." Mrs Rushworth's pleased surprise was everything Elizabeth could wish for.

~ ~ ~ ~ ~ ~ ~ & ~ ~ ~ ~ ~ ~ ~

Sir Walter slid out of bed and padded to the door. Very carefully, he opened it. He stood there for a few minutes listening. There were voices below: Wilson's and his daughter Mary's. She was, he knew, headed for church with Lady Russell.

It was well that he had taken breakfast in his room this morning, for he had avoided Mary's conversation. As it was, he overheard quite enough of her fussing: her hat was not right, or her hair, or some such thing. That was the trouble with small houses like this—no privacy. All the more reason to return to his rightful residence at Kellynch Hall. Presently, he heard something more satisfying: the deep click of the main door as it closed. Sir Walter promptly reached for the bell pull.

The truth was, as much as he despised physicians and their meddling ways, he had been impressed by Mr Savoy's advice. The more he thought about it, the better it all sounded. He needed the proper atmosphere in which to heal, an atmosphere which would be in keeping with his station and with his sensitive, creative nature. How delightful it was that Mr Savoy recognized this about him! Under such a physician's care, he would thrive.

However, there were difficulties in following the path to his heart's desire. There were responsibilities to maintain, especially in regard to Elizabeth. He released the bell cord, frowning. Elizabeth, the daughter after his own heart. He had made any number of sacrifices on her behalf, and how had she repaid him? In his hour of need, she hadn't thought of him at all. She left Bath to pursue her own pleasure. Heartless, she was. No wonder Lady Russell did not care for her company. All at once he came to his decision and gave the bell pull a series of tugs. He was going out!

Some thirty minutes later, Wilson handed him into a sedan chair. He was, as usual, impeccably attired. Today he carried an additional accessory: a fine Malacca cane.

"Tell my daughter," he said, settling carefully into the seat, "that I have gone to call on Mr Savoy. A social call, mind! I shall return within the hour."

"Very good, sir."

"Oh, and Wilson!" Sir Walter called him back. "Would you send a note round to Shepherd, my man of business? Tell him I need to discuss, right away," Sir Walter paused to cough, "the terms of lease for this house." His bit his lip, thinking. "Best to send it express, then, as the matter is urgent. That will be all."

As the chair moved forward, Sir Walter extracted Mr Savoy's card from a pocket. "The Citadel," he mumbled, reading the address. "Therein lies the key to my recovery."

~ ~ ~ ~ ~ ~ & ~ ~ ~ ~ ~ ~ ~

Elizabeth quelled an unladylike impulse to dig an elbow into Caroline Bingley's side. The pew was uncomfortable–anyone would agree to that–but it did not give Caroline leave to squirm so! Elizabeth folded her hands piously over her mother's open Testament and turned her attention to the sermon.

> For God hath not appointed us to wrath but to obtain salvation by our Lord Jesus Christ ...

Elizabeth stifled a yawn. Miss Bingley twitched once more. Perhaps because of her own recent misfortunes, or perhaps because she was in church, Elizabeth chose to be charitable. No doubt Caroline's bony posterior was the cause of the trouble. She gave Caroline a sidelong look. That one should be thin, pigeon-breasted, and devoid of all taste were heavy burdens for anyone to bear. Elizabeth's pity was short-lived, for she then remembered that Caroline was arrogant, opinionated, and possessed of a truly handsome independence.

The rector continued with his reading.

> ...who died for us that, whether we wake or sleep, we should live together with Him.

Whether we sleep? The man should take a hint and finish up! Another text was announced, and Elizabeth directed her attention to her mother's Testament. What a very good thing it was that she'd thought to bring it. It was obviously well used, as Mrs Rushworth had no doubt noticed. A folded square of paper fell from its pages. It was the note she'd received at breakfast. Elizabeth slowly unfolded it.

My Dear Miss Elliot,
It appears that you were right. Overzealous suitors are
everywhere, it seems—even in a moonlit garden.
I cannot issue you a cutlass, which you would doubtless
handle with aplomb, but this should do the job in a pinch.
Aim for the eyes, Miss Elliot, and do not hold back, no
matter who your opponent may be.
Yours,
P.M.

"My dear, what have you there?"

Elizabeth looked up. Caroline Bingley's fingers were fastened on
a corner of the letter. She pulled playfully at the page. "Eliza," she
whispered. "What is this?"

"Nothing! Nothing at all!" Elizabeth tightened her grip. But her
gloved fingers could not keep hold; she felt the paper slip.

"Don't keep secrets! Let me see!" Caroline pulled harder.

Elizabeth flushed, aware of curious looks. "Caroline, please!" she
whispered back. "You are causing a scene!"

"You are causing the scene, dearest. Let me see!"

The rector brought his sermon to a close. "In the name of the Father, and of the Son, and of the Holy Ghost." Out of habit, Caroline
and Elizabeth joined the congregation in saying, "Amen," before
resuming their tug-of-war.

After the hymn was announced, the congregation stood. Caroline
gave another pull. Elizabeth held on with all her might. There came
a tearing sound and an audible gasp. The rector glanced up with a
look of reproof.

Elizabeth kept her gaze focused on the altar as she sang, leaving
Caroline to fumble with the hymnal. Let Caroline be blamed for
tearing up a prayer book! After all, she was the one holding the torn
paper! One question burned in her mind: exactly which portion of
that letter did Caroline have?

~ ~ ~ ~ ~ ~ ~ & ~ ~ ~ ~ ~ ~ ~

Sir Walter was in good spirits when he returned to Camden
Place. After surrendering his coat, gloves, and hat into Wilson's care,
he studied his reflection in the looking glass. Yes, he was definitely
on the mend.

His visit with Mr Savoy had been most enlightening. Mr Savoy had spoken of a new medical discipline—the study of brain development relating to the skull, or some such thing. Sir Walter could not remember what it was called. A physician from Vienna, who had the extreme misfortune to be named Gall, espoused it; that much Sir Walter knew. At any rate, Mr Gall's theory was taking the Continent by storm. Mr Savoy believed it was the most important medical discovery of modern times.

Presently, Sir Walter left off gazing at himself, climbed the stairs to the drawing room, and found his favourite chair. He dropped into it with a heavy sigh and sent the foot-boy for tea. Soon, however, he recovered enough strength to begin feeling his forehead again, tracing its features with eager fingertips.

"The only true science of the mind," he murmured, repeating Mr Savoy's enthusiastic description. According to Mr Savoy, his striking forehead was not only handsome, it was an indication of the development of Wit (which was hardly a surprise). Also, it seemed that the back of his skull rose to a prominent angle, thus displaying the quality of Self-Esteem, which as anyone knew, was no bad thing. Sir Walter massaged the telltale bulge fondly, regretting (for once) the mass of attractive hair that covered it.

"Alas," he said aloud, "I was destined for greatness, and yet, here am I, reduced to..."

What was he reduced to? This rented house? He eyed the drawing room resentfully; it was not at all worthy of the name. A glorified parlour, this was! Two adjoining rooms separated by a sliding door! When compared with the magnificent proportions of Kellynch Hall, this house was laughable!

"Absolutely laughable!" Sir Walter repeated, reaching for the lap robe that hung on the arm of the chair. His frown deepened when he noticed a pile of clutter in the corner of the room. It was made up of wrapping paper from Mary's purchases, which no one had bothered to clear away.

"This is what happens when I am not up and about to supervise," Sir Walter complained to the empty room. "It is not worth having this house if I must forever be scolding the staff for inattention! Or," he added, "my negligent daughters!"

At length, Wilson brought in the tea tray and received a reprimand for Mary's rubbish. The man departed quickly enough, leaving Sir Walter to hang over his cup. He was feeling worse by the minute; the curious burning sensation in his chest had returned. For a moment he wondered whether he should get himself into bed but abandoned the idea as soon as he remembered his dreary, prison-like bedchamber.

As Mr Savoy pointed out, there was an alternative: he could lodge at Mr Savoy's facility, The Citadel. This, of course, was absolutely out of the question. That ladies and gentlemen came from all over the kingdom to enjoy its healing benefits was all very well, but for Sir Walter Elliot, no! He had been genuinely impressed by the accommodations, and he would, of course, recommend it without hesitation to any who had need of–how had Mr Savoy described it?–"A civilized place of healing for those desiring rustication from the exigencies of modern life."

Sir Walter took a sip of tea. He had certainly had his share of exigencies lately.

"Actually," he muttered into his cup, "the only reason I keep this house is for Elizabeth. And how has she repaid my kindness? Bah!"

He managed to finish his tea, grumbling all the while. Elizabeth would find things to be different upon her return, there would be no mistake. But it would not do to think about Elizabeth anymore; he hadn't the strength for it. Amanda Russell had spoken of making a search; it was best to leave the matter in her hands. Sir Walter set the cup in its saucer, leaned back, and closed his eyes.

"Amanda is capable, always capable," he murmured drowsily, drawing the lap robe to his chin. "She will find Elizabeth. Which is her duty, as godmother, yes…"

Some time later he awakened to see the drawing room door open slowly. "I won't disturb him if he is sleeping," he heard a woman's voice say.

Sir Walter closed his eyes. It was probably the maid, wishful to do the dusting. Never again would he consent to hire a house! He opened an eye. Anne stood just inside the door. "Hello, Father," she said.

~ ~ ~ ~ ~ ~ ~ & ~ ~ ~ ~ ~ ~ ~

Mary Musgrove turned to wave at Lady Russell as her carriage pulled away. Attending church with her godmother was a great bore, for she had no interest in anything important. Lady Russell would talk about the sermon. Mary didn't see the point in that–it was always the same, wasn't it? Lady Russell was perfectly willing to discuss the music as well–but what good was Bach to anyone? What excited Mary's imagination were the people—and wasn't it one's Christian duty to pay attention to them? Her particular interest was, of course, what the ladies and gentlemen were wearing. This morning Mary's attention was captured by the astonishing variety of bonnets. Everything Mary brought from Uppercross was sadly provincial.

Wilson took her hat and cloak, prosing on about something or other. Her father had returned from his outing and was with a caller in the drawing room. And Captain Benwick and someone else were partaking of a very late breakfast. It took Mary a full minute to realize that Wilson meant Charles. "Bless me, why didn't you say so?" she said, and made for the dining room.

The two men at the table looked worn to the bone, Captain Benwick in particular. He was nursing a cup of coffee with his elbows rudely planted on the table. "What are sixty miles of good road?" he was saying. "Nothing but pain and discomfort!"

Neither of them appeared to notice Mary's entrance. She sniffed loudly to attract their attention and wandered to the sideboard to peek under the covers. Her father's cook was rather better than most. Mary took up a plate and began to fill it.

Charles raised tired eyes. "My dear Benwick," he said, "we are vastly in your debt, for you have made the journey three times over!"

Captain Benwick raised a hand. "Don't mention it, Musgrove," he said. "Line of duty."

"Duty?" said Mary. "Well, I like that! No one ordered you to make the journey, Captain Benwick!"

Charles turned sharply in his chair. "He means duty to family. Hello, Mary."

Both men slowly got to their feet. Charles pulled out a chair for her.

"I understand exactly how you feel, Captain Benwick," said another voice. Anne came forward to the table. "Forgive me for breaking in like this. I've been visiting Father. Wilson told me you were here."

"So that's what he meant by a caller," said Mary. "Why didn't he say so? But then, what else can one expect of Bath servants?" Mary waited until the others had exclaimed over Anne and welcomed her to the table. "Well?" she said at last, unable to contain her curiosity. "Let's see the ring!"

Anne, blushing a little, removed her glove. It was only a simple gold band. Poor Anne! Was this the best Gretna had to offer?

Of course there were the usual bits of news to be gone over. Anne was not forthcoming with details about her wedding trip, though Mary plied her with questions. She was longing to know what a flight to Gretna was like. In books it was romantic. Anne made it seem commonplace.

Anne was most interested in what had become of Elizabeth. "For," she said, "I am beginning to wonder if Father knows where she is. His answers to my questions were unusually vague."

Charles shrugged. "Perhaps there is no need to be concerned."

"I thought so too, at first, but Father mentioned Lady Russell and something about launching a search. He mentioned a family named Bingley."

"Bingley?" Charles took up his coffee cup. "Did your father say anything about them?"

"From what I gather, they live in London. But how shall we find them? How can anyone be found in a place like that?"

"It is not so very hard," said Benwick, "if one knows where to begin."

"What if a person does not wish to be found?" Anne leaned forward. "Father told me about Penelope Clay's disappearance. Charles, I think Elizabeth has run off to join Mrs Clay!"

Mary spoke up. "Oh, surely not!"

"Apparently, Mr Shepherd wrote to Father. That's where he thinks his daughter is–adventuring in London. Father says she did the same thing years ago and came back married to Mr Clay."

"Well, that settles it!" said Captain Benwick. "If this Mrs Clay is busy entrapping some fellow into marriage, I doubt your sister would be welcome."

"But Mrs Clay could hardly turn away my sister if she found her on the doorstep!"

"Mrs Clay might not," said Charles, "but your cousin certainly would!"

"My cousin?" said Anne. "Do you mean Mr Elliot?"

"Charles, really!" cried Mary.

He shrugged. "That's what they're saying in Crewkherne. Apparently Mr Elliot and Mrs Clay disappeared from Bath at the same time. It's the talk of the town."

"What does anyone know in Crewkherne?" scoffed Mary.

Captain Benwick spoke up. "Perhaps we should see whether Elizabeth left a letter. Or there may be other clues lying about."

Anne rounded on Charles. "Why in the world would Mrs Clay be with Mr Elliot?"

"Oh, please!" said Mary. "You saw the way she used to look at him, Anne."

"No, indeed, I did not! Mrs Clay had designs on Father!"

"And Mr Elliot is his heir." Charles took up his fork and speared a piece of potato. Between bites, he said, "If I were in her place, I think I would rather have him, too. More money for one thing."

"The whole idea is preposterous!" cried Anne. "But I agree, Captain Benwick. We should certainly look for clues."

~ ~ ~ ~ ~ ~ ~ & ~ ~ ~ ~ ~ ~ ~

Anne led the way to Sir Walter's book room. Wilson, who clearly did not approve, gave a loud sniff. Anne pointed to the stack of letters on the desk. "Has my father been receiving *any* of his correspondence?"

Wilson bristled. "The master has requested that his letters be retained here, ma'am. He does not wish to be troubled by unnecessary unpleasantness during the term of his illness."

Captain Benwick began sorting the letters. "How convenient," he murmured.

Anne faced the butler squarely. "Thank you, Wilson. You will please inform me when Father awakens from his nap. Well?" she said, as soon as the door was closed. "Have you found anything useful?"

Captain Benwick's face was grim. "There are several here from some sort of bank which have never been opened. They look rather important."

"Ha," said Charles. "What do you bet he owes them money?"

Anne closed her eyes. It was beginning again, just as she suspected. "And Elizabeth? Is there anything from her?"

"Here's a letter with her name on it," said Charles. "Although it looks like it was never posted." He held it out to her. "Addressed to her at Chalfort House, Richmond. Could this be the Bingley residence?"

Anne frowned at it. "That's odd," she said. "This is written in Elizabeth's hand."

"That can't be right," said Mary. "Why would Elizabeth write a letter to herself?"

Anne boldly broke the seal. "Father mentioned that he and Elizabeth were invited to spend the week at Chalfort House," she said, unfolding the letter, "but his illness changed their plans. And now we have this, written by Elizabeth, to herself. Look here," she said, pointing. "It is signed by…Father."

Mary looked over her shoulder. "But that is not Father's signature!"

Anne spread the letter on the desk so that Charles and Benwick could see. "Charles, she went without him. Elizabeth went to Chalfort House without him! She must have!"

"And summoned Mary to care for him in her absence?" said Charles. "Of course! We had a letter begging Mary to come!"

"She would," said Anne. "Oh, she would! How very like Elizabeth to be so selfish! But why this letter?"

"Presumably to show to her hosts by way of explanation," said Benwick. "Look here. After he tells her that his illness has worsened, he says he'll be arranging to bring her home later in the week."

"Ha!" crowed Charles. "I wonder how she planned to manage that?"

"Merciful heavens, what presumption!" said Anne. "Father even tells her to enjoy herself!"

"Well, certainly," said Charles.

She eyed him doubtfully. "What shall we do?"

"Do?" Charles grinned. "Absolutely nothing. Let Elizabeth explain his absence and find her own way home."

"Oh, surely not!"

"On the other hand," said Benwick, studying the letter again, "we could easily follow these instructions and have this delivered to Elizabeth tomorrow by express. Charles and I could travel to up to Richmond on Tuesday. That would give her a nasty shock, eh?"

"But Captain Benwick," said Anne, fighting an impulse to smile, "you cannot show up at Chalfort House and force Elizabeth to come with you! It would be, well…kidnapping! Unless–" Anne swallowed a gurgle of laughter. "Oh, but we couldn't! Elizabeth would be so angry!"

"Ah! Now we're getting somewhere!" said Charles. "What mustn't we do?"

Anne looked from one man to the other. "Why," she said, "take Lady Russell with you."

~7~
That's What Friends Are For

M y dear, *who* is he and *what* did he give you?"
Elizabeth merely smiled and moved away. There
was little to fear from Caroline. Admiral McGillvary's
initials had been torn from the letter. But that did not stop Caroline
from teasing her about it. She had the letter with her now, in fact.

As it turned out, the presence of the Rushworths was a godsend.
Elizabeth had sought them out this morning, requesting a tour of the
portrait gallery. This was a wearing task, but rewarding, for it kept
Caroline at bay for quite some time. Mrs Rushworth was happy to
oblige. She rattled on about every one of her odious relations, so
much so that Caroline could hardly get a word in edgewise. Her son,
by contrast, behaved so well that Elizabeth's opinion of him softened
markedly. However, the problem of retrieving Admiral McGillvary's
letter from Caroline still remained. Elizabeth knew she must act, but
how?

"A cutlass is a sword; I know that," Caroline whispered, as soon
as Mrs Rushworth was out of earshot. "Did he give you a sword,
Eliza? That would be so excessively romantic!"

"I wish he had," Elizabeth replied truthfully. "I would have run it
through his wretched heart!"

"Good gracious!" This remark came from Mr Rushworth, who
was standing quietly by.

"So I am right!" A smile of triumph lit Caroline's face. "This *is* a
love letter!"

Elizabeth winced at her slip. Thinking fast, she summoned up an
attitude of wounded dignity. "You, of all people, should know better
than to tease about such a thing, Miss Bingley. You know first-hand
what it is to have a broken heart."

Caroline's eyes went round with interest. "Were you in love with this man, dear Eliza? You never breathed a word of it to me!" She lowered her voice. "Did he break your heart?"

A strangled sound came from Mr Rushworth. Elizabeth shot a glance in his direction. No doubt he had suffered at the hands of his wife. Could Caroline's question be put to good use?

"I suppose I thought I was in love with him," Elizabeth said slowly, aware of Mr Rushworth's attention, "but he proved to be an insolent cur!" There was no need to dissemble. Memories of Mr Elliot and his insulting preference for Anne lent her the bitterness she needed. "He used me very ill, with gallant words and promises. And then, having made a fool of me, he was gone! I hope I never set eyes on him again!"

It was Mr Rushworth who broke the silence. "My dear Miss Elliot," he said. "I am so terribly, terribly sorry…"

Elizabeth lifted a hand as if to brush aside a tear. She turned to Caroline. "Might I have my letter, please, Miss Bingley? I wish to burn it. Now."

With obvious reluctance, Caroline brought it out. "I do wish you will tell me what he gave you," she said, unfolding the letter for one last look. "I've been wondering all afternoon, and…"

Mr Rushworth stepped forward and plucked it from Caroline's grasp. "Miss Elliot," he said, presenting it with a little bow, "I believe this is yours."

"Th-thank you," said Elizabeth. "Mr Rushworth, I—"

A door at the far end of the gallery opened noisily. "Miss Elliot?" Lady Claverling's musical voice carried the length of the gallery. "Here she is, Carlton," she called over her shoulder. "I have found her." As she drew nearer, she said, smiling, "Gracious, my dear, we have searched everywhere for you!" In Lady Claverling's hands was a flat packet.

"This has come, just now, by express," she said, as all eyes fixed on Elizabeth. "Dare we to hope it contains news of your father, dear?"

Elizabeth blinked. She had forgotten all about *this* letter! Bracing herself to appear worried, Elizabeth took the envelope.

"Well? Open it, Eliza!" Caroline urged. "What does it say?"

Elizabeth could only stare at it. The direction had been crossed out and re-written in a hand she did not recognize. And it had been sent by express! But by whom? The sender had signed it in the bottom corner, but she could not make out the name.

Aware that every eye was upon her, Elizabeth tore it open and pretended to read the words she had worked so diligently to compose. "My father is ill," she managed to whisper. "He will send a coach to bring me home, although when that will be, he does not say…"

Amid the expressions of sympathy, which included an offer of smelling salts from Mrs Rushworth and her son's kind offer to conduct her to a chair, no one noticed that Elizabeth paid far more attention to the envelope than to the letter itself.

~ ~ ~ ~ ~ ~ ~ & ~ ~ ~ ~ ~ ~ ~

There seemed to be no evading Caroline Bingley. Ever loyal, she trailed after Elizabeth, offering consolation and a continual trickle of uninteresting conversation. Although weary of such company, Elizabeth tolerated it, keeping her ears open for tidbits of gossip that Caroline let fall from time to time. Tuesday afternoon was no different. Caroline stood in Elizabeth's bedchamber and stroked the fabric of her ball gown.

"So, this is your dress for this evening," said she, in a hushed, almost reverent voice. "It is lovely, Eliza. And it is so...so." She paused, searching for the perfect word. At length she gave it up, and shrugged. "It is nothing at all like mine."

Elizabeth's lips curved into a smile of agreement. The dress was very beautiful. It was of vibrant red silk with glittering black beadwork at the neckline and sleeves. Caroline bent to examine the hem, which was adorned with a wide band of the same intricate beadwork.

"Altogether lovely," she repeated. "And dancing slippers to match. What lovely tassels these are."

Elizabeth bit her lip. Those wretched shoes! She had not forgotten about the concert and that odious missing tassel! Both had been replaced, but Admiral McGillvary had obviously not forgotten their meeting! Elizabeth's toes curled around his clasp knife, which was concealed in her shoe.

"You have such a flair for couture, Eliza," Caroline continued, straightening. "Your emerald gown caused a sensation last Season; who could forget it? In fact, I have followed your lead, somewhat. My gown for this evening was designed to match my yellow diamond necklace. It is simply divine." She caught Elizabeth's eye and smiled archly. "Wait! I'll fetch it!" Before Elizabeth could utter a word, Caroline had run away. Within moments she was back with a primrose-coloured gown draped over her arm.

"What do you think?" she said, spreading it out on Elizabeth's bed. "Isn't it perfect?"

It was perfect—for a much younger woman. Pink rosettes cascaded from one shoulder to cross the yellow bodice and skirt. Miss Bingley's costly diamonds would be better placed against a darker, more sophisticated gown, but Elizabeth could hardly say so.

"And my mask! I forgot to bring the mask! It matches the gown exactly." She dimpled. "Do you think I shall be able to keep my identity a secret?" Caroline practically hugged herself in excitement. "Wouldn't it be romantic not to be recognized at all? And to fall helplessly in love with a wonderful stranger?"

Caroline Bingley would be recognized all right, as a plum ripe for plucking! With that necklace, every fortune hunter in the room would be following her about! At one time, avoiding such men mattered very much to Caroline. But now?

"I don't see that at all," said Elizabeth. "How can a masked ball be romantic?"

"Surely you know, you simpleton! A handsome, charming gentleman appears who will dance only with you..."

"How will you know he's handsome if he has a mask covering his face?"

"Dear me, the mask conceals only the smallest bit! Would you miss such a delightful opportunity for romance?"

Now it was Elizabeth's turn to stare. "Have you run mad? Fall in love with a man who isn't at all suitable? I call that a complete waste of my time!"

Caroline plaited the folds of her skirt. "Any gentleman at Lady Claverling's ball will be suitable, I am sure. Besides, I am becoming rather weary of suitable men."

"But what about the man from Derbyshire? The friend of your broth—"

"Oh, *him*," interrupted Caroline. She shrugged. "He was not so suitable after all. I found him to be cold—and heartless."

"Oh." Elizabeth lapsed into silence. "Indeed," she said at last, "I think men—all men—are thoroughly disagreeable!"

"Sir William tells me that Admiral McGillvary will be at the ball tonight. What do you think of that?"

Elizabeth managed a blank look. "Who?"

"Admiral McGillvary. The delightful man I met at dinner on my first evening here."

"Oh yes, the man from Bath. I remember. How very nice for him, I am sure."

Caroline's eyes widened. "Don't you care to see him again?"

"Not particularly," lied Elizabeth.

"Well, *I* do." Caroline eased herself onto the edge of the bed and lowered her voice. "No matter what Louisa says, I want to meet a man, a real man. Not a spineless, drawing-room-nothing like Mr Hurst or my brother's friend from Derbyshire! I want a man who is daring and brave, a commanding man, who carries all before him!"

Elizabeth brought forward a chair. "I know all about naval officers, Caroline," she said frankly, "and let me tell you, they are not worth your consideration. Most of them are so terribly ill-mannered and lowborn—what my father calls mushrooms! Fortune hunters of the worst sort! And I know what you think of *them*."

Miss Bingley picked at the fabric of her skirt. "I do not care so very much anymore," she said slowly. "So long as a gentleman is decent and has a passion for me, I..." She looked up. "I would never marry a brute, Eliza, but one must be practical. Some gentlemen, younger sons, perhaps, must seek a wealthy wife."

"And you are willing to oblige? But truly, you have your hopes set too high if you expect to find happiness with some officer or other. The men I have met are not at all daring or brave. My new brother for instance, Captain Wentworth—"

"Captain? Is he a sea captain?" Caroline's eyes were shining. "Oh, delicious! Is he very dashing? Has he fought...*pirates*?"

Elizabeth blinked; what on earth had come over Caroline? "Dear me, I rather doubt it. Except..." Elizabeth frowned in an effort to remember. "I recall hearing him say that the worst thing about pirates was their stench..."

Caroline dissolved into giggling. "Oh, horrible! And I thought being captured by pirates would be thrilling and romantic! But not if they *stink*!"

"Yes, Captain Wentworth said they have rotting teeth, or some such thing." Elizabeth's calm deserted her. "Can you imagine? Men of the Navy pride themselves on cleanliness! Cleanliness!"

"Admiral McGillvary is a lovely man. What a pity his hair is not darker. I do so adore dark men."

"It is brown; is that not enough?"

"Brown?" An odd look crossed Caroline's face. "You are very kind to say so, Eliza." She dimpled. "Sir William says Admiral McGillvary is bringing a group of officers with him tonight from Whitehall. Perhaps one of them will be the man of my dreams..."

The conversation kept returning to Admiral McGillvary! "It is most unfortunate, then, that Sir William is not dark-haired," said Elizabeth. "I hear that he is hanging out for a rich wife. Although, he is rather elderly."

"But he is only a baronet, Eliza, and I–"

"Only a baronet?"

Caroline's face puckered. "Oh, how can I make you understand my position?" Before Elizabeth could answer, Caroline jumped up and rushed out of the room. She came back with a book. "This," she said soberly, "has changed my life." She pushed the volume into Elizabeth's hands.

Elizabeth opened the cover and turned to the title page. "*The Captain's Cabin Mate*," she read aloud. "A novel? This has–"

"–changed my life? Yes." Caroline spoke seriously. "There was a time when I thought a woman of breeding must read only dry, prosy, mind-improving books. Louisa would have hysterics if she knew, but I don't care! Let me tell you, my eyes have been opened to the truth! I now know what a *real man* is like!"

"But this is a work of fiction."

"Not entirely! This luscious book is absolutely authentic. A sea captain's wife wrote it; it says so in the preface. Here, let me show you."

Caroline began hunting for the reference. "Bah! I cannot find it; you'll have to take my word for it. Oh, don't look like that, Eliza! It is the most *wonderful* story! A young Englishwoman, who is stuck in some foreign port or other, is forced to hide aboard a naval ship to escape the French–"

"What sort?"

"What do you mean, what sort? I haven't the faintest idea. Are there different sorts of ships?"

"According to my brother-in-law, yes. I believe his first command was a very small, horrible type of ship. No one could hide there. I think it eventually sank. But please, go on."

Caroline resumed her synopsis. "To keep the heroine's reputation intact and to save her from, oh, did I mention the lecherous admiral? There is a lecherous admiral who lusts after her, ah, womanly charms."

"Is he ugly?" Elizabeth was warming to the story. "The lecherous admiral, I mean."

"Very!" Caroline cried. "As I was saying, the captain of the ship allows the young woman to pose as his wife. She can't actually become his wife, of course, because they are perfect strangers and because she is engaged to her odious and boring cousin, who is presently in India—"

"Is the captain married to somebody else?"

"No!" Caroline squealed. "And he falls hopelessly in love with the heroine! Although, being a man of extreme honour, he won't admit it. They share his cabin, but very decently. It is very awkward for them, but, oh, so amusing, because everyone else thinks they are married! Imagine, a strong man like that, blushing!"

Elizabeth could hardly keep a straight face. "And he is handsome, naturally."

"A god in the flesh," said Caroline solemnly. "Except for the scar. He has a dreadful sword cut on one cheek, but only half of his face is involved."

"A half-handsome hero, then. He must take care to present the proper profile in company. And, I take it there are pirates in the story?"

"Of course there are!" cried Caroline. "And a naval battle with the French, and a mutinous lieutenant, and a hurricane, too! But my lips are sealed; I won't spoil it for you, dearest. The ending is splendid, though. He takes her into his brawny arms, and they share the most passionate kiss imaginable. And then they are married at sea and can share his cabin in earnest." Caroline's eyes closed in rapturous remembrance.

The clock chimed the hour. "Good gracious, look at the time!" Caroline gathered her book and the pale yellow dress and went out.

Elizabeth watched her go with a smile. "*The Captain's Cabin Mate*," she murmured, shaking her head. If ever she saw that title at a bookseller's, she would certainly buy it, if only to read about the lecherous admiral.

And now she intended to take a nap in preparation for the late night ahead. She kicked off her kid boots and rang the bell to summon Elise. Just in time, she remembered to remove the clasp knife from her shoe.

~ ~ ~ ~ ~ ~ ~ & ~ ~ ~ ~ ~ ~ ~

Anne arrived at Camden Place to hear voices coming from her father's book room. She went to the open doorway. Mr Shepherd, her father's solicitor, stood beside the desk. He looked most uncomfortable, as he was having to endure a cross-examination by Lady Russell. Anne listened carefully to the exchange. She gathered it had something to do with Sir Walter's copy of the lease for this house that Mr Shepherd had been studying.

After a few minutes of this, Charles Musgrove and Captain Benwick came in. They shared a look. "I beg your pardon, ma'am," Charles broke in, "but as we now have the card of invitation, perhaps we'd best not waste any more time here?" He winked broadly at Anne.

Lady Russell broke off mid-sentence to glare at him before finishing what she had to say to Mr Shepherd. With another look at Charles, she abruptly took herself out of the room.

"That's scotched her," said Captain Benwick. "Nice work, Musgrove. Now we've no choice but to ride outside with the driver!"

"Wouldn't have it any other way," Charles replied gaily. "Good thing it's not raining! Cheerio, Shepherd," he added, before shutting the door behind him.

It was with a sour face that Mary watched Lady Russell's carriage pull away. She turned from the window and cast herself on one of the drawing room sofas. "Lady Russell has no leave to be so disagreeable," she said. "I would gladly go in her place! Let her remain behind with Father! A pretty pair they'd make!"

"Has he been troublesome this morning?"

"Oh, dear me, no. Father has been simply delightful!" Mary's face darkened. "It was a complete waste of my time to come, for he'll have nothing to do with me! Here I am, ready to read to him or bear him company, or help him with his meals; but does he want me?"

Anne opened her mouth to speak, but Mary continued on.

"And to think I gave up Henrietta's wedding and left behind my two sweet babies to attend to him! Well!" She dabbed at her eyes with her bare hand. "I do not intend to kick my heels in this empty house, waiting on his good pleasure! I daresay he isn't ill at all!"

Anne found a handkerchief and passed it to Mary. "I've a better notion," she said. "Put on your hat and come with me. I've some shopping to do this afternoon. When I am finished, we'll take tea together."

"Shopping? And tea?" The words worked like magic; Mary's head came up. "Oh, certainly!" she cried. Her bonnet was snatched up with astonishing speed. "What sort of shopping, Anne?" Mary said, as she tied a bow under one ear.

"Clothing. After his spell of duty is over, Frederick would like to visit his brother in Shropshire. I have nothing fit to wear for a holiday."

"You have nothing fit to wear for any occasion," said Mary in a low voice. "But if you're planning to leave very soon, there'll be no time for new dresses. Unless..." Mary's eyes narrowed in suspicion. "You aren't planning to purchase a made-up gown, are you?"

Anne's lips curved into a smile. "Would it be so very bad of me?"

"No one in our family has ever done so, I am sure. It is not at all the thing."

Anne kept her voice steady. "I was hoping to purchase several muslin gowns for the summer. Frederick has given me a generous allowance. If they are reasonable enough, I don't think he'd object to you having one as well."

Mary's eyes went wide. "Muslin gowns?" she said, in an altered tone of voice. "Well, I suppose it wouldn't hurt to look at them." She drew her arm through Anne's. "Of course, anyone knows that a muslin gown is perfectly acceptable, regardless of its maker..."

~ ~ ~ ~ ~ ~ ~ & ~ ~ ~ ~ ~ ~ ~

Elizabeth slewed round in her chair. "A gentleman wishes to see me? *Now?*"

The girl bobbed a curtsey. "If you please, milady, he says it's urgent."

"And what is this gentleman's name?"

The girl's face paled. "If you please, milady," she stammered, "it was Robert as gave the message. It's one of the gentlemen as is staying here. He didn't say a name."

Elizabeth digested this bit of news. It was excessively inconvenient to see anyone just now, let alone a gentleman! Only one man would be impertinent enough: Admiral McGillvary! "Bind up my hair, Elise, and fetch the bronze silk! It appears I have no choice but to speak with this gentleman." She turned to the serving girl. "And where am I to meet this person?"

"In the rose garden, milady. Under the arbour."

"Out of doors?" This was becoming worse and worse! Admiral McGillvary deserved to be roasted!

Sometime late, Elizabeth emerged from her bedchamber. "Urgent. It is urgent, ma'am," she muttered, descending the broad staircase. "I'll show him urgent!" She was not one of his sailors to be ordered about!

When she reached the final landing, she paused to take herself in hand. It would never do to arrive in the garden looking flustered. Besides, it would do him good to wait. Hot-headed men such as he needed to learn patience. Elizabeth resumed her descent in very much the grand manner. The main hall was bustling with activity. Elizabeth brushed past the servants to stand before one of the large mirrors.

She surveyed her reflection with critical eyes. Her hair was terrible, and her face looked lined and old. But there was nothing for it; Admiral McGillvary had ordered her into the garden, so to the garden she must go. She secured her curly-brimmed bonnet, making a very respectable bow. This accomplished, her reflection again underwent scrutiny. She smiled a little. The hat made a great improvement to her appearance, and her gown—a hard-won victory over her much-too-opinionated French dressmaker—was perfection itself. Few women could wear a bronze striped silk, but for the handsome Miss Elliot, nothing was impossible!

The handsome Miss Elliot. Today these words stung with unusual force. At the time of her coming out, she was said to be pretty, and the years had mellowed pretty into beautiful. But now she was reduced to being merely handsome!

As for Admiral McGillvary, what was it he had said? Something about Sir Henry and 'coming about'? Elizabeth lifted her chin. Never again would that man be given an opportunity to insult her! If Admiral McGillvary so much as opened his mouth this afternoon, he would be annihilated!

~ ~ ~ ~ ~ ~ ~ & ~ ~ ~ ~ ~ ~ ~

Meanwhile, a nervous James Rushworth paced beneath the arbour in the rose garden. He glanced over his shoulder at the house. If his mother knew what he was about, he would be done for! He considered the structure of the arbour. The rose vines were thorny and bare; he doubted that the arbour could conceal his bulky person from curious eyes. He resolutely turned his back to the house.

Again his timepiece was brought out. Nearly thirty minutes gone! Surely Miss Elliot had received his message by now! Presently, a crunching of gravel caught his ear. Mr Rushworth's eyes went wide; he dared not turn around. He knew that gait. It was his mother! Sure enough, the footsteps halted at the arbour.

"You desired my presence, sir?" a cool voice said. "Behold, I have come."

James Rushworth spun around. "M-mother?" he stammered.

"Mr Rushworth?" cried Elizabeth. "What are you doing here?"

Poor James Rushworth's heart was hammering; he had never seen Miss Elliot like this, so grim and terrible!

"Good gracious, do you mean it was *you* who sent the message?" she said. "I beg your pardon! I thought it was someone else, for the girl gave no name..."

Mr Rushworth felt a wave of relief. "Oh, servants!" he said, thankful to shift the blame. "One can never trust them to get it right! But," he paused to peer anxiously over Elizabeth's shoulder, "are you sure my mother did not follow you?"

Her brows shot up. "I imagine she is occupied with her toilette, Mr Rushworth, as are all the ladies of our party."

"I knew it! This was my one chance to speak to you, while she is busy making up her face! Though it seems a dashed waste of time, if you ask me, since we will all be wearing masks, you know!"

"Ah!" said Miss Elliot, smilingly, "but do not forget the unmasking at midnight. That is a crucial moment to be looking one's best!"

Mr Rushworth had never thought of that. He thrust this observation aside. Now that he had Miss Elliot to himself, he must speak. But how to begin? She was so very beautiful that at first all he could do was smile. "Miss Elliot," he said, reaching for her hand. "My dear Miss Elliot..."

She took a step back and cast an anxious look at the house. "Would you prefer a more private location for our discussion, Mr Rushworth? Under those trees, perhaps?" She indicated the grove of elms.

"But Moth–" He looked back at the house. One never knew who might be looking out. Yes, he would feel much better being away from prying eyes.

"I'll go first," she suggested. "Perhaps you could take a round-about path and meet me in the grove in, say, five minutes?"

Mr Rushworth was overcome. "You are a clever one, Miss Elliot." He took hold of her hand in order to kiss it.

"Later!" she said, with a sly smile.

Elizabeth pulled her hand out of James Rushworth's plump clasp and made for the garden path. That Mr Rushworth wished to speak to her was incredible! And privately! From his shy, admiring looks, Elizabeth could guess what was to come. But if he proposed, should she accept him?

Did she have a choice?

The path took her toward the terrace beside the river. Here she halted, gazing at the water. How different it had appeared that first night, dancing silver in the moonlight! Sir Henry Farley had found her here that evening and so had Admiral McGillvary. But this afternoon, the sky was blue with streaks of white. The water sparkled cheerfully, and neither Sir Henry nor Admiral McGillvary was anywhere to be seen. In a few minutes, she would have an appointment with a very different sort of man.

"Mr Rushworth has blue eyes," murmured Elizabeth, considering the river's hue. She had noticed his eyes for the first time today, as the slanting rays of the sun had caught them. This was a surprise; she had always though his eyes were dark. Blue eyes were very appealing.

And Mr Rushworth had been kind; she had not noticed that before, either. That he had so honourably given her the Admiral's letter spoke volumes.

"He is wealthy, he is considerate, and although he has no title, he is related to Lady Claverling," she said, listing his good points. "And, although he is ugly, he is easily led."

Elizabeth's throat constricted. This was no time to give in to sentimentality! Was it so important to marry a handsome man? Did it matter that Mr Rushworth was a little foolish? Her own father was rather foolish. He was not hard to manage, either. Whereas, a man like Admiral McGillvary....

Elizabeth closed her eyes. These days at Claverling had taught her this: she had no use for a spirited, opinionated man. In fact, he would be very much in the way! This meant she must choose a man like Mr Rushworth.

The minutes were passing; it was nearly time to meet him. Elizabeth turned to cast an appraising look at the mansion, shining golden in the slanting rays of the sun. A house like this, servants, gardens—

the ability to do and buy exactly what she wished—all of these could be within her grasp. When he asked, she must say: 'Yes, thank you.' The life she was meant to live, bred to live, could be hers, if she would only say three little words.

Three little words. Elizabeth's eyes strayed to the river. Its beauty tore at her heart. There were three other words—little words—that she knew she could never say to him: I love you.

To her horror, Elizabeth discovered that tears were rolling down her cheeks. To weep was unthinkable! She gathered up her skirts and the remnants of her dignity, and fled down the path toward the grove.

~ ~ ~ ~ ~ ~ ~ & ~ ~ ~ ~ ~ ~ ~

As the dinner things were being cleared away, Mary gave a sharp sigh. "Anne," she said, setting down her wine glass, "pining over him won't bring him back any sooner. Honestly, you're nearly as bad as Henrietta."

A smile pulled at the corners of Anne's mouth. Mary was right; she had been staring dreamily at one of the empty chairs. Very sorely did she miss Frederick. As her gaze returned to her sister, her smile slipped a bit. Anne suspected she was still feeling offended at not being asked to travel to Richmond.

"Am I as bad as all that?" Anne spoke pleasantly, determined to overcome Mary's sullenness.

Mary thought for a moment. "No," she said at last, "Henrietta is very much worse. She moons over Charles Hayter dreadfully."

Anne laid her napkin on the table. "Now that they are married, perhaps she will learn to overcome the fault?"

"Oh, certainly. Now that they are married, he'll begin to neglect her soon enough."

Anne dimpled. "I cannot believe all husbands to be neglectful."

Mary shrugged a careless shoulder. "Charles certainly is. He never notices me anymore." There was a pause. "I wish he would."

"He notices that you are unkind to his mother." Anne caught her breath. The words were out before she could stop them!

"Unkind to Mama Musgrove?" cried Mary. "Never!"

Anne sought for a way to soften the sting, but it was hopeless. She had spoken the perfect truth, a truth Mary did not wish to hear. There was nothing for it; having begun she must speak. "You do not mean to be unkind, Mary, and yet..." Anne hesitated, then plunged boldly ahead. "And yet, it is unkind to insist on taking precedence over Mrs Musgrove, as you did when I was last in Uppercross."

"Oh, is that all?" Mary took up the wine glass.

"She is Charles's mother. He is bound to notice the slight."

"Slight? What slight? Perhaps you have forgotten who you are, Anne, but I have not! And it is not unkind to insist on the recognition that is rightfully mine!" Mary tossed her head. "I suppose you will have me be humble and lowly and remind me that the meek shall inherit the earth! Well, I tried that, and it doesn't work! I was slighted and ignored, and it will not do! I'll not change my ways for Charles or his family!"

"But what will others think of you? Wouldn't it better to be—"

"What they will think," interrupted Mary, "is that I am the daughter of Sir Walter Elliot! If I do not remind them, who will? And I think you are unkind to throw it in my face, Anne! I do not care for your snippety hints!"

"I thought you wanted your husband to notice you." Again the blood rushed to her cheeks. This was exactly the sort of outrageous thing Frederick would say! Was she becoming so like him already?

Mary's lower lip began to tremble. "Must you be so like Elizabeth?" she cried, and took refuge in the folds of her napkin.

Unfortunately, Wilson chose this moment to re-enter the dining room. One look at Mary and he quickly withdrew. Anne took a long breath. One way or another, she must bring Mary around. "Oh, I doubt anyone can be as bad as Elizabeth," she said mildly. "Unless it is Lady Russell, when she is very angry. And I think she will be very angry with Elizabeth."

Mary gave a loud sniff.

"Do you know," continued Anne, "I am very glad we were not asked to accompany Charles and Captain Benwick to Richmond. Can you imagine how dreadful it will be?"

Mary raised her head and hiccupped. "But I wished to see Chalfort Hou—"

"—to see Lady Russell give Elizabeth a scold?" Anne maintained an innocent front. "Yes, she shall certainly give her that, a good long one, I imagine. And all the while, there we would be, having to listen to all of it, jolting along in her carriage, smashed up against the two of them. Elise, too! We mustn't forget her."

Mary sat upright. "Elise?" she said. "Good heavens, what a terrible squeeze!"

"And once we left Richmond," Anne said, "we would be forced to spend the night together in some dreary roadside inn."

"With Lady Russell, cross as crabs? Oh! Insupportable!"

Mary said nothing more, and for some moments silence reigned. Presently, she turned her attention to the near-bare table, as though seeing it for the first time. "Anne," she said, quite composed now, "why do you suppose our dessert has not been served?"

Anne reached for the small silver bell. "I must suppose poor Wilson had not the courage," she said. "Seeing that we were...cross as crabs."

~8~
Keeping Poise

Elizabeth pulled the candle nearer. Squinting, she made another attempt to fasten the clasp of her pearl bracelet. It was an awkward, one-handed process, and one that she must work at alone. Elise would have fastened the clasp straightway and without asking questions, but her eyes would have said much. Elizabeth was not strong enough to face that, not yet. Again, her fingers lost hold of the clasp; the bracelet slid to the dressing table. With weary patience, Elizabeth began again, for she must display his love-token or risk offending him.

Offending him! After all she had been through, Elizabeth was not fool enough to do that! Still, it was an awkward circumstance. Any other woman would have worn such a thing on a chain about the neck, pleased and proud of the secret triumph it represented. It was a triumph, but Elizabeth was hardly proud of the part she had played.

At length, the clasp was fastened. Suspended along the row of pearls, shining gold against the white of her evening glove, was a gift from Mr Rushworth: a watch fob seal. He had wanted to give her one of his many rings instead, but Elizabeth had been adamant; he was not to make such an obvious display. This had not been difficult. His lively fear of his mother worked very much in her favour.

The seal was a heavy, mannish piece, a green stone with red flecks, deeply engraved with his initial. He told her the stone was a heliotrope, which Elizabeth knew was another name for a bloodstone. Indeed, it was a fitting emblem for her cold-blooded choice.

At her elbow was the mask for that evening's masquerade. It was black and very ugly. Reluctantly, Elizabeth took it up. Was such a mask the portent of romance, as Caroline Bingley claimed? If so, Caroline was welcome to it. Elizabeth had never allowed romance to have a place in her life, save for a few flutterings over William Elliot, and she was not about to begin now.

A soft scratching at the door told her Caroline had come. It was time to go down. Elizabeth drew on her remaining evening glove, took up the mask, and blew out the candle.

"Why, my dear," Caroline said, when Elizabeth came out. "What has happened to your beautiful red gown?"

Elizabeth smoothed the golden fabric. She'd rejected the red dress because of Admiral McGillvary. Thinking of him made her remember something else. Gracefully, she bent down and removed a small object from her shoe. With an apologetic smile to her companion, Elizabeth slipped back into her bedchamber and tossed the clasp knife onto the dressing table. What did it matter if Elise found it? Why had she worried about its discovery?

She and Caroline were almost to the staircase when Caroline gave a cry. "Eliza! Your mask! You've forgotten to put it on!" Elizabeth grimaced and handed over the hateful thing.

"Have you heard from your father, Eliza?" Caroline enquired, as she fastened the mask in place. Without waiting for an answer, she turned and continued her descent. "I have the liveliest fear that you will be snatched away from us before Wednesday's concert. Lady Amcott says it is to be held here, for a very select company—rather like a command performance! Won't that be wonderful?"

"I—" Elizabeth moistened her lips and said in a rush, "I will be leaving for Bath on Thursday morning. Mr Rushworth has offered to see me home."

"You don't say!" Caroline's mask could not hide her saucy smile. "What a sweet gesture." Below, the entrance hall was filled with guests. "Poor boy," she said loudly, over the chatter of the others. "I hear he's had a rough time of it. You do know that he and I are neighbours?"

"He has mentioned his house on Grosvenor Square, yes." Elizabeth did not know what else to say. Soon, they would be officially engaged; she must begin to speak of him sometime. "His mother owns a house in Bath, as well," she heard herself say. "We were introduced this past winter. As you say, James is very...sweet."

Caroline looked back with an amused smile. "I had no idea the two of you were acquainted so intimately! Do I sense the tender stirrings of romance?"

Now Elizabeth began to feel ashamed in earnest, as she was forced to confess him before Caroline Bingley. The dead feeling within her disappeared; revulsion took its place. With all her being she longed to shout, "In love with him? Never!"

Instead, she forced a coy smile. "Perhaps. One never knows where love may bloom."

Miss Bingley's answer was lost in the crowd. Elizabeth knew what she was thinking simply by the tilt of her head. However, before she could compose a reply, the Grand March was announced. It was time for the ball to begin.

Elizabeth found herself taking her place in the line, but very near to the end. In a party this size, it was only to be expected. Still, it was a little hard that Miss Elizabeth Elliot, who had opened every ball in the vicinity of Kellynch for years, should be so abased. Unfortunately, she was also forced to admit that as Mrs Rushworth, she would likely be no better. There was only so much precedence that twelve thousand a year could buy!

And so it was with bright eyes and a lump in her throat that Elizabeth danced at the much-anticipated ball at Claverling. Her partner she barely noticed, save for those moments when the dance brought them together. A glance was enough to tell her that he was impeccably dressed. He moved with particular grace, unusual in one so tall. His black mask hid his features well. Indeed, the only distinguishing marks about him were a head of thick auburn hair and a dimple in his well-formed chin. If he would only smile, she thought, perhaps she might have a chance of recognizing him, but he never did. Presently, Elizabeth gave it up. His identity was a mystery…and so was hers. She was content to have it so.

~ ~ ~ ~ ~ ~ ~ & ~ ~ ~ ~ ~ ~ ~

"What the devil does she mean, 'a veritable vortex of dissipation'?" Charles kicked at a stone in the coaching yard. He and Captain Benwick were finishing their cigars, watching the stable boys bring out the team of fresh horses for Lady Russell's carriage.

"A vortex is an eddy," said Benwick. "You know, a whirlpool which pulls down and engulfs anything floating in its path." The ashes at the end of his cigar glowed orange; he blew a stream of smoke. "I don't suppose her ladyship approves of society balls like the one we're to pull Elizabeth from."

Benwick was silent for a moment before adding, "Having seen my share of naval balls, I can almost agree. It isn't a place I'd like a daughter of mine to be without a chaperone."

"Elizabeth isn't young; she doesn't need a chaperone," said Charles. "She can take care of herself, all right."

"Undoubtedly. But, she is a beautiful woman and an unprotected one—a circumstance that often leads to disaster. I've seen it often enough." Benwick puffed meditatively on his cigar. "The beautiful, lonely wife, free for the taking. The charming officer, most willing to oblige. Her ladyship has reason to be concerned."

"Not Elizabeth! She'd set up a screech and send the blighter packing!"

"Perhaps," was all Benwick would say. Presently, the stable boys finished their work; the ostler ambled off, presumably to fetch the coachman. Benwick examined the butt of his cigar, then extinguished it on the ground.

"Where's her ladyship got to, anyway?" Charles wanted to know. "They're nearly finished here."

"Still inside the inn, I imagine."

"All alone and unprotected, James? For shame!"

"Lady Russell isn't young; she doesn't need a chaperone," said Benwick, with a grin. "And you're right; I ought to return and bear her company. But Charles, as this is our final leg, I think we should finish the journey inside the carriage."

"Inside? Oh, lord. Lady Russell will nag and natter these two hours and more! Or," he added, "sit silent as a stone, answering 'Yes' and 'No' like she did at dinner!"

"Think of it as priming the pump," Benwick suggested over his shoulder. "For your dear sister-in-law's benefit."

~ ~ ~ ~ ~ ~ ~ & ~ ~ ~ ~ ~ ~ ~

Amid such a crush, Elizabeth felt overwhelmed. Most of the guests were unknown to her, but as all faces were concealed, she hadn't a prayer of recognizing anyone. Nevertheless, it was a merry crowd, bent on amusement. Never once did Elizabeth lack for a dancing partner. The orchestra was excellent, the refreshments, superb. Supper was to be served at eleven, which had been promised to James Rushworth. Sometime after midnight would come the unmasking. The dancing would likely continue until the wee hours.

Elizabeth was rather depressed by it all. The ball ground on, dance after dance, and between each set, the eager, bobbing form of James Rushworth would appear from nowhere, pleading for her

hand. She refused him, of course, for nothing could be more preju-
dicial than to be seen with the same partner for the entire evening.

But although she was accustomed to dealing with unwanted attention, she had trouble finding enough gracious excuses to satisfy
the puppyish Mr Rushworth. She was now grateful for the ugly
mask, for it concealed her growing disdain. At last, fatigued and
overwhelmed by the overheated, stifling air of the ballroom, Elizabeth sent him away to procure a glass of punch with the promise of a
private interview on the portico.

It was all so disappointing. She had plotted and connived and
lied to be here, and in the end, it was not worth the trouble. And
now she must face a tender tryst with Mr Rushworth. With all her
heart, Elizabeth prayed that the portico would be crowded, as were
the other public rooms of the mansion. Unfortunately, it was not.
Those who lingered there kept to the shadows.

Elizabeth wandered between the columns, pressing gloved hands
to her flaming cheeks. After the vile mix of odours in the ballroom,
the fresh air was delicious. But even here there was no peace. As she
began to recover her composure, the strains of an old country dance
drifted out to mock her. Elizabeth must wince, for she knew the tune
by heart: *Dissembling Love.*

"James," she said, after they had finished their punch, "you must
return to the ballroom. Your mother would be most displeased if she
were to see–"

"My mother be hanged!" he protested. "I've held off all evening
from you, save that one dance. Burn it, I'll not be denied my rightful–"

"Mr Rushworth, please!" Elizabeth cried, aghast. "Lower your
voice, for heaven's sake!" With her prettiest smile, she added, "This
is the first event of the Season. We don't wish to provide grist for the
gossip mill, now do we? Gossip can be very hurtful, as well you may
recall…"

"Curst gossipy snoops!" He pulled out his handkerchief to mop
the sweat from his brow. "And curse this blasted mask! Dashed
uncomfortable things, masks!" He began to pull at its strings.

"Mr Ru-James! What are you doing?" cried Elizabeth. He flung
his mask aside and reached to loosen the strings of hers. "Have you
gone mad?" she said. "We must wait for the unmasking!"

"But how will I kiss you?" His face was awash with love and admiration.

"Kiss me?" The mask fell away from her face, but that was not the worst of it. She felt his arms come round her, pulling her close against his sweaty person. There was no shyness in his manner now.

As his face came nearer to hers, Elizabeth realized she had no choice but to submit. Were they not practically engaged? Closing her eyes, she saw a fleeting image of the prodigal son, reduced to eating pig-slop. Prodigal daughters, she now realized, had to kiss the pigs.

Someone coughed. "Rushworth! I say, Rushworth!" a voice called. "Someone's asking for you inside."

With an ill-concealed oath, Mr Rushworth broke off the kiss. Elizabeth grasped at the interruption as a drowning man would a piece of planking. "Your mother!" she cried, in a ragged voice.

That was enough. Mr Rushworth shied off and made for the ball-room. Elizabeth wiped her lips with the back of her gloved hand. If only she could wipe away the memory of that first, horrible kiss!

"Well, well, well. What have we here?" The same voice that called to Mr Rushworth now spoke to her.

Elizabeth froze. This was not the voice of a stranger.

"Do you know, Miss Elliot," the man said, as he emerged from the shadows, "perhaps I ought to have issued that sword after all."

~ ~ ~ ~ ~ ~ ~ & ~ ~ ~ ~ ~ ~ ~

"And there it is. Chalfort House." Charles' head was practically hanging out of the window, so great was his curiosity. Lady Russell's carriage swayed a little as it navigated the torch-lit sweep of the drive.

Captain Benwick glanced up, but only for a moment. He did not share Charles Musgrove's interest in the estate. Nothing about this journey had been pleasant, but this last confrontation with Miss Elliot would likely cap all. In the seat opposite sat Lady Russell, black-clad and silent. For most of the journey, she had maintained an erect, unyielding posture. Benwick sighed. She would handle her goddaughter, all right, most certainly with an ungentle hand. Was Miss Elliot prone to hysterics? He would find out all too soon.

Again his mind traced through the events that had led him to this place, and again he was brought to the same unhappy conclusion. Having begun, there had been no way to shirk his duty in helping Charles Musgrove fetch Elizabeth Elliot home.

~ ~ ~ ~ ~ ~ ~ & ~ ~ ~ ~ ~ ~ ~

With all her might, Elizabeth struggled to maintain composure. The only thing to be done was to maintain a dignified silence and hope Admiral McGillvary would go away.

But the man did not go. "I find it most unusual," said he, strolling nearer, "that you are often in the garden at night, Miss Elliot. And tonight is no exception." He paused, as if awaiting a response.

"And, it seems to me," he continued, unflustered by her silence, "that whenever you are here, you are never alone! On that first night, let me see, you were with Sir Henry, were you not? And tonight? Why, tonight I find you with another gentleman."

Elizabeth kept her attention fixed rigidly ahead.

"Tell me, Miss Elliot, are you always such a hellion at house parties?"

Elizabeth whirled to face him. "A hellion? How dare you!"

He spread his hands. "But what else am I to think?" Behind his mask, his eyes were shining. "Loving words and a tender embrace under the portico! With Rushworth, of all people. I am shocked, Miss Elliot, shocked!"

Elizabeth's eyes narrowed. He was mocking her, of course. Heaven only knew what he thought of her! Looking at him more closely, Elizabeth suffered a shock of her own, for this was the man who had been her partner for the opening of the ball. She had actually danced with Admiral McGillvary!

"Appearances can be deceiving," she said sweetly, "for even now, I am not alone, am I? But do you suppose your presence pleases me, sir?"

He placed a hand over his breast, feigning a wound. "Alas, I am as all the others, a hapless victim of your charms. No better than poor Rushworth, whom you lured into your lair."

"Lured?" cried Elizabeth. "Do you suppose that dreadful scene was my fault?"

Admiral McGillvary remained unperturbed. "Why, certainly. Who else is there to blame?"

She answered nothing, but he was not disconcerted by her silence. Indeed, it seemed as if he were enjoying himself.

"Come now, Miss Elliot, where is your fighting spirit?" he challenged. "You submitted to Rushworth without a struggle. And I took such pains to see that you were properly armed."

"Do you truly think," she demanded, "that I wished to be mauled by that person?"

"No, no more than I wished Boney to escape Elba!" he countered swiftly. "And yet, by your estimation, mine was the blame!"

So this was the crux of the matter: she was being punished. Elizabeth was loath to admit a fault, but this time there was no escaping it. "I beg your pardon, Admiral McGillvary," she said stiffly. "You are entitled to your revenge. Now you have it. Undoubtedly, this is why you sought me out. I bid you a good evening, then."

"Actually," he said, smiling, "I came to invite you to go riding with me tomorrow. What do you say?"

"I do not make it a practice to accompany any gentleman who insults me, sir!"

"Now that I will not believe. How could you be in Rushworth's company for even five minutes and not be insulted?"

Elizabeth had to smile; was the man never at a loss? But of course she could not accept his invitation. "I-I brought no horse," she said.

"Come now, Lady Claverling must have any number of mounts you may ride. You'll never convince me you are not an intrepid horsewoman."

Elizabeth was nothing of the sort. Her father did not approve of riding, so she had never learned. She suddenly became aware that the music had stopped. She heard her voice bleat into the silence, "I...I brought no riding dress."

This checked him, but only for a moment. "Then join me for supper."

Elizabeth could only stare at his outstretched hand.

"Come, come," he urged. "You owe it to me, you know."

Elizabeth did not know what to do. To accept Admiral McGillvary's request was to offend Mr Rushworth. "I...cannot! Not tonight!"

The door to the house opened; a shaft of light crossed the terrace. Although the mask hid his expression, Elizabeth had the impression that he was rather hurt by her refusal. "No, you...don't understand," she stammered, blushing furiously. "Tonight's supper is promised to—"

"There she is!" The musical voice of her hostess carried clearly. "Yes," the voice continued, "I see her now!"

Elizabeth turned sharply toward the door.

"Cousin, you are an absolute gem!" she heard Lady Claverling say. Behind her stood a small knot of people, James Rushworth among them. "Miss Elliot, here are your godmother and your brother, come to fetch you home. We are indebted to dear cousin James for knowing exactly where to find you!"

Elizabeth was nearly overcome. "My father? Is he...well?" she said, noticing Lady Russell's black gown and forbidding expression.

"We have come to fetch you home," was Lady Russell's only response. "Elise is packing your trunk as we speak."

"I do hope you will join us for supper before you go," said Lady Claverling. "You must be famished from your journey."

"I thank you, no," said Lady Russell. "Elizabeth, come! We must leave at once!"

"But–"

Lady Russell marched forward and grasped Elizabeth's forearm. She lowered her voice. "Elizabeth, how could you? In addition to everything else, I find you here, alone, with this masked person." She eyed Admiral McGillvary wrathfully.

Elizabeth felt the blood drain from her face; surely he had heard every word! "Lady Russell!" she whispered.

"No missish airs with me, if you please!" Lady Russell looked around with displeasure. "A Masked Ball!" she said scornfully.

"Don't forget to mention the kiss," he murmured.

"What?" cried Lady Russell.

It was now Elizabeth's turn to take hold of her godmother's arm. "Never mind him," she said, pulling her away. "He's only funning."

"He? And, pray, who might *he* be?"

Captain Benwick held the door as Elizabeth pulled Lady Russell into the house. "It's only Admiral McGillvary, Lady Russell," Elizabeth whispered. "It is best to pay him no mind."

"Admiral McGillvary!" Lady Russell halted abruptly on the threshold. "Patrick McGillvary of Belsom Park? Good gracious, Elizabeth, are you lost to all reason? How could you allow yourself be alone with that man! Don't you know anything about his reputation?"

"Reputation?" Elizabeth cast a fleeting look over her shoulder at the figure on the portico. "Has he a repu–"

"This is neither the time nor the place to discuss this." Lady Russell gave her arm a tug. The door was closed by a man Elizabeth did not recognize. His coat proclaimed that he was an officer of the Navy. "Has he a...a reputation, Lady Russell?" Elizabeth asked later, as she prepared to enter Lady Russell's coach. Lady Russell did not answer. The unknown man coughed. His expression, barely visible in the light of the lanterns, told Elizabeth all she needed to know.

~9~

An Unjust Recompense

Rain drummed against the window of the bedchamber; Elizabeth lay listening to its music. Then she remembered and came fully awake. This was not Chalfort House. She was in Bath, at Lady Russell's house on Rivers Street. She pulled the pillow over her head.

But it was fatal to lie in bed. If sleep did not return, memories would, and memories of her trip to Richmond—certain memories, in particular—were dangerous. Elizabeth got up, found her robe, and padded across the room to her open trunk. There was work to be done.

There were letters to be written to her hostess, to Miss Bingley, and to Mr Rushworth. The sooner these were posted, the better. All would be variations of the same theme:

> I am very sorry to have been called home so suddenly, but I have good news. My father is not as ill as was previously thought.

Lady Russell had said nothing about his condition, so she was free to assume all was well. One by one, the letters were copied out. It took some courage to add:

> Under the circumstances, I cannot blame dear Lady Russell for becoming overwrought and fetching me home.

Elizabeth laid down her pen. Oh, Lady Russell had done her work very well and in such an odious, overbearing way! She did not look forward to breakfast this morning, for there would doubtless be more of the same. Elizabeth ended each letter with:

In spite of everything, I am not unhappy to be with poor
Father in his hour of need. Please, will you do me the
honour to call whenever you are in Bath?
I remain,
Very sincerely yours,

Elizabeth signed her name with a flourish. However, when it
came time to seal Mr Rushworth's letter, she hesitated. Ought she to
include a personal note? It could be enclosed in Caroline Bingley's
letter quite easily. In fact, Caroline would delight in being party to a
secret delivery.

For now that they were parted, she must not allow James Rushworth to forget his promise. Lady Russell's interference made her
even more determined. Whatever the cost, she must have her own
establishment, free from interference from her family—especially
Lady Russell! Elizabeth pulled forward another sheet of paper. She
wrote slowly:

My dear Mr Rushworth,
I am terribly sorry to have been called away so suddenly.
We never even had a chance to say good-bye! When next
you are able to come to Bath without arousing suspicion,
please know that I eagerly await your visit.

Elizabeth studied her handiwork, substituting the more truthful
anxiously for *eagerly* in the last sentence. Even so, the message was a
safe one. This note could be entrusted to Caroline Bingley's care
and, if discovered, would give nothing away. Even so, it was not
very lover-like. Elizabeth suspected she should do more—sprinkle the
page with scent or write an endearment.

She sat for some time considering the more commonplace expressions.

I long to be held in your arms again.

This was not at all true! Could she convey the same idea without
actually writing the words? She thought some more.

If only we had had one more dance together.

This was better, but only a little. James was a clumsy dancer; she
would rather not dance with him ever again! For that matter, she
would rather not write anything sweet or kind or endearing! Eliza-

beth had never met Mr Rushworth's former wife; what if she had been a romantic? Mr Rushworth might have expectations.

Elizabeth decided not to risk it. There were several standard modes for declaring passion. A love-token, such as the one he had given her, would do the trick. She could scarcely bear to look at his watch fob seal, yet it was a solid reminder of their agreement. At length she hit upon the very thing. It was romantic, yet impersonal; she would send him a lock of her hair.

It took a few minutes to locate the scissors. It took even longer to decide which section of hair would be the least damaged by the loss. Finally the choice was made, and with determination, Elizabeth lopped off a curl. She wound it round her finger, thinking. And the more she thought about it, the more revolting it became. An impersonal token? Not at all! It was horrible, sending him a lock of her very own hair! In her mind's eye she could see the awful James stroking it, gloating over it, bringing it to his cheek and kissing it tenderly. The thought of his lips made her shudder.

But how foolish, to risk her future because she was squeamish over a few strands of hair! What was important was to maintain appearances. She must appear to be in love with James Rushworth. Still, it would be much nicer to merely appear to give him a lock of her hair. Lady Russell's late husband had been quite the huntsman; at one time he had an animal skin displayed in his study. Whatever it was, it had long, shaggy hair almost the same auburn colour as her own. Elizabeth laughed to think of James Rushworth tenderly sighing over a lock of bear's hair!

But such a thing was not to be. The rug must have been discarded long ago. Elizabeth took up the pen and, remembering how Admiral McGillvary had closed his little note, signed:

Yours,
E.

Mr Rushworth's love letter was promptly sealed up, enclosed in Caroline's (with a note), then all were set aside to be posted later. There was another matter of business that required attention: her precious ledger needed work. Each night at Claverling, she had carefully added her comments about what had gone forward that day. Now it was time to add notations about the masked ball, with detailed observations about each one she had seen or spoken with. This occupied her for some time.

Finally she turned to the page headed *Admiral McGillvary*. This page she had avoided all week, but she could do so no longer. What could she say about him? Volumes!

Arrogant. Overly-opinionated. Conceited. Vengeful. Has a Reputation.

Justice forced her to add:

Well-dressed. Conversant. Said to be handsome. Dances well.

He wished me to go riding with him. This thought came before she could stop it, but she did not dare to write this in her book. Would she have gone riding with him? Heady visions assaulted her: galloping full-tilt over open fields, soaring over hedges with the wind in her face. The exhilaration of freedom, perfect freedom...

Elizabeth tightened her hold on the pen. It was ridiculous to think about what could never be! She continued with her entries. She wrote next:

A horseman. Sensitive to insults about the Navy. Retalia-tory. Never at a loss for words.

She hesitated, then added:

Saw me on the portico with J.R. Thinks I am a coward.

This last was all too true, and it bothered Elizabeth greatly. Why it mattered that Admiral McGillvary thought ill of her she could not say. There was another thing that troubled her. In all this time, she had never had a good look at him. A moustache, a smile, a strong chin, eyes that sparkled behind a mask—she could not remember anything more. Since the man owned a house in Bath and presuma-bly moved in polite circles, she would certainly see him again. How humiliating it would be not to recognize him! She would then appear not only to be a coward but stupid as well!

Elizabeth applied the blotter to the page with unnecessary force. More than anything, she hated to be thought stupid!

Before long, the door opened and Elise came in. She paused, ob-viously surprised to see Elizabeth awake and busy. After murmuring

a greeting, she set about the business of laying out Elizabeth's clothing. Elizabeth closed the ledger and rested her elbows on it, still
thinking about the Admiral. A motion caught her eye: a folded
paper, inscribed with her name, now rested on the dressing table.
The handwriting was all too familiar. This was a message from her
godmother.

> I have had a note from Anne. For some reason (which she
> did not explain to me), she feels it is crucial that you and I
> see your father this morning. As you know, I had hoped to
> put this off for a few days to give his vexation time to
> abate. However, you might as well get the unpleasantness
> over with. We depart for Camden Place promptly at ten.
> Elise will bring your breakfast. Please do not be late.

Elizabeth descended to find her godmother standing in the entrance hall tying the ribbons of her hat. "Good morning, Elizabeth.
You are late," was all she said, before nodding to Longwell to open
the door. Lady Russell went directly to her waiting carriage, and
Elizabeth was left to snatch up her bonnet and follow as best she
could.

When they arrived, they found Anne and Mary waiting in the
drawing room. Soon Sir Walter came in, carried by two footmen. He
glared at her. Elizabeth looked the other way. Obviously, he wished
to make her feel guilty about her trip to Richmond. He succeeded.

But he was changed, Elizabeth could see that. He looked thinner;
his face was more lined than before. As Sir Walter was lowered onto
one of the sofas and a blanket arranged on his lap, Elizabeth looked
more closely at him. Sure enough, there was a sparkle in his eyes.
He was up to something.

Sir Walter held up a hand. "My dears," he began, in a frail and
trembling voice Elizabeth knew was put on, "I have called you here
this morning to put a period to this chapter in our lives; that is to say,
our chapter regarding this brief, pleasant residence at Camden
Place."

Sir Walter's voice grew stronger, assuming the lordly tone he
used on Public Days at Kellynch. "As you know," he continued, "we
removed to this city in September as a means of retrenchment. My
decision was made from motives of the most disinterested selflessness. That is, not only as a means of economization, but also out of
concern for the welfare of my two eldest daughters. To say truth,

they were in desperate need of the benefits of a larger social circle."
He nodded to Anne. "One of those daughters has married. And let
us hope," he added, with a small, tight smile in Elizabeth's direction,
"that the other will follow suit in due time."

Elizabeth's hands clenched into fists.

"Nevertheless, the time has come for me to put selflessness aside.
I must begin to consider myself. I find that for reasons of health, I
must do a little retrenching of my own. For this, I owe an inestima-
ble debt to dear Mr Savoy, who has shown me the way." Sir Walter
paused to acknowledge the physician, who stood in front of the
drawing room door. "Under his care, I shall be restored to my
former robustness." Sir Walter paused again in order to cough–a
deep, wracking cough, which seemed to weaken him.

"And now," he said, more softly, "the time has come to say good-
bye to you, my daughters, and to this house. I have left cards with
my new address with Wilson. Mr Shepherd will handle the rest. You
will, I am sure, wish to visit your poor father from time to time?" He
smiled benignly. "Anne, as you know, has very nice ideas about
charity and visitation. You would do well to imitate her example."
He motioned for the footmen to come forward.

Elizabeth struggled to find her voice. Lady Russell beat her to it.
"Merciful heavens, Sir Walter!" she cried, as the men lifted him.
"You are quitting this house? But where shall you go?"

"To The Citadel, madam," he said. "If I am to become well, I
must be entirely independent of all unpleasantness, all encum-
brances! My spirit must be free to soar!"

"But," said Lady Russell, "when do you plan to return?"

"To this house? Never. I am giving up the lease."

"But what about Elizabeth? She will have no home!"

The footmen carried Sir Walter to the doorway. "Elizabeth is a
resourceful girl and an independent one," he said, over his shoulder.
"She may stay with either of her sisters for the duration of the Season. At summer's end, we shall resume our residence at Kellynch
Hall, as befits our station."

"Well, I never!" cried Mary. "What am I to do with her at Uppercross Cottage?"

"But what about the Crofts?" said Elizabeth. "Surely they are not
leaving Kellynch Hall!"

Sir Walter looked uncomfortable. "Admiral Croft will not be re-
newing the lease. He prefers to live in Bath."

"But the retrenchment!" cried Lady Russell. "What about the retrenchment? Surely you cannot return to Kellynch Hall so soon!"

"Ah, the retrenchment. The retrenchment is now finished!" Sir Walter gave a slight, graceful wave. "Farewell, my dears!"

Mr Savoy made a bow before closing the door. The three women were left alone.

Mary pulled the door open; together they rushed out to the landing. "Well!" she cried, watching the men exit the house. "Of all the high-handed, odious things! And look, he is gone! Just like that!"

Elizabeth stood rooted to the spot. "I shall remain here," she said. "And you need not fear, Mary. Not for anything will I impose upon you." She turned to find Anne at her elbow.

"I am sorry for this, Elizabeth" said Anne, in her quiet way. "Apparently you will need to be out of this house by Monday. According to Mr Shepherd, it has been let to others."

"So soon?" cried Lady Russell. "Mr Shepherd must negotiate for more time! Why was I not told of this before?"

"It was arranged yesterday morning during your absence," said Anne. "I, too, was told nothing until it was too late. The papers have been signed. There is nothing we can do."

"Yesterday?" Lady Russell struck her hands together. "Yesterday, while I was chasing after Elizabeth! And now he has gone off, poor lamb, captive to that horrid doctor!"

"Poor lamb?" cried Elizabeth.

"Your father is victim to a cruel ruse and deserves our pity," said Lady Russell. "And the two people who could have stopped him, who *would* have stopped him, were away on that fool's errand in Richmond! Now you see what has come of your wickedness, Elizabeth!" She caught sight of Mary. "And where were you, Mistress Mary? Surely you saw what was going forward! You were in this house all that time! Why didn't you stop him?"

Mary blanched. "I...I was shopping."

"For every moment of every day? You allowed that physician admittance to this house! How could you?"

"How was I to know what was going on?" Mary pulled out her handkerchief. "No one tells me anything!"

"Father was very secretive about his plans," said Anne. "We ourselves saw Mr Shepherd here, Lady Russell, with the lease for the house in his hands. How could we have known what Father had planned?"

Lady Russell folded her arms across her chest. "What is to be done about Elizabeth?"

"I shall remain here," Elizabeth said. "According to Father, I am quite the old maid! I am not a child!"

"As we have seen by your behaviour of late," said Lady Russell. "You will stay with me, Elizabeth, until I depart for Muriel Stanhope's next week. In the meantime, your personal belongings, and your father's, will need to be packed up and stored somewhere."

"Anne has the largest house," Mary put in.

"Anne has the most cluttered house," countered Anne. "To be honest, I have not begun to settle in. I don't see how I can possibly accommodate a guest! At least, not right at the moment."

"Very well, I shall find room for your father's things at Rivers Street," said Lady Russell. "And next week, Elizabeth, you shall either come with me to Mrs Stanhope's, or go to one of your sisters. Is that understood?"

"I shall do neither!"

"My dear, you do not have a choice in the matter! The house is let to others."

"Lady Russell has several empty bedchambers," offered Mary. "And even you cannot be ashamed of her house, Elizabeth."

Lady Russell gave Mary a quelling look. "In the meantime," she continued, "we shall do what we can to rescue your father from this Citadel. Although why he would consign himself to such a place is a mystery to me!"

"Is it?" said Elizabeth. "To me it is plain as day! It is his excuse! Don't you see? He is not able to appear in London this Season, as he has done every year of his life, so he must be seen to be violently ill! Incapacitated, in fact!"

It was not until later that she remembered the letter she had burned. Was he hiding as well?

~ 1 □ ~
Till the Storm Be Overblown

They reminded him of beetles, these men who sat around the makeshift conference table. Even their names were weevil-like: Sturmer and Lonk. Hervy and Snape. And they'd scuttled about all that long morning as McGillvary went through his list of grievances.

This visit was particularly galling, for no member of the family had ever come to the premises. Old Billingsley had handled everything with a firm hand. But Billingsley had passed on last autumn, as had the elder McGillvary. His son was now at the helm, a man who had plenty of experience with entrenched bureaucrats and functionaries.

"To a man, you deserve to be flogged," he muttered.

"Sir?"

"Under your leadership, a profitable lending institution has become a Hurrah's Nest." Admiral McGillvary's gaze shifted to his riding crop on the table. The men, who were watching his every move, flinched.

McGillvary pushed back his chair and stood. "Gentlemen," he said, "these accounts will be brought into compliance before the next Quarter Day. Is that understood?"

Mr Lonk moistened his lips. "Certainly, sir!" he said. "As your Honour will be pleased to recall, we have been engaged doing just that! In fact, only this week we–"

"Furthermore," continued McGillvary, looking hard at Mr Lonk, "no new loans will be made without my express approval. Lonk, you will report to Mr Starkweather."

Beads of perspiration dotted Mr Lonk's forehead. "Yes, your Honour, sir!"

128

McGillvary eyed the men one by one. Their faces registered a pleasing degree of strain. "I would like to remind you of a proverb, gentlemen: *Never confuse motion with action.*" He paused. There was a long silence. "Action brings results. I want results, gentlemen, not excuses. By the next Quarter Day, let us hope that these unfortunate errors," he indicated the stack of ledgers littering the table, "will be corrected." McGillvary smiled slightly. "After all, these are difficult times in which to begin a new career." The tension in the room was now palpable. "That will be all, gentlemen," he said.

As the men filed out McGillvary took his seat, grimacing at the unsteadiness of his chair. Was everything about this business falling to bits? He selected a pen from the standish. "Sturmer," he said, without looking up, "where are the drafts I must sign? And Snape, bring in some coffee. Fresh coffee." McGillvary glanced up; the man was staring stupidly. "Now, Snape, if you please."

Mr Snape and Mr Sturmer exited the room, leaving McGillvary to sign the drafts. Faulty equipment made this a challenge. By the time he got the inkpot uncorked, his right cuff was stained with ink. He swore under his breath and went on with the signing.

Presently, the coffee was brought in. A raw-boned clerk came in with the cup; Mr Snape followed with the coffee pot. Unfortunately, the boy lost his footing and stumbled against Mr Snape, who dropped the pot of steaming coffee onto the table. The cup toppled into McGillvary's lap, along with a generous spray of hot coffee.

With an oath, McGillvary jerked away. This proved too much for the ancient chair. It collapsed, sending McGillvary sprawling.

Mr Snape stood by, clasping and unclasping his hands, his stammered apologies interrupted by a string of oaths from McGillvary. Trembling, Mr Snape assisted him to rise, unaware that his foot was planted on the tail of McGillvary's coat. There followed the unmistakable tearing of fabric and another round of oaths.

"Jeffreys," moaned Mr Snape, looking to the boy who had caused the disaster. "Get me Higgins's spare frock coat! Immediately!"

~ ~ ~ ~ ~ ~ ~ & ~ ~ ~ ~ ~ ~ ~

Alone in a hired hack, Elizabeth emptied the contents of her purse into her lap. Carefully she counted out the coins. There were precious few of them. Saturday had been Lady Day, but her father had said nothing about how—or if—he would pay her quarterly allowance. For the last three weeks he'd refused to see anyone, even

Mr Shepherd. Today, Elizabeth was acting on her own, for another of those letters had come. She'd sent the others to Mr Shepherd, but apparently he was away for he never responded. She brought out today's letter and read again its troubling message:

> Regarding the overdue account: Would Sir Walter Elliot, or his man of business, be pleased to call upon the Financial Commissioner at Madderly, Kinclaven, and Planque at his earliest, most immediate convenience? In this matter, time is of the essence.

Surely the misunderstanding was the bank official's fault. Her father was gravely ill; he could not be expected to attend to his business as he lay dying! But, of course, she knew her father would never bother to explain himself, so nothing would be solved.

Thus, she had decided to handle this matter on her own. She would forward this letter to Mr Shepherd, again, and she would explain the situation to the bank official, whatever his name was. Elizabeth glanced at the signature: *Lonk.* Almost, she laughed out loud. To have a conversation with someone named Lonk would not be difficult at all! The man would blush and bow and wash his hands and apologize profusely for involving her in the matter. The letters would stop arriving, Mr Shepherd would come to Bath, and all would be well. Elizabeth folded the letter. "I certainly hope Father appreciates all I do for him," she murmured.

At length the hack jerked to a stop, and the door came open. Elizabeth climbed out, ignoring the driver's offer of assistance. He looked grubby and disreputable. She had never dealt with such a person before, and she was not about to begin now. As it was, he had to repeat the fare three times before she understood what he was saying.

This was a crowded area of Bath, with tall, undistinguished buildings on either side of the street. Worse, common pedestrians filled the sidewalk. But there was nothing for it; Elizabeth must finish her business, especially since it had cost her something to get here. She straightened her hat, squared her shoulders, and stode to the door bearing the name Madderly, Kinclaven, and Planque.

~ ~ ~ ~ ~ ~ ~ & ~ ~ ~ ~ ~ ~ ~

The last shreds of his patience gone, McGillvary strode out of Lonk's office. "There must be a decent pen somewhere in this hovel," he said under his breath. He came into the front office. A row of clerks sat at tall desks copying out documents. The reception area was empty.

So much the better, thought McGillvary. He was wearing someone's ancient brown coat, which was too short in the shoulders and arms. His cuffs were splotched with ink; his waistcoat was generously stained with coffee. But there was no time to think about his appearance; he must find a pen. There were none on the counter, so he began pulling out drawers. One stuck fast, so he tugged at it. And of course it came suddenly free—both the drawer and its contents went flying. However, among the items on the floor were several pens. McGillvary knelt to gather them. He never heard the chime when the outer door opened.

A faint cough and an "I beg your pardon," caused him to look up. A woman's face peered down at him—a lovely face, framed by a charming hat with curled feathers. It was all he could do not to stare. What the devil was *she* doing here?

Mr Snape came into the front office and found McGillvary kneeling on the floor. He threw up his hands. "Gracious me, Mr McGil–!"

McGillvary's glare silenced him. "We have a customer, Snape," he said quietly. He climbed slowly to his feet, aware that his face was flushed.

Miss Elliot presented a calling card. "I beg your pardon, Mr…Gill," she said. "Would you be so kind as to inform Mr–" she broke off to consult a paper, "Mr Harold Lonk that Miss Elliot is here to see him?"

Patrick McGillvary's eyes never left her face. Could it be that she did not recognize him? And then he remembered the moustache. What luck that Pym had lost yesterday's bet, for the moustache was gone and, by all appearances, his identity was safe! He took the card she offered, planting an inky thumbprint in the process. Miss Elliot's brows rose. She reached into her reticule. "Let me give you another," she said.

"That will not be necessary, thank you," said McGillvary. "Was Mr Lonk expecting you, Miss Elliot?"

"Not precisely." She indicated a folded letter. "I am calling on behalf of my father who is ill."

"I'll tell him you are here," he said. In the hallway, McGillvary collided with the unfortunate Mr Lonk. "Miss Elliot has come to see

131

you, Lonk," he said, taking the man by his shoulders and propelling him back into his office, "although why the devil you asked her here is beyond me!"

Mr Lonk stared at her card. "But I didn't!" he squeaked. "Admiral, sir! Sir Walter Elliot's account is one of *those accounts!* Delinquent!"

"Give her a thirty-day extension."

Mr Lonk gaped at him.

"A thirty-day extension, no questions asked," repeated McGillvary. "As a courtesy to a valued client."

"But, Admiral. Sir Walter Elliot is hardly a valu–"

"Just do it, Lonk." McGillvary took up his hat, crop, and leather satchel. "And send those drafts to Belsom," he said. "I'll sign them tonight. Starkweather will return them in the morning. And Lonk. Order some pens–decent, functioning pens."

Still, McGillvary lingered in the doorway, a slight smile pulling at his lips. Mr Snape escorted Elizabeth Elliot to Lonk's office in very much the grand manner. The door was kept open, he noted with approval. So, her father was ill–that was hardly a surprise. But why the devil had he sent her to do his business? And what a fortunate thing she hadn't recognized him! Still smiling, he let himself out of the building.

Since he hadn't instructed Henry to wait, he'd have to take a hack. No matter, the hacking stand was only a few blocks away. As McGillvary put on his own hat, he noticed that the elbow of his borrowed coat was split. In fact, not only his waistcoat but also his fawn trousers were generously splashed with coffee. His appearance was worse than he thought. He was, in fact, the spitting image of Simple Simon!

Grinning, McGillvary turned the corner and strode along George Street, wondering whether anyone else would fail to recognize him. A crack of thunder caused him to glance overhead. The clouded sky was becoming darker by the minute. Lightning flashed, thunder rolled–and before he'd gone another block, the rain began to come down in earnest. A gust of wind took away his hat and rolled it into the street. Patrick McGillvary threw back his head and laughed.

But this was no spring shower. Pedestrians went running for shelter and McGillvary with them. He opened the door of the nearest shop and ducked inside. The sign on the door read *The Cytherean Garden Tearoom.* The reception area was crowded. McGillvary pushed through, for a small table by the window was vacant. He tossed his riding crop onto the chair.

"And will you be wanting The Special, sir?" A woman in a mob-cap and starched apron bobbed a curtsey. She went on to recite: "Curried chicken sandwiches, cucumber sandwiches, biscuits, and Scottish scones with jam and clotted cream, a slice of seedcake, and a pot of tea."

McGillvary was not fond of tea, but the food sounded wonderful. He pulled out the chair and sat. Smiling, he spoke his thought, "I don't suppose you have any sherry?"

"Beg pardon, sir?"

He recalled his attire. Simple Simon, after all, was a man of humble tastes. "The Special will do nicely," he said.

~ ~ ~ ~ ~ ~ ~ & ~ ~ ~ ~ ~ ~ ~

Elizabeth found Mr Lonk to be most understanding about her father's situation. She didn't know what an extension was, but it seemed to be a good thing. Out of his office she sailed, very pleased with her abilities as a businesswoman. The interview had proceeded just as she'd foreseen.

The street was wet; vehicles rumbled past at an alarming pace, spraying mud and water. Elizabeth watched them with trepidation. How could she tell which ones were for hire? She decided to walk on for a bit. Perhaps she would find a gentleman to ask, or perhaps she could find her way back to Rivers Street on her own. There were many persons on the street, but no one looked trustworthy. Then again, she wasn't excited about spending any more money. She struck off in what she hoped was the right direction.

By the time she reached George Street, Elizabeth was thoroughly confused. How different Bath appeared when one was riding inside a carriage! Rivers Street might be very far away, or it might be quite nearby. If only she could decide which streets to take!

And then the rain began again. As people ran for shelter, Elizabeth was swept along. She found herself in a shop surrounded by damp, unsavoury persons. The man standing beside her smelled strongly of sweat; a stray child trod upon her foot.

"Here now! Patrons only!" A sharp-eyed woman in a ruffled cap herded the 'refugees' to her tables. Elizabeth looked the other way. She was not about to part with any more of her precious coins, not even for a place to sit.

"Miss Elliot!" a voice called. Elizabeth pretended not to hear. There was no one she knew in this rabble. Besides, it was a man's voice.

The woman in the mobcap looked hard at Elizabeth. "Patrons only, ma'am!" she repeated.

A hand touched Elizabeth's elbow. Reluctantly she turned. It was the freckled clerk from Mr Lonk's. "Over here!" he insisted.

When seen at close quarters, he was even worse than she remembered. She nodded politely and turned away, but his fingers kept hold of her elbow. "I have a chair for you! Come quickly before the Gorgon returns!"

Elizabeth hesitated. "I thank you, sir," she began to say, but the door opened, and a fresh wave of people trooped in. Rain lashed at the windows, thunder made the china dance. Somewhere a child began to cry. "Oh, very well," she said. She allowed him to lead her to a table by the window.

"It's Mr...Gill, is it not? From the counting house?" she said, as he held the chair for her—his own, it seemed. That she had taken the only chair did not seem to trouble him; he simply found another.

"Please," he said, sitting down, "share my tea." He hailed the serving girl, and before Elizabeth had time to refuse, a fresh cup and plate were being placed. She removed her damp gloves and her ruined felt hat. She could think of nowhere to put them but the floor.

Meanwhile, Mr Gill filled her cup and passed the plate of sandwiches. "Beastly rainstorm," he remarked, with a nod at the window.

"Er, yes." She took a sip of tea. Politeness forced her to make conversation with this scruffy man, so she must think of something. At least he spoke clear, comprehensible English! But what sort of things did a clerk converse about?

Fortunately, Mr Gill began to talk—about rain in different parts of the world, of all things. Apparently he had travelled, for he spoke of hurricanes at sea and of the tropics, where the rainfall was unusually intense. Elizabeth smiled and nodded at what she hoped were the appropriate moments. Really, it was too much. The sandwiches, however, were delicious. She helped herself to another.

This Mr Gill could never be called handsome, of course, not with freckles and ruddy hair. For some reason the skin above his upper lip was paler than the rest of his face; she hoped he did not have a disease! But for the most part, he was passable. His chin was well shaped, and when he smiled his cheek showed a dimple. He was smiling now.

His hair was wild, and his clothing was no better. But that was to be expected, even without the rainstorm, for a clerk wouldn't have a manservant to look after his clothes. He probably lived in the lower city, too, poor creature. Elizabeth looked away. But soon she was back to studying him. His eyes held an alert, intelligent look. Were they blue—or were they green?

And then Mr Gill did an odd thing; he tapped a biscuit sharply against the tabletop. Her gasp must have been audible, for he quickly apologized. "Old habit," he said, grinning. "This reminds me of a nibby."

Elizabeth looked at him with narrowed eyes. He'd apologized, but he did not appear to be at all sorry. In fact, his eyes were twinkling. "A what?" she said.

"A sea biscuit. Navy issue."

"Oh," she said. "The Navy."

Mr Gill's brows went up. "You disapprove of the Navy, Miss Elliot? You will find yourself alone in that opinion."

Elizabeth rolled her eyes; where had she heard this before? "Let us say, rather, that I have little love for the officers of the Navy."

"Ah," he said. "So you are a champion of the common seaman. I salute you."

"I have absolutely no use for the common seaman." Elizabeth raised the teacup to her lips.

"No use for any of them?" He leaned forward. "And I thought all ladies adored Admiral Nelson! But then, that was a number of years ago. Perhaps I am behind the times."

"I suppose Admiral Nelson's sea-faring skills were acceptable," she admitted. "But honestly, to carry on with Lady Hamilton in that odious way was the outside of enough!"

Mr Gill's eyes were dancing. "Carry on? What do you mean?"

She set the teacup in its saucer. One needn't mince words with a clerk. "To speak plainly," she said, "Admiral Nelson was what my brother Musgrove would call a *loose fish.*"

Mr Gill gave a shout of laughter.

Elizabeth saw nothing amusing. "I suppose Lady Hamilton was a loose fish, too," she said, reaching for the teapot.

"Oh, officers of the Navy are excellent *fishermen,*" he gasped, between gusts.

"So I am given to understand. Would you care for more tea, Mr Gill?"

~ ~ ~ ~ ~ ~ ~ & ~ ~ ~ ~ ~ ~ ~

McGillvary finished the last bite of his "nibby" with particular relish but only after dunking it in his cup. He made sure that she could see his ink-stained fingers, too. A raised eyebrow was the only sign of Miss Elliot's disgust. McGillvary was disappointed; he was hoping to provoke one of her wrathful outbursts. So far, he had not had much luck; the lady was obviously on her best behaviour.

Still, the afternoon was young, and he had nothing to do. The delight of Miss Elliot's company was clearly in the challenge. Rarely had he been in the presence of such a beautiful woman who was so patently uninterested. The temptation to tease her was overwhelming. He lowered his napkin and gave her one of his most charming smiles.

She looked away. "Will this rain never stop?"

McGillvary nearly laughed outright. Obviously, flirting with a clerk was taboo! When she looked his way, he poured the last of his tea into the saucer to cool. This was clearly outrageous; his mother would have boxed his ears! As it was, he had to bite his lip to keep from laughing at the expression in Miss Elliot's eyes. He lifted the saucer and took a long, gleeful draught.

Replacing it, he remarked, "A nice brew, but I prefer coffee. As you can see," he indicated his waistcoat, "we had a little a mishap with the coffeepot."

"Do you mean today?" she said.

He stiffened. Did she think he would wear a stained waistcoat all week? He decided to retaliate. "By the bye, I am sorry about your hat. Is there a way it can be repaired?"

At that, her chin came up. "I rather doubt it," she said. "But if it rains in Bath as much as you say, what is the point?" She coughed politely. "Have you lived in Bath long, Mr Gill?"

"My family owns a house here, but I have been abroad for much of my life."

"Of course. Your time at sea. I forgot." The look she gave told him plainly what she thought that he had been transported to Australia on a convict ship—and was only newly returned to England!

"So, tell me," he said, determined to even the score. "How was your meeting with old Lonk? I trust he behaved himself. The old boy cuts quite a dash with the ladies, or so he thinks. A prime matrimonial prize, in fact!"

He was rewarded with a stunned look. "You must be joking!" she said. "Him, a prize? For whom?"

McGillvary leaned forward, unable to resist. "Did he offer you a thirty-day extension?"

"Yes. But what does that have to do with–"

"You see?" he interrupted. "He's smitten! For a banker, the thirty-day extension signifies passion. However," he added, in a lowered voice, "if Lonk invites you into the office again, Miss Elliot, you'd best bring a chaperone."

But she did not react to this last bit. "A matrimonial prize," she marvelled, shaking her head. "Men have the oddest notions."

McGillvary put both elbows on the table, cupping his chin in his palms. "Such as?"

"A man needs three qualities in order to be considered a matrimonial prize, Mr Gill." She counted the points on her fingers. "Good breeding, good looks, and a good income. And he should not be too old. My father and I disagree on that last point."

"And if he has only two of the three?"

"To which do you refer?" She was smiling now. "They are not valued equally."

"Tell this to my daughter," he said, ruefully. "She thinks that if a fellow is young and good-looking, it is enough!"

"Have you a daughter?" Miss Elliot looked genuinely surprised. "She must not be very old."

"She is but fifteen."

"A difficult age," she said. "If you must know, to be well-born comes first. At least, it must be so with me, as my father is a baronet. Therefore, I must marry a titled gentleman. Perhaps your daughter has more freedom in this area." She paused to take a sip of tea. "And," she continued, "one must have something to live on. Thus, financial resources must come second. Again, your daughter's requirements are very different from mine, but the principle is the same."

"But you have not mentioned the things dearest to her heart!" he cried. "Charm, a handsome face, a ready address–"

"–and, no doubt, the ability to dance well," she finished, smiling. "Certainly, attractiveness has its place, but you may tell your daughter this: The more charming the suitor, the more ineligible he is certain to be. Surely, your wife has told her as much."

"My wife has been dead these three years. But please, say that again: The more charming the suitor–"

Miss Elliot cut in. "You are raising your daughter alone?"

"With help from my wife's sister, yes."

"Do be careful!" she said earnestly. "My own father...handled my upbringing rather badly! I was just sixteen when my mother died."

"Shut you away with a duenna, did he?"

"Not at all! I was taken from school and thrust into my mother's role. Playing hostess to his dinners, opening the local balls, that sort of thing."

"Did you dislike it?"

"Not after I became accustomed," she said. "But later..."

"Did you tell him how you felt?"

She did not answer but gazed beyond him to the window. "The rain has stopped," she remarked.

McGillvary leaned forward. "Did you tell your father how you felt, Miss Elliot?"

She began to draw on her damp gloves. "Certainly not," she said. "You do not know my father, Mr Gill. Of course not, how could you?" She smiled a hard, tight smile. "Here is another truth I have learned: It is fatal to admit a weakness." She bent to retrieve her hat.

McGillvary sat back. There was more to Miss Elliot than he'd supposed. Her comments about raising a daughter rang very true. She rose, and so, of course, did he. I wonder, he thought, studying her.

"Miss Elliot," he said slowly, "I realize this sounds presumptuous, but..." She looked at him. He smiled. "We've hit upon a fascinating topic. Might we continue another day? I am interested to hear your opinions. I take my tea here on–" He paused to think; what day was this? Ah, Wednesday. "–on Tuesdays and Thursdays at two o'clock. If you are in the neighbourhood, I'd be honoured if you would join me."

She said nothing as he paid the bill and escorted her to the door. Once on the sidewalk, he waved to hail a passing hack. "What do you say, Miss Elliot?" he said, as the driver jumped down to open the door. He gave her his most adorable smile, the one that never failed to melt even the sternest matron's heart. "Join me for tea on Tuesday?" He dropped the fare into the driver's hand, making sure Miss Elliot noticed.

"I'll consider it," she said quietly. "Thank you."

"The devil you will," McGillvary muttered, as the carriage rumbled away. "And yet, I wonder..."

~ ~ ~ ~ ~ ~ ~ & ~ ~ ~ ~ ~ ~ ~

Sir Walter gazed into the mirror above the mantelpiece. His reflection brought a smile. For the first time in weeks, he felt truly alive. His good looks were indeed returning. For this, Mr Savoy was wholly responsible. The man's painstaking care, along with his plan for physical and emotional convalescence, was working.

Sir Walter drew a long breath and let it out slowly. "I welcome the blessings of this universe," he said aloud, repeating the words Mr Savoy had made him memorize. "I cannot deny who I am. I am in no way obliged to lead a monotonous existence." He straightened his shoulders.

"In fact," he stated, more firmly, "I am the greatest miracle in nature! I deserve the best of life! And from this day forward, only the best will come to me!"

A knock sounded at the door. "Come," he called.

A serving girl entered; she held a calling card. "If you please sir," she said, bobbing a curtsey, "you have a visitor."

Sir Walter held up a hand. "No visitors at this time!" he said.

The girl backed away. "But sir," she said.

"Mr Savoy has been most insistent." Sir Walter turned away and began hunting through his pockets. Where had he put that slip of paper?

"And so have I," said another voice.

Sir Walter spun around. Lady Russell stood in the doorway. "I have come to bid you farewell," she said. "And I have brought your mail."

"No interference!" squeaked Sir Walter. "I am to have no interference during this delicate time! Including the mail!"

Lady Russell did not go. Instead, she closed the door and sat in a chair. "Really, Sir Walter," she said. "You must be practical. Some of these letters look to be important."

"Forward them to Shepherd. I must be free to think on more exalted matters."

"Such as your daughter's welfare?"

He knew to whom Lady Russell referred, but he said, "Mary? Is Mary still in Bath?"

"She and her husband returned to Uppercross weeks ago. No, I refer to Elizabeth."

Sir Walter felt his face pucker into a scowl. Scowling, as anyone knew, was extremely detrimental. Surely this negative atmosphere was not good for his looks!

"You've seen no one these three weeks," continued Lady Russell. "I have had to postpone my visit to Muriel Stanhope, which was most inconvenient, in order to look after Elizabeth. Surely it is time for you to resume your responsibilities."

Sir Walter became occupied with the button on his sleeve. "Elizabeth," he said, "is well able to look after herself."

"As she has proven. Well! Since you have gone into seclusion, several decisions have been made."

He brightened. "There, you see? The blessings of the universe have come...without exertion or fuss."

"Anne has taken a house on St. Peter Square. She and Captain Wentworth have kindly invited Elizabeth to live with them while I am away."

Sir Walter nodded. "That is Anne's duty, yes," he said. "But I was not aware that there were any boarding houses on St. Peter Square."

"Nor are there! Captain Wentworth and Anne have taken an entire house, Sir Walter. It belongs to a fellow officer who is out of the country." She presented the stack of letters. "Where shall I put these?"

Sir Walter looked at them with distaste, for they represented the troubles of the world. "On the mantelpiece, I suppose," he said, shrugging. "I've no time for them now. Or, perhaps, ever."

Lady Russell looked at him strangely. "Mr Shepherd has called several times. When will it be permissible for him to see you?"

"That," said Sir Walter, "is for Mr Savoy to decide." He saw Lady Russell's lips compress. His gaze shifted to her eyes. Yes, the crow's feet were now even more pronounced. How harmful to one's looks were the troubles of the world!

"I bid you farewell, Sir Walter, for the present," she said. "I shall be away for at least the next fortnight." Her expression softened. "I must say, you do look to be much improved."

"Oh, but I am!" cried Sir Walter. "You have no idea!"

After Lady Russell left he grew thoughtful. Lady Russell's visit was proof indeed that he was not yet strong enough. Now then, what was he doing before he'd been interrupted? Ah, yes. The recitations. Sir Walter found the slip of paper.

"I vibrate with enormous happiness," he read aloud, "in a magnificent body sculpted by the incredible power of my own intellect and creativity!" The smile returned to his lips, along with the feeling of buoyancy and freedom. Sir Walter sent the paper sailing. "I let go of the past!" he cried jubilantly. "I now live completely and utterly in the present!"

~ ~ ~ ~ ~ ~ ~ & ~ ~ ~ ~ ~ ~ ~

Elizabeth returned to Rivers Street just after Lady Russell did. She paused to look up at the front of the narrow house. What a life was now hers! Surely, living in a convent would be an improvement! But she did not live the life of a hermit with Lady Russell; it was worse! She was, in fact, becoming a bluestocking! Lady Russell must take her to philosophical lectures and concerts of ancient music, and she was forever pressing on Elizabeth this book or that. Nothing lively or entertaining–these were history books or mind-improving books, the kind Caroline Bingley had spoken of so bitterly. Elizabeth did not see why she needed them. After all, she had Lady Russell at hand to guide her every thought and action. But when she'd shared this sentiment, her godmother had not been best pleased.

Sighing heavily, Elizabeth went into the house. Was this to be her life, then? Sharing a dwelling with her godmother and following her about like a shadow? Mr Rushworth, who was now in London, was looking better and better. Even the clerk with whom she'd shared tea was preferable!

~ 1 1 ~
A Doubtful Point

It was not easy for Penelope Clay to concentrate on what was going forward. Never had she been to such an elegant milliner's shop. And the thought of choosing hats made her giddy. Still, the stout young man and his mother were too comical to be ignored.

"I say, that's a jolly hat," he told her. "Have it wrapped up and sent along home."

The woman frowned at her reflection. "Well now, I don't know." She made a slight adjustment to the brim. "I think it a bit too girlish."

"Girlish? Well, of course! Just the thing to make you feel young again, Mama!"

The woman flinched. "That will be quite enough, James. Young again, indeed!" She addressed the milliner. "Is there anything else in this shade? The brim is rather wide–but I do admire the lace trimming."

"The *passementerie* is most attractive, madam. If you will allow but a moment…"

"Hang it all, Mama, who gives a rip about a hat? It isn't as if anyone we know will see you in it!"

"James!" the woman said. "Hush!"

"Buy the thing and be done with it. And then we can clear out of here and get something to eat! I'm starving!"

The woman continued to study her reflection. "You'll live," she said.

He flung over to the window, casting dark looks at her now and again. He dug out his timepiece and fingered the many fobs dangling along the chain. "Mama," he said, turning, "when do we return to Bath?"

"Whatever for? Nobody is in Bath at this time of year." She looked to the milliner. "What sort of feathers did you say these are? Egret?"

"Yes, madam. *Aigrette.*"

The young man shuffled over. "Not all of your friends are gone from Bath," he said. "Besides, I *hate* London, Mama! I am never comfortable here!" He thrust his hands in his pockets. "I want to go to Bath."

She sighed heavily. "Tiresome boy!"

"If you must know, every place we go reminds me of...you know. *Maria.*"

The woman pursed up her lips. "I suppose I'll take this one," she said, passing the hat to the milliner. "Very well, James, you may choose where it is we shall eat."

Penelope Clay turned to her companion with a smile. "Bath is the very last place *we* wish to be, isn't it, dearest?"

There was a pause. "Look," he said. "The girl is bringing your hat."

Penelope twisted round to see. It was a round-crowned hat trimmed with ostrich and pheasant feathers. "Oh, William!" she said, taking it from the attendant. "It is so stylish!" She smiled up at him. "I can scarcely believe it is to be mine!"

"Nothing but the best, my dear."

Penelope turned this way and that, delighted with the image in the mirror. "You are too, too good to me!"

William Elliot withdrew to the window, frowning to himself. He pulled out his timepiece. How long did it take to choose a hat? And why must she use his Christian name in public? Truth to tell, Penelope's ready smiles and agreeable chatter, so pleasant during their first weeks together, were becoming tiresome. Why, she hadn't the first idea how to conduct herself in company! He had invited a few friends to spend an evening at cards the other night. But did she know how to comport herself? Of course not! Sophisticated flirtation and insouciance were beyond Penelope's grasp. Oh, there were smiles aplenty. But even those did her no credit, for there was the matter of that projecting tooth!

His gaze travelled back to her. There was only one woman who could wear a hat like this, and that was his cousin Elizabeth. Penelope had plenty to say about her! At first, her abuse of his cousin was quite entertaining. But now–

A slight smile crossed Mr Elliot's face. Elizabeth would have known exactly how to behave the other night. And she would have dazzled them with her beauty!

He dug his hands in his pockets. If only Wallis hadn't written. But he had, and a very good thing it was, for his news about Sir Walter was important. Unfortunately, it was beginning to look as if the only prudent thing to do was to investigate the matter himself.

Mr Elliot frowned some more. Naturally, Penelope wouldn't like it—what mistress would?—for he meant to travel to Bath alone. *Alone.* He turned the word over in his mind. Indeed, it would be delightful to be alone. His gaze wandered back; she was still taken up with selecting the hat. He shrugged. Such was the lot of the mistress. Did she expect him to spend every minute of the day with her?

Naturally, he had a part to play in this little arrangement. Penelope's new wardrobe, which she insisted he help her to choose, was his part of the deal. He took another turn about the shop, studying the hats on display. He selected a black one draped in fine veiling and finished with curled quills. It was a sophisticated hat, worthy of Elizabeth. He waited until the attendant stepped away.

"What about this one, my love? A woman can never have too many hats, I'm told. And," he leaned nearer to whisper in her ear, "you may wear this one to the theatre. *Tonight.*"

She twisted round in her chair. "Oh, William!" she cried. "Are we truly to go *out?* I thought you'd never ask!"

She would have embraced him, but he stepped away. She caressed the feathers and smiled lovingly into his eyes. "Imagine," she whispered. "The theatre."

~ ~ ~ ~ ~ ~ ~ & ~ ~ ~ ~ ~ ~ ~

Lady Russell's house was like a tomb, Elizabeth decided, and Longwell, her butler, was the spider that lived there. He watched her every move as if he resented her presence in the house. The feeling was entirely mutual, but things had taken a turn for the worse, if that could be possible. Elizabeth was leaving to stay with Anne for an undetermined period. Her trunks now stood in Lady Russell's small entrance hall. Longwell lurked in the shadows, his face expressionless, but Elizabeth knew what he was thinking just the same.

Well! She would show them! Once she was mistress of Sotherton, they would sing a different tune. In fact, if the divorce decree was finalized this summer, perhaps she could host a grand and glorious

Christmas celebration for her family. At the house in Grosvenor Square? Or the fine Elizabethan manor house at Sotherton? Sotherton would be best, she decided. There was more scope for the imagination on an estate. And more at hand to keep her future husband occupied.

~ ~ ~ ~ ~ ~ ~ & ~ ~ ~ ~ ~ ~ ~

Anne said nothing until she and her husband were well away from the building. As they neared the front wall with its wrought iron gate, her steps slowed. She turned and looked back at The Citadel, taking in its ivy-covered facade and sweep of lawn. "This is a beautiful location," she said quietly. "Under other circumstances, I'd be pleased to see Father living in such a place."

Captain Wentworth reached to open the gate. "I wonder how much this 'elegant convalescence' is setting him back?"

"I don't dare think about it," she said, allowing him to guide her through the opening. "Father has always been so irresponsible with money."

Wentworth gave a derisive snort. "And when he's run off his legs? What then?"

"I don't dare think about that, either." Anne lowered her eyes. "I suppose when that happens," she said, in a small voice, "he must live with us."

"He supposes it too, obviously!"

"Oh, was there anything like it?" They began walking down the street together. "I was never so mortified, Frederick! He was actually gloating that we have taken an entire house." She thought of something else. "And Elizabeth. She comes to us today."

"That settles it, then," said Wentworth, hailing a passing hack. It came clattering to a stop a few feet ahead. "We leave for Shropshire tomorrow."

"But we cannot go off and leave Elizabeth!"

"Why not? She's a grown woman. One accustomed to adventures, it seems. If Sophia can fend for herself in the Indies, Elizabeth can manage very well in Bath. And," he added, more seriously, "if Elizabeth is to live with us, she will need to adjust to our whims, not vice-versa." He helped her into the carriage.

"Yes, I know," said Anne. "But we cannot leave her alone in the house."

"Do you mean without a chaperone? That can be remedied."

Anne struggled to put her thoughts into words. "I am not entirely comfortable leaving her because, well, Elizabeth is accustomed to being in command. Who knows what she will do to our house while we are away?"

"Ah," said Wentworth, smiling. "You, my dear, have underestimated the abilities of our new butler. In Naval circles, Yee's reputation is legendary."

"What do you mean?"

"Merely that Yee is a relentless, unyielding opponent."

Anne shook her head. "What Elizabeth will do is give orders about, oh, things. Little things."

Captain Wentworth laid a hand on her knee. "Anne, in that house, our word is law—your word is law. Elizabeth will change nothing."

Anne digested this. "What do you think Yee will do when she tries?"

"Nothing. And with the most icy, patronizing condescension imaginable."

"Condescension? Frederick, Elizabeth will be furious! She'll demand you dismiss him for impertinence!"

"Which I shall refuse to do—with the most patronizing condescension imaginable."

~ ~ ~ ~ ~ ~ ~&~ ~ ~ ~ ~ ~ ~

Elizabeth was not happy to be deposited on Anne's doorstep like so much baggage, but what could she do? Over a belated breakfast, she had the leisure to reflect on the past week. Indeed, there was little else for her to do! Her father was still shut up at The Citadel, Lady Russell was gone to Stourton, and just this morning Anne and Captain Wentworth had deserted her for Shropshire! Trust Anne to be so abominably rude—and selfish—as to leave a newly arrived guest to fend for herself! She'd tried to point this out, but this only made matters worse. Captain Wentworth put his oar in then, informing her that she was family and not a guest at all. As if he knew anything about manners! How in the world was she to get on with a man who was next door to a barbarian?

At length, Elizabeth tired of breakfast and removed to the sitting room. She moved quietly so as not to catch the ear of her sister's butler. He was every bit as bad as Longwell. Being a Chinaman, his expressions were even more impossible to read. In fact, every member of Anne's staff set her on edge. Captain Wentworth had allowed her to bring Elise into the household with the proviso that she teach Anne's girl, Gloria, to become a lady's maid. What could Elizabeth do but accept? But it was most inconvenient.

The doorbell sounded. It was probably Miss Owen calling again. The woman was a neighbour of Anne's and very well meaning, but such a funny one! Anne had taken to her right away, though Elizabeth could not see why. Miss Owen's clothing was painful to behold, and her hair was even worse. Elizabeth strolled to the fireplace. She did not wish to witness Miss Owen's awkward entrance.

Sure enough, after a few minutes she heard Yee come in. She did not look in his direction.

"Mrs Henry Stevenson-Bragg," he announced.

Elizabeth turned to face her visitor. She took in the woman's impossible flowered bonnet, flaxen hair, and ermine-trimmed spencer.

With both hands extended, Elizabeth's caller came rushing forward. "Why, Cousin Anne!" she cried. "How delightful to meet you in the flesh at last!"

Elizabeth stepped back a pace. Stevenson was the name of her mother's family. Was this woman a relation? She found her voice. "I am Anne's sister, Elizabeth. Anne is not at home. Won't you sit down, Mrs Stevenson-Bragg?"

Elizabeth's invitation went unheeded. Mrs Stevenson-Bragg roamed about the room, eyeing the furnishings. "Dear, oh, dear," she murmured. "I wonder if Anne has the pair of Sèvres vases? Uncle Roland claims he gave them to his sister ages before she died. I hope they haven't been lost or broken."

"I beg your pardon?" said Elizabeth.

Mrs Stevenson-Bragg looked up. Her eyes were china blue, edged with outrageously long lashes. The woman's lips formed into a perfect pout. "I took such pains to come quickly, as Captain Wentworth requested," she said. "And Anne is not here to welcome us?"

"Us?"

"My children and me. Captain Wentworth said we were to come straightway, and so we have." The woman's blue eyes widened. "Surely, Anne told you we were coming?"

Elizabeth did not know what to say. "I suppose Captain Wentworth mentioned it to Yee..."

"Yee? Oh, you must mean the butler." Mrs Stevenson-Bragg sank onto a nearby sofa. "Come sit beside me, Cousin Elizabeth, and tell me all the news. How is your dear father? Captain Wentworth said in his letter that Sir Walter was unwell."

Elizabeth found a chair. "I believe he has improved a great deal."

"Oh, famous! Now I can be easy!" Mrs Stevenson-Bragg removed her bonnet and shook free her golden curls. "And as we are cousins, I must be Estella to you, my dear. How delightful it will be to spend the entire season in Bath! So fashionable! And a house in St. Peter Square, too! It was not easy for me to leave Mr Bragg at this time in the year—Mr Bragg is my husband, you know—but how could I refuse the offer of a holiday?" She draped her arm along the back of the sofa.

Holiday? Elizabeth's eyes narrowed. And what was this? Was the woman lounging?

"To say truth," she continued, "I am famished. Do you suppose the old Chinaman knows how to make a proper cup of tea?"

Elizabeth was stunned to silence. She had to listen to a good deal more before she was able to escape. She found Yee in the dining room laying another place at the table.

"Who is that woman? And why was I not told she was coming?"

Yee deftly folded a napkin into an elaborate fan. "Perhaps," he said, "it suits Captain Wentworth to remain silent?" He placed the napkin beside the plate. "As I understand, Mrs Stevenson-Bragg has come as companion."

"For me?" cried Elizabeth. "I need no companion! And what nerve, to bring her children! Without so much as a by your leave! We have no accommodations for children here! Who will look after them?"

"We shall manage, Miss Elliot."

"If she thinks she can stroll into this house, as if it were an inn, and take over–!" Elizabeth walked to the window and back again. "She had the effrontery to enquire whether *you* knew how to make tea!"

Yee's lips twitched. This, apparently, was the closest he came to smiling. "We shall manage, Miss Elliot," he said. "We always do." He lowered his voice. "It is not becoming to allow a guest to ruffle one's dignity."

Elizabeth turned away. "She is an upstart, that's what she is!" she muttered, speaking more to herself than to him. "A vulgar, presuming upstart, come to Bath to enjoy an elegant holiday at my sister's expense! I'll give her elegant!" Elizabeth rounded on Yee. "What are you serving for dinner tonight?"

Before he could answer, she said, "Whatever it is, I want it and the time changed." She drew a deep breath, considering her line of attack. "We shall dine at an excruciatingly fashionable hour. Listen carefully: I want braised escargot, and lobster, the latter served *inside* the shell, if you please. Never mind that it is difficult to eat. And then, crisped duck set off with port sauce and toasted brioche garnished with *foie gras*–let her think she's eating stale bread! Then asparagus, truffled potatoes, and slices of pear drizzled with…" She paused to think of something appropriate, "balsamic vinegar. And for dessert, let me see." Elizabeth's face grew intent. "A flute of cassis sorbet would be perfect…with some of those dismal lemon jellies on the side. And we'll finish with chocolate-dipped figs. Mrs Stevenson-Bragg will think they're supposed to be delicious. Yes."

Yee took this in without batting an eye. "Very good, Miss Elliot," he said. "And will you require a formal setting? Using *all* of the silverware?"

"But of course," she said, with a lift of her eyebrow. "I'll wager she hasn't the least idea of the proper uses for each! Well, we shall see, won't we?"

When Elizabeth swept into the sitting room, she felt much better. "My dear Mrs Stevenson-Bragg," she said, "I've a lovely dinner all arranged. We dine at nine."

Estella's face fell. "Nine? My goodness."

"I find it convenient to keep Town hours," said Elizabeth. "So fashionable!"

And then Elizabeth noticed the time–and recalled that this was Tuesday. Her heart gave a little jump–wasn't it fortunate? She had a prior engagement!

"My dear Cousin," she said, "I would so *love* to hear all about your *wonderful* husband and his *marvellous* school–Brookside? Brookfield?" Elizabeth paused to let the snub sink in. "But, unfortunately, I have an appointment at two o'clock. And as you can see…" She spread her hands.

Mrs Stevenson-Bragg's head came up. "You are leaving? But I have only just arrived!"

By this time, Elizabeth had the sitting room door open. "Since you are to be here for the entire Season, we won't stand upon ceremony. Yee will bring in refreshments shortly, I am sure," she said. "And the housekeeper will show you to your room. And your children to theirs, of course." She frowned. "I wonder where your children could be?" She went out before Estella could answer.

The closet in the entrance hall contained a variety of hats. Elizabeth chose one. "Oh, Yee!" she called, wrapping an old shawl of Anne's around her shoulders. "Would you kindly summon a carriage for me?"

~ ~ ~ ~ ~ ~ ~ & ~ ~ ~ ~ ~ ~ ~

Miss Owen stood before the door to the Wentworth's house. She was not at all comfortable with this arrangement. During the late Mrs Norman's long illness, she had used the service entrance and had run in and out whenever she chose. But now, of course, things were different. The Wentworths had come, and Mr Yee had been firm. The door remained unanswered. Winnie was distinctly relieved, and turned to go. And then, of course, it opened.

"Ah, Miss Owen." Old Yee greeted her with his precise formality. "It is Tuesday, yes. Please, come in."

Winnie shyly presented two of her newly-printed calling cards. "Is Mrs Wentworth at home?" she enquired, with what she hoped was a proper degree of politeness.

Yee took the cards and examined them carefully, a little smile pulling at his lips.

Red-faced, Winnie hastened to explain. "One card is for Mrs Wentworth. The other is for your wife. And for Gloria."

Yee raised an eyebrow, but made no comment. He put one of the cards carefully into a pocket and moved to close the door. "Captain and Mrs Wentworth have left Bath, Miss Owen. I shall ascertain whether Miss Elliot is at home."

At this, Winnie's courage deserted her. "Oh, no, Mr Yee, please!" she begged. "Please, don't disturb Miss Elliot! I'd never wish to presume! That is—" She broke off in confusion.

Both of Yee's eyebrows went up. "This is your afternoon for calling on the neighbours, Miss Owen, is it not?" he asked mildly. "Miss Elliot is now a neighbour." He lowered his voice. "And you must now be calling me Yee."

Winnie reluctantly went ahead of him into the sitting room. "Yes, I...I know, but..." She took a seat on the very edge of an upholstered chair. "Please don't snub me, Mr Yee," she said quietly. "I don't think I could bear it."

"It is not a snub to correct for an unfortunate lapse. This house has a mistress again. We must now observe proper distinction when you call."

"But I-I'd so much rather use the service entrance, as before."
She lowered her gaze, as if to examine the button on one of her
gloves. "I do so miss the fellowship of your kitchen table, Mr Yee,"
she admitted. "Mrs Wentworth is very kind, of course, but...Miss
Elliot!" Her face grew pinched. "She is so beautiful and so refined
and elegant! I cannot think of even one thing to say to her!"

"Look for areas of commonality," Yee suggested.

"Commonality? Mr Yee, I have nothing–absolutely nothing–in
common with Miss Elliot! Why on Sunday at church..." Winnie
lifted her gaze to Yee's face. "I am not a fit acquaintance for Mrs
Wentworth either, if the truth be known."

"You must let Mrs Wentworth decide this for herself. You are her
closest neighbour. And now that Mrs Stevenson-Bragg has come, she
might be pleased to find a friend in you."

"Mrs Stevenson-Bragg." Winnie smoothed an unruly strand of
hair, tucking it behind her ear.

"There will be opportunities to converse."

Winnie gave a great sigh. "I suppose you think I need the practice."

"But of course." Yee's voice took on a fatherly tone. "Miss Elliot
has lived in the country, as have you. Perhaps you have more in
common than you think." He raised an eyebrow. "This house con-
fines Miss Elliot. She escapes to the garden when she thinks I do not
see. Before long, she will learn of Mr Norman's gate and escape into
the park."

"If many more of us go sneaking back there, Mr Yee, Mr
McGillvary's son will be upset."

"You are a neighbour; what harm do you bring?" Yee replied
mildly. "Without you, his swans would go hungry in winter."

This brought a smile. "Mr Yee, since when has a handful of
week-old bread crusts kept anyone alive?"

"Ah, yes. *Man does not live by bread alone...*" Yee quoted. "But perhaps," he continued, with a twinkle, "perhaps the swans do."

~ ~ ~ ~ ~ ~ ~ & ~ ~ ~ ~ ~ ~ ~

Meanwhile, Patrick McGillvary was reading through a summary
of Sir Walter Elliot's account. "This knocks the gilt off the ginger-
bread and no mistake," he muttered. The extension he had unthink-
ingly authorized Lonk to offer was going to cost him plenty. Last
September, Lonk had allowed the Baronet to borrow far more than

his collateral could support. Aside from several hundred acres adjoining his ancestral estate (which was entailed) and various personal possessions, Sir Walter Elliot owned nothing.

And his daughter said he was ill. McGillvary did some rapid calculations. If he seized every cent of Elliot's income for the next eight years, it could be repaid, minus the interest. No interest would mean no profit, of course, but that could not be helped. The alternative was bankruptcy. But Sir Walter had to be alive for that. Exactly how ill was he?

McGillvary ran a hand through his hair—again. His appearance today was almost as bad as before. Pym had found another tweed coat for him, but insisted on making alterations. "For homespun is homespun," he'd said severely, "but you haven't no call to have it set so poorly across the shoulders, sir!"

His shirt was one of his oldest, though a brown waistcoat hid most of it. His neck cloth was an unfashionable hunter green. He'd taken special pains with his hair, much to Pym's chagrin. He'd wetted it down and combed it over his forehead so that it covered his eyebrows. While it was still damp, he'd mashed his hat well down. Now that the hat was removed and the hair ruffled, he looked like a wild man.

"Will you be wanting anything else, sir?"

McGillvary looked up. "Nothing, thank you." He folded the paper and returned it to his satchel.

The girl refreshed his cup of tea. "I'll be on the watch for the fine lady, sir, just as you said," she promised.

The fine lady. McGillvary flicked open his timepiece. The lady was late.

In point of fact, it would be a miracle if she came at all. McGillvary shook his head. At first glance, he'd been overwhelmed by her beauty. He later discovered her wit. But then she shunned Wentworth's dinner and revealed a shrewish tongue. Now he thought her snobbish and expensive. Very expensive.

The bell on the door made a tinkling sound; McGillvary looked up. In an instant he was on his feet, guiding Miss Elliot to the table and then holding her chair. It was not until after she was seated that he realized his mistake. Mr Gill would have made awkward work of it, allowing her to stand or seat herself. Long years of training had taken over, unfortunately. He resolved to do better. Or rather, worse.

Meanwhile, Miss Elliot was removing her gloves. "Would you care for fresh tea?" she enquired, laying them aside.

"Please," he said, and held out his cup and saucer. In the light of the window her complexion fairly glowed. He'd forgotten how stunningly lovely she was. And could it be that she was blushing?

"You wished to continue our conversation from last week," she said, expertly adding more tea to his cup. "Where shall we begin?"

McGillvary could not take his eyes from her. She was charmingly dressed, if one did not count the ratty shawl. A smile tugged at his lips; he had a good idea of how much her get-up had cost. But the only thing he could think to say was, "Tell me about your morning."

Elizabeth settled the teapot. "I was hoping, rather, to forget it."

"All the more reason to talk. Get it off your chest, so to speak."

She gave a tiny shrug. "My wretched cousin has come for an un-expected visit...with her two children, no less. Apparently, my new brother-in-law invited them as company for me!"

New brother-in-law? Did she mean Wentworth? McGillvary hid his smile. "Well then," he said, lifting his cup. "Here's to celebrating the siege of Gibraltar!"

Elizabeth looked at him with an odd expression. "Do you know what a mushroom is, Mr Gill?" she said at last.

"A kind of fungus that grows in the woods? They are good in soup."

"No, I mean people, lowly people, who presume too much and who have social ambitions to better themselves beyond their station. Estella, my delightful cousin, is one of those."

"Social ambitions," he repeated. "And you mean to say that you have no such ambitions? Excuse my ignorance, Miss Elliot, but I thought all ladies had social ambitions."

She looked at him fixedly. "Ah, but I am not lowly, Mr Gill. Would you care for a sandwich?" She passed him the plate.

McGillvary could barely manage a reply. Here she sat, in debt up to her eyebrows, having tea at the expense of an underpaid clerk with perfect *sangfroid!*

"My cousin's husband recently inherited ten thousand pounds, apparently." Elizabeth selected a sandwich. "As if that were a whop-ping fortune."

"Try paying it back," he said, before he could stop himself.

She ignored this. "And because of it," she continued, "dear Estella now feels that the world must make way for her. Can you imagine? As if money could purchase gentility! I always thought my mother's father was a gentleman, but his niece is no lady. You should see the clothing she wears! She is rather pretty, in an obvious sort of way, but—"

"Fairer than the tongue can name, eh?"

Elizabeth frowned at him. "I did not say she is beautiful, Mr Gill. I said that she is pretty, which is altogether different! Pretty fades. Beautiful does not."

"I stand corrected," he murmured.

"But I shall even the score, never fear." Elizabeth's smile became ingenious. "Tonight we are having the most outrageous dinner. I could hardly keep a straight face while giving orders to the butler."

While giving orders. Yes, he could picture the scene. Elizabeth Elliot was one born to command.

She leaned forward, continuing her narrative. "We shall dine with the most excruciating formality at the long table: a six-course meal using every utensil imaginable! I do wish," she added, "that strawberries were in season. I'll have to ask about that. I daresay she's never seen a strawberry fork."

McGillvary had to laugh. "A what?"

"And, my sister has the most hideous epergne—I've seen it on the sideboard—which will quite dominate the table and keep Estella from following my lead with the courses."

"Next time, serve Fisher's Eyes," he suggested. "That's what sailors call tapioca. And, Tiddy-Oggy. That's Cornish pasty."

Elizabeth laughed, obviously delighted. "Why, I believe I shall, Mr Gill. And oranges. Unpeeled."

"And don't forget grapes. They slide off one's plate at the worst moments!"

Elizabeth seemed to recall her surroundings. "Dear me," she said, smiling, "I've quite monopolized the conversation! As I recall, you had questions about your daughter. She has contracted a fancy for a hopeless ineligible, am I right?"

Cleora had done no such thing, but McGillvary was too intrigued to contradict this. "I fear so," he said mildly. "Have you ever made such a mistake, Miss Elliot? Lost your heart to some poor, ineligible fellow?"

She looked at him with a blank expression. "Certainly not," she said. "To fall in love with the wrong sort of man is extraordinarily stupid, unless one is very young…like your daughter."

McGillvary's brows rose. This beautiful woman, so keenly aware of her own worth, was very much in need of a set-down—much like her father. "Never fall in love with an ineligible," he repeated, lifting his teacup in a mock salute.

Very well, he thought. Let us see if you can be made to change your tune, Miss Elliot.

~ ~ ~ ~ ~ ~ ~ & ~ ~ ~ ~ ~ ~ ~

Later that evening, some miles away in London, a not-so-ineligible suitor sat working on a letter. Scattered on the floor were crumpled pages, evidence of a difficult correspondence. He laboriously wrote the salutation once again: *My Darling Elizabeth,*

Here James Rushworth hesitated; was it proper to be so bold? Then, recalling that this was a private letter, he shrugged and continued with his task. Writing was always an awkward business for him, but this was important. He must answer her letter. He bravely soldiered on.

> Today I saw the solicitor myself, while Mama was calling on Mrs Pangborne. He had quite a bit to say about the divorce—how these lawyers can talk! I cannot remember all of it. The main thing is, the business at Surgeon's Commons is all finished up. And so is the suit against Maria in the Court. Any day now he expects Parliament to grant the divorce. Mama has said she'll be happy if everything is wound up by the end of the session. But that will be August!
> Such happiness as ours should not have to wait for an act of Parliament! I'll contrive to get to Bath somehow, as soon as possible, within the next two weeks.
> I remain,
> Most truly and sincerely yours,
> J. R.

~ ~ ~ ~ ~ ~ ~ & ~ ~ ~ ~ ~ ~ ~

Penelope knew it was impolite to stare, but tonight she could not seem to help it. Even after the play was underway there was so much to see! An evening with William Elliot at one of London's largest theatres—could anything be more wonderful? At long last, her fashionable life in London was beginning. However, she knew better than to display an attitude of triumph. There would be plenty of time

155

for that later, after she became Mrs Elliot. For now it was enough to be seen with him.

Her gaze dropped to the beaded reticule on her lap. Like her darling black hat, this was a gift from William. She bit back a smile. Not even Elizabeth Elliot owned something so fine! As for her evening gown, why, it was perfection itself! Actually, it was a copy of a red gown of Elizabeth's, which was adorned with hundreds of tiny black beads. Her version was similarly decorated, but instead of red she had chosen a lively shade of green. She wore long kidskin gloves of the same colour, richly scented, and a bangle bracelet at each wrist. Around her neck, she wore a string of jet beads. As for the splendid feathered hat William had chosen—she raised a hand to check its angle—the milliner had added green quills, the better to match her gown. Penelope gave a sigh of contentment. How delicious it was to be so well attired!

She stole a look at her companion. He turned slightly and, noticing her gaze, returned the smile. Just in time she moved her hand away from his knee. William was very sensitive about public displays; her embraces would have to wait.

However, *Macbeth* could not claim her attention for long—the first act was so dreary and went on forever. Soon she was back to thinking about him and the life they shared together. Surely she had made the right choice?

The force of this thought nearly took her breath away. What was this? Of course she had made the right choice! There was no question as to the rightness of her actions! She cast a withering glance at the stage. Macbeth's wretched cowardice was to blame for her doubts, for William Elliot was a prize worth any price!

Penelope became intent on smoothing the wrinkles from her skirt. True, he was not as easy to manage as Sir Walter. The Baronet's moods had been easier to read, and he was more forthcoming with information. Then too, he did not hesitate to present her in polite company. She eyed William's profile. This man had just as much pride as Sir Walter and a great deal more reserve. Their relationship was at an awkward stage, that was all. Things would be much more comfortable after they were married.

Again Penelope sighed, this time not so contentedly. As nice as it was to have a private box, she was under no illusions. The ladies and gentlemen in attendance this evening would not be introduced to her, or she to them. Although, she longed to walk about during the Interval, she knew she must remain closeted in the box. There had been limitations when she was Elizabeth's companion. Now that she was William's, there were many more.

And then, there were the children...

Penelope winced–this was a fine time to think of them! Naturally, she had not written to her father about her present situation. That would come later. Her mother would care for her children, she was sure of that. And one day she would be able to send for them. What she did now was for their future as well as her own. Soon enough nature would take its course, just as it had with Henry Clay. Now that she thought about it, she'd been feeling rather light-headed this week. Penelope cast another glance at William. Yes, before long she would be in a position to appeal to her father.

At last the curtain fell, and the lights came up. William Elliot excused himself and left the box. He came back some time later with a glass of ratafia for her. "My dear," he said, taking his seat, "I wonder if you have thought over what Wallis said in his letter. Unfortunately, I see no way around it." Over the rim of his glass, his eyes were watchful. "I fear I must look into the matter myself."

Why did he look at her like that? Something was wrong, but what? She knew she must keep her voice pleasant. "Letter, William?" she said. "Have you a letter from Colonel Wallis?" She turned her attention to the empty stage below, feigning unconcern. "This is the first I've heard about it."

He clapped a hand to his head. "My dear, I am so sorry! I thought I had mentioned it–read the whole curst thing to you, in fact!" He leaned forward and placed a hand on her knee. "The thing is," he said, "I've got to return to Bath."

"Return to Bath?" she said quickly. "For how long?"

"Now, now. Let me explain," he said. "Wallis told me Sir Walter's been ill. Very ill. And what's more, he's changed his residence. It bears looking into."

"But William, consider!" She lowered her voice. "Surely, Sir Walter knows about us!"

"Ugly rumours," he said, "are best met head-on. However, as I don't intend to see Sir Walter myself, I won't hear a word about it!" He looked at her for a moment before adding, "Elizabeth can tell me all I need to know."

Elizabeth? Penelope could no longer conceal her panic. "You don't mean to see Elizabeth! Surely she suspects! William, be reasonable, please! Think of my reputation!"

It seemed to her that his smile slipped a bit. "Oh, but I think I must," he said. "You needn't fret, my love. And once my business in Bath is completed, I'll stay clear of London for a few weeks. Travel about the country. Look in on some friends in Brighton."

Penelope swallowed. His eyes, why, they were so cold! She dared not say any more—at least, not now. She moved her hand to cover his. "I'll miss you terribly," she whispered.

"I know," he said, and drew his hand away.

~12~
The King's Hard Bargain

The days following Estella's arrival were anything but easy—Elizabeth simply could not escape her cousin! What was worse, she knew that sooner or later she'd be forced to take her to the Pump Room. What if the woman's public manners were no better? If only Captain Wentworth hadn't invited her! However, Elizabeth knew who was behind this scheme: Anne. Anne must be helpful, always, which meant interfering with matters that did not concern her. And why must Anne correspond so faithfully with each of their relatives? The Stevensons were not at all worthy of her notice!

Just when Elizabeth was at her wit's end, Yee approached with an idea. She ought to take Mrs Stevenson-Bragg and the children to church. Elizabeth seized on this with a secret relish. And so, come Sunday morning, she followed every one of Yee's suggestions, beginning with being on time for breakfast. Estella, of course, was late. Nevertheless, promptly at half-past ten, two hired carriages arrived to take the household to church.

Elizabeth allowed Estella to lead the way, with her two children and their nursery maid following behind. To Elizabeth, who had very strict ideas about what was appropriate for church, Estella's attire was simply ridiculous: a pink-and-white striped gauze gown with a heavily ruffled flounce, topped with a leaf-green spencer. Her frilly hat, all but smothered with silk roses and trailing pink ribbons, was tied under her chin with a huge satin bow. Elizabeth glanced at her own sombre-hued gown and smiled. Considering where they would be worshipping this morning, she knew hers was the better choice.

The trip across Bath was wearisome. Estella's children, a boy and a girl, were not good travellers. They kicked at the seat and kept up a running list of complaints, silenced only by a bag of sweets brought out by their mother. Elizabeth bit back a smile as they crossed the Pultney Bridge. Soon, the carriage came to a stop. The driver opened the door and let down the steps.

"But …my goodness!" cried Estella, craning her neck to see. "This isn't the Abbey! We've been brought to the wrong place!"

"Do you think so?" said Elizabeth.

Estella scrambled out and stood on the sidewalk, blinking at the building. "There must be some mistake, Miss Elliot. I wish to attend services at the Abbey! Not here!"

Elizabeth fought to maintain an innocent face. Argyle Chapel was perfectly dreadful, but the expression on her cousin's face was worth it. "The minister is said to be a brilliant pulpit orator. I expect we'll have a most interesting sermon."

"But I wish to go to the Abbey! Not this nonconformist place! Besides, what is the point of attending services here?" Estella gestured to the parishioners who were filing in. "Look at all this rabble! There is no one of quality, surely! This is a complete waste of our time!"

Ignoring the fact that she had felt exactly the same way, Elizabeth merely said, "That shows how much you know. Nevertheless, it is best to avoid causing a scene. Therefore, I suggest–"

"Causing a scene?" interrupted Estella. "What does that signify? No one knows me here!"

Elizabeth gave her a measured look and made a slight gesture. Yee, the butler, stood apart with the other servants.

"Mercy me, Cousin Elizabeth, you cannot mean the servants! I care nothing for their opinion!"

Elizabeth lowered her voice. "My mother taught me not to offend the sensibilities of inferior persons. It so happens that I asked Yee for a recommendation, and he directed us here. And as he is the one who sees to your meals–and orders the hot water for your bath and any number of other things–I suggest you do nothing to offend him."

Estella met her look with a pout, but said nothing more.

Coward! thought Elizabeth. In Estella's place, she would never have given way!

The four of them entered Argyle Chapel and filed to a pew near the front. The nursery maid, Elizabeth noticed, chose to sit with the servants at the back, leaving the children to be supervised by their mother. Elizabeth knew that Calcutta would freeze over before she would!

Sure enough, Estella was taken up with smoothing her gloves and making adjustments to her silly hat, all the while stealing glances at the congregation. She was, in fact, looking for compliments and admirers. Never mind that on many a Sunday Elizabeth had done the same!

Presently she spoke, more loudly than Elizabeth thought seemly. "At Brookfield, our family pew is at the very front of the chapel. Which is only fitting, you know, since dear Mr Bragg is Headmaster."

By now Elizabeth was ready to strangle dear Mr Bragg, the Headmaster! Meanwhile, dear Mr Bragg's son, Johnny, had collected several hassocks and was stacking them. His sister kicked at the hymnal rack. Elizabeth looked the other way. What a very good thing it was that no one knew her!

Or did they? Mr Gill lived in this area of Bath; would he attend a church like this one? Much like Estella, though with more subtlety, Elizabeth turned to scan the congregation. Many of the men were dressed in the same outmoded fashion Mr Gill favoured, but she could not discern his face among them. The organ began the introit. Elizabeth brought out her mother's Testament and, turning a deaf ear to the children's commotion, pretended to read.

As it turned out, the sermon was not bad. The minister, William Jay, lived up to his reputation as an earnest Christian speaker. Elizabeth wasn't certain what his sermon topic was—something about Jesus' earthly ministry—but she was mindful to look up every scripture reference he gave, mostly to shut out what was going on beside her. From the sound of things, the children were giving their mother plenty of trouble.

"Matthew eight, verse twenty," Mr Jay announced, and Elizabeth's fingers went racing through the pages.

"No fair!" Johnny whispered loudly. "I want more! Pig!" He made a lunge for the bag of candies and missed. They fell to the granite floor and went rolling. Estella swatted at her son's knee. Elizabeth kept her gaze piously focused on the text while Mr Jay read:

> And Jesus saith unto him, "The foxes have holes, and the birds of the air have nests, but the Son of Man hath nowhere to lay his head."

Elizabeth blinked at the words on the page. That's me, she thought. She lifted her eyes to gaze at the people around her. These people had homes. Even Estella had a home, the awful Brookfield. The animals had homes, even foxes. Whereas she ...

Elizabeth grew very still. She no longer had a home. She had nowhere to lay her head, except as a guest. It became impossible to read, for the text swam before her eyes. She quietly closed her mother's Testament.

After the service, there were more challenges. Quite naturally, Estella gloried in introducing herself to all who came to greet her, prattling on about her husband and how delightful it was to be in Bath. Elizabeth smiled and nodded, wondering all the while how to get Estella out of the door and into the waiting carriage.

A quiet voice intruded on her thoughts. Startled, Elizabeth turned. Who would know her here? At first, she saw only the ugly brown hat and straw-coloured hair. But beneath the hat's brim, the woman's eyes were smiling. Green eyes, of an unusual shade. Of course, Elizabeth realized. This was Anne's neighbour, Miss Owen.

"Perhaps," Miss Owen said shyly, "it would be best if I took the children for a little walk? They seem a bit restless, and it looks as though you'll be occupied for a while longer."

Elizabeth heartily agreed, and this time her smile was genuine. In truth, she owed Winnie Owen rather a lot. Over the past days, Miss Owen had very kindly taken the children for what she called "rambles"—long walks through a nearby park to feed the ducks in a pond. Elizabeth would never go there, but it seemed like a perfect place to entertain two noisy, energetic children.

At last they were able to leave. Estella began talking as soon as the carriage pulled away. "So very like home!" she said. "At Brookfield I can never seem to get away, simply because of the many well-wishers."

"Since Mr Bragg is Headmaster, yes," murmured Elizabeth. By now her head ached, and she was hungry, but there was more to come. After dropping Estella and the children at St. Peter's Square, she planned to continue to The Citadel to visit her father. Wouldn't that be a pleasant way to end her afternoon?

Sir Walter appeared pleased to see her until he realized she had not brought the post. Apparently Mr Savoy was now allowing him to have letters. Her omission kept him from a favourite occupation, collecting invitations. "It's all very well for you, who may come and go as you please," he complained, "but what about those who are not so fortunate? You might have had a little consideration!"

He was being unreasonable again. Did he think she could afford to hire transportation whenever she pleased? "You ought to have your letters delivered here, instead of Lady Russell's. It would save me a world of trouble. As well as fare for the carriage. Or perhaps you could have them delivered to Anne's house."

Sir Walter's brow furrowed. "But is St. Peter Square a more fashionable address than Rivers Street? That is the question." This was a matter requiring much thought. "No," he decided, "for a man of my station, Rivers Street is preferable. I daresay Lady Russell's residence will be dignified by the delivery of *my* letters. So," he continued, "tell me how you are faring."

Elizabeth shrugged. "There is not much to tell. Anne is away, and my busy cousin Estella is not."

"Does Mrs Stevenson-Bragg suit you as well as Mrs Clay?"

Elizabeth did not answer right away. Hadn't she told him never to mention Penelope's name? "It would be a help to have your tickets for the assembly this week."

"I think not," he said. "There is no telling what sort of wild scrape you might get yourselves into." He grew thoughtful. "I believe I'll offer them to Mr Savoy, instead. You ought to choose a more pedestrian form of entertainment. What about a Breakfast Promenade at Sydney Park? And a ride in one of those leaky rowboats?"

Elizabeth sighed. Thursday's assembly would have been perfect, as the tickets were already paid for. She rose to take her leave. "Very well, Father, I'll collect your letters tomorrow—or Tuesday—and bring them by." She hesitated. "There's one more thing. I've had a few unexpected expenses, and as last quarter's allowance was not fully paid..." She did not finish her sentence.

Sir Walter rubbed his hands together. "So you've come to a standstill already, eh? Mr Savoy said you would."

"I *beg* your pardon?" Elizabeth was coming to hate Mr Savoy.

"You've run short of funds, haven't you?"

"Certainly I have! With having to run here and there, hiring a carriage every time I wish to go anywhere—"

Sir Walter sat back. "I suggest you apply to your new brother for assistance."

"And so I would, if he were not away in Shropshire! It is bad enough to be fed and housed by him while you are here!" she said. "Am I reduced to begging for charity as well?"

He blinked. "No," he said. "We are not yet reduced to that." He dug in the pocket of his waistcoat. "Here," he said, holding out a bill. "This should tide you over, as the saying goes."

It was a five-pound note. Elizabeth didn't know whether to laugh or cry. She longed to throw it in his face and run from the room, but she did not dare. Five pounds was rather a lot of money.

~ ~ ~ ~ ~ ~ ~ & ~ ~ ~ ~ ~ ~ ~

Monday came and went but Elizabeth did not stir from the house, as it did not suit her to collect her father's post on that day. Tuesday was much better. She could hire a carriage, collect his letters, and continue on to George Street in time to meet with Mr Gill. Shortly after one, Elizabeth came into the hall, pulling on her gloves.

"There you are!" called Estella from the landing. Elizabeth finished tying her bonnet and pretended not to hear. Estella came down the stairs. "Where are you going? Might I join you?"

"It's nothing you would like. I've some errands to do, and then I'm to visit Father." Elizabeth bit her lip, for Estella looked interested. "He's been feeling poorly and is grouchy."

Estella's mouth quivered. Elizabeth looked quickly away, before the beautiful pout appeared. "But what am I to *do* while you are gone?" cried Estella. "This house is like a tomb!"

Wasn't it, though? Elizabeth glanced at the clock. "Perhaps you could read," she suggested. "There are plenty of books in the library. My sister, Anne, is a great reader."

Estella's expression showed what she thought of that!

Hiring a hack was no longer so difficult, now that Elizabeth was more accustomed to it. Yee had exchanged her five-pound note for coins of smaller denominations. She now carried nearly a pound–it seemed a fortune. At length, the hack came to a halt before Lady Russell's narrow house.

"Please wait," she told the driver. Longwell answered the door. "I have come for my father's letters," she told him.

Longwell opened the door fully. "If you will be pleased to step inside, miss," he said, "I'll ascertain whether her ladyship is at–"

"Do you mean my godmother is here? But I cannot come in! I have no time–"

"Her ladyship has just arrived and will be pleased to see you, miss, if I may say."

"Longwell, no! Wait!" The last thing she needed today was her very busy, very inquisitive godmother!

"Elizabeth! My dear!" Lady Russell came out of the salon with both hands extended. "Do come in. Give your things to Longwell."

Elizabeth made a hopeless gesture. "But I've a carriage waiting, Lady Russell, and–"

"Send it away," she said, smiling. "I'll have my own out and will take you home myself, for I simply must hear everything that has happened while I've been away." She drew Elizabeth toward the door of the salon. "Tell me, how is your father?"

Elizabeth blanched; this was worse than anything! "Really, Lady Russell," she stammered, "I have an appointment on George Street in a few minutes, and I..."

"An appointment?" Lady Russell looked at her fixedly. "What sort of appointment, dear?"

Elizabeth worked to keep her tone light. "Oh, it's nothing. I'm meeting a friend."

Lady Russell's brows went up. "It wouldn't happen to be Mr Elliot, now would it?"

Elizabeth gave her godmother a look. "Why would I meet Mr Elliot? He's still in London!"

"Ah, but Longwell tells me he called twice yesterday. Both times he enquired about you. He was most insistent."

"Did he? I cannot imagine why."

Lady Russell's hold on Elizabeth's arm tightened. "I think we need to have a little talk about Mr Elliot, Elizabeth." She turned. "Longwell, why are you standing about in that foolish way? Oh, the post. Elizabeth, here are your father's letters."

Elizabeth knew better than to object. "Please don't send the carriage away, Longwell," she said, as she gave him her gloves and hat. "And whatever you do, don't bring in refreshments!" She glanced at the tall clock. There were only fifteen minutes to spare.

"As you wish, Miss Elliot," Longwell said, but his eyes held a smirk.

Elizabeth lifted her chin. What a horrid man he was!

~ ~ ~ ~ ~ ~ ~ & ~ ~ ~ ~ ~ ~ ~

It was not until Elizabeth was well away from Rivers Street that she began to consider what Lady Russell had said. It was all such a jumble. To begin with, there was her reaction to Elizabeth's dress. It was one of her oldest gowns, but it was not unattractive. There was no need to dress exquisitely for Mr Gill, but she could hardly say this to Lady Russell!

And then there was Lady Russell's ranting speech about Mr Elliot. What on earth had he done to offend her? It must have been something dreadful, but Lady Russell did not give details. She only said that he was guilty of infamy and was a disgrace to the family. Still, it was interesting to think about him. After all, that he was in Bath and enquiring about her was something. Not that Elizabeth trusted the man. He showed his true colours when he threw her over for Anne. Nevertheless, he was her father's heir. It would never do to alienate him.

At last the hired carriage reached George Street. Elizabeth had the fare ready. Moments later she was out and hurrying toward her destination. She went to open the door of the tearoom, but it would not budge. It was locked.

Elizabeth did not know what to think. She was more than a little late, but why would the tearoom be shut?

"Miss Elliot!"

She looked up to see Mr Gill coming toward her. He pointed to a sign on the door: *Closed until three o'clock.* She felt her face grow hot. How could she have missed such an obvious notice?

"I have an alternative," he said. "If you don't mind walking a bit." He bowed and offered his arm. Elizabeth said nothing, but he was not deterred. He took hold of her gloved hand and placed it on his arm. "Good!" he said. "I'm glad you agree! Shall we go?"

Elizabeth found herself propelled down George Street at a brisk clip. He turned onto Gay Street. "Where are we going?" she demanded.

"You'll see."

"But," she protested, "we're nearly at Queen's Square! Is it as far as that?"

"I'm thinking of a little place on Cheap Street, actually. Not far from the Abbey."

"The Abbey! But that's blocks and blocks away!"

Mr Gill grinned down at her. "You look to be a strong enough walker."

"Of course I am strong enough!"

They crossed several more streets. Mr Gill began humming a tune. Then Elizabeth thought of something. "I served your Cornish pasty the other night," she said. "It was brilliant! You should have seen the look on Estella's face! I told her it was a delicacy."

"*Pâté en croûte*, eh?"

"You know French?" she cried. "Where did you learn French?"

"In France, of course. What else have you done to your cousin?"

Elizabeth struggled to keep a straight face. "You'll never believe it. I took her to service at Argyle Chapel."

"No!" He wanted to hear all about it, so she told him. "But I must admit," she added, "the sermon was better than anything old Dr Stuart ever preached. So as long as Estella remains, this is where we'll go to church. And tomorrow..." She dissolved into giggling.

"Yes?"

"Tomorrow Estella wishes to visit Sydney Park and go round the canal in one of those horrid little boats! Can you imagine?"

"Hah! Capsize it! That'll fix her!"

"Capsize?"

"Overturn the boat."

"Good gracious!" she cried. "What about *me*?"

He shrugged. "You look to be a strong swimmer."

"But I'm not! And I refuse to drown myself on account of Estella!"

The dimple appeared in his cheek. "But surely, you've been to float in the hot baths with the rest of the ladies. Swimming is similar."

"Don't be ridiculous!" she shot back. "Immerse myself in all that filthy water?"

He gave her gloved hand a friendly pat. "I quite agree, Miss Elliot."

At last they drew near to the Abbey Churchyard. Elizabeth's steps slowed. "This is Cheap Street," she said, looking about. "Where exactly is this tearoom?"

"Just there," he pointed. "I must warn you, most of the patrons are old ladies coming from service."

"Old ladies?"

"Yes, but consider how respectable."

"I don't believe there is such a place, respectable or not."

He came to a stop. Elizabeth glanced up. Patrick Gill's blue eyes looked directly into hers. "Trust me," he said softly.

Elizabeth compressed her lips. "Why?"

~ 13 ~
Touch and Go

Patrick McGillvary nearly laughed outright. Never had that line elicited anything but the most heartfelt sighs from women! Not so with Elizabeth Elliot. She must ask why.

Nevertheless, that she'd come was a triumph. By this time, they were directly in front of the Abbey. McGillvary wracked his brain. He had taken tea once with Cleora and her friend at this place. Where was it? They walked a block more—and he breathed a sigh of relief. "And there we are," he said, pointing. "Just at the corner. Do you see?"

Miss Elliot read the sign: "Bailey's Tearoom." She wrinkled her nose. "It's very small."

And it was. Worse, the place was packed. They must wait for a table to become available, and they were not the first in line. But Miss Elliot made no complaint.

"How unusual," she whispered, after a few minutes of standing. "I believe this establishment is run by a man. What do you think?" She indicated the fellow in question. "Could that be Mr Bailey?"

McGillvary took a look. A harried fellow, balding and definitely on the wrong side of forty, wound his way between the tables, bowing and scraping. "Look there," he said, touching her elbow. A group of matrons had just finished and were putting on their wraps. "There's our table." He drew out his wallet.

Miss Elliot made an impatient movement. "Are you going to *bribe* that man?" she whispered.

"How else shall we get a table?"

She laid a restraining hand on his arm. "Put your money away, please." She removed her shawl. "Hold this," she said. She then drew off her gloves.

"What are you going to do?" he whispered.

168

She smiled and looked him full in the eyes. Hers were dancing. "To display my bare fingers, of course." She held up her ring-less left hand. "Do you think he'll mistake me for a tradesman's daughter?"

"You must be joking," he whispered back.

"I am an Elliot," she said, lifting her chin. "We do not pay bribes for tables, Mr Gill. Let me show you how it's done."

"Elizabeth..." he protested, catching at her arm.

She shook him off. "Watch and learn," she said.

McGillvary saw it all: Miss Elliot's perfect smile, the adorable blush and modest flutter of the lashes, her musical voice enquiring oh-so-sweetly about the table. The poor proprietor looked dumbfounded at first, but before long he was smiling. Within moments, she was being escorted to the now-vacant table. After she was seated, she shot him a look of pure triumph.

"Termagant!" McGillvary said under his breath, as he took the chair opposite hers. "That," he said, "was the worst thing I have ever seen! The poor man! Tradesman's daughter, indeed!"

Miss Elliot handed him the menu. "I don't know how you can say that, Mr Gill," she said serenely. "After all, it was you who taught me to appreciate tradesmen. Remember Mr Lonk? The man who is so admired by the ladies?" She gave him an arch smile. "Besides," she added, "you called me a coward back there."

McGillvary bit back a grin. "I did no such thing."

"Ah, but I think you did. Not aloud, perhaps. But the challenge was there, just the same."

McGillvary's lips twitched. "And is it your practice, Miss Elliot, to take up every dare that is issued?"

She dimpled adorably. "Only when I am certain to win."

McGillvary threw back his head and laughed.

At length, Elizabeth returned her cup to its saucer. She had tarried here longer than was wise, but somehow she could not bring the conversation to a close. Mr Gill, who was never at a loss, just kept talking. It was odd that a clerk could be so entertaining.

This tearoom was just as dowdy as he said it would be, but the food was excellent. They even had a table by the window, just like they'd had at the place on George Street. By now, every one of the sandwiches had been consumed, and the teapot was empty. Slowly, Elizabeth brought her reticule from her lap and placed it on the table. Her father's letters, which were stuffed inside, made an unattractive bulge. She covered it with her hands.

"I'm afraid I must be going," she said at last. "I must deliver these letters to my father. He will likely be wondering what has happened to me."

But Mr Gill did not take the hint; he made no move to rise. "And how is he feeling?"

"Better," she said. "At least, I must suppose he is better. I haven't much experience with the sickroom. If men become crabby as they recover, which I've heard is often the case, then Father is restored to perfect health!"

Mr Gill leaned back in his chair. "My father was the devil himself whenever he was on the mend."

"The devil himself," she repeated. "That describes Father perfectly. And then," she continued, "there's the evening to spend with Estella." Her fingers traced a pattern on the table. "Such delights await me. I do wish Father had given me his tickets for Thursday's assembly."

He looked amused. "So that you may exhibit her to all of Bath?"

"No, so that I might entertain her cheaply! Father's subscription is paid for, and Estella spends money like–" She broke off, smiling in spite of herself. "Like I used to do! Which means she is shockingly expensive."

"Excellent! A lesson in pecuniary management!"

Elizabeth did not understand the word he used, but the twinkle was delightful. "I do not mean that I will never be shockingly expensive again, Mr Gill. It's just that I'm doing a little...retrenching...at the moment."

"And just what do you know about retrenching?"

This was said with such a direct look that Elizabeth did not know what to say. "I am not wholly without resources, Mr Gill," she blustered. "I am not without a plan! One way or another, I shall make a recovery. You'll see."

"Does it involve entrapping our friend, the proprietor?" he said, with a nod in the man's direction.

"What are you talking about?"

"I think you know very well," he replied. Pointing to her bulky reticule, he added, "Speaking of letters, has your father received mine? About the extension?"

"You wrote to my father?"

"That is to say, the letter from Madderly, Kinclaven, and Planque," he said. "Has he received it?"

She pulled them from her bag, one by one. "It does not seem to be here," she said, sorting through them. And then she discovered one with her name on it—and froze. It was from him. He had written—he had actually written!

Elizabeth could feel Mr Gill's curious gaze; her cheeks grew hot. She resumed sorting. "Ah, here it is." She forced a smile. "I shall make certain Father receives it, Mr Gill."

"But what about the other? Does your father see that one, too?"

Elizabeth gathered the letters together. "What do you mean?"

"That one near the bottom, which gave you such a start. Will you show that letter to him?"

She pushed back her chair.

Mr Gill was on his feet in an instant to assist her. "Speaking as a father," he said, "may I point out that I find your lack of filial respect unnerving?"

"No," she said tartly. "You may not."

There was an uncomfortable silence. She stole a look at him. The expression in his eyes made her wince.

"Forgive me, Mr Gill," she said quietly. "My father has put me in a wretched situation, but that is no reason to snap at you." She lifted her chin as if to ward off pity. "You need not fear for me. I expect this letter," she patted her reticule, "brings good news."

Mr Gill raised an eyebrow but did not press her. As he reached for his wallet, he said, "Is this location convenient for Thursday, Miss Elliot?" There seemed to be no question that they would meet again.

Elizabeth hesitated. "Perhaps it would be better," she said slowly, "now that Lady Russell has returned. And the prices here are quite reasonable. You see? I do know something about retrenching."

McGillvary was about to reply, but his attention was arrested by the condition of his wallet. He turned away so that she would not see and quickly sorted through the bills. His smile disappeared.

He checked a second time. There was nothing smaller than a five-pound note. He searched his pockets for stray pennies. There were none. Out of the corner of his eye, he saw Miss Elliot place something on the table. It was a handful of coins.

"Let this be my treat today, Mr Gill. It is only fair, after all." She smiled brightly. "A lesson in, how did you say it? Pecuniary management?"

McGillvary was struck speechless. Yes, she was paying with his money, but that did not remove the sting.

And then he heard Elizabeth catch her breath. She was staring out at the Abbey courtyard. "Oh no! He cannot be here!" she cried.

McGillvary joined her at the window. "What's wrong?"

"My cousin, William Elliot," she said. "He's over there."

McGillvary knew the name. "Which one is he?"

She pointed. "That's his carriage, the one with the crest," she said. "I'd heard he was in Bath, and I know he's been asking to see me. But I had no idea he would find me toda–"

The gentleman in question looked up. His gaze shifted to the window and held. Suddenly, he smiled.

Elizabeth backed away. "Mr Elliot must not find me here! Not like this!"

"Why not?"

She made an impatient gesture. "Look at me! Dressed like a–"

"Like a tradesman's daughter?"

"It makes no difference to you; why should it? But Mr Elliot's good opinion means quite a lot to me!" she said. "He is my father's heir. And," she added, "he is unmarried."

McGillvary stiffened. "Is he the solution to your 'wretched situation'?"

"My cousin is very rich," she said. "I must keep my options open." Miss Elliot's gaze was fastened on the tearoom door. "He is coming in! What can I do?"

McGillvary snatched up his hat and caught her hand. "Come on!" he said.

"But my gloves!"

"No time!" He pulled her through the dining area, dodging tables, to the doorway at the rear. McGillvary parted the curtain, and they plunged inside.

Elizabeth was aghast. "What are we doing?" she cried.

"Looking for the service door," he said. "Here it is. Come on!"

"But, Mr Gill!"

McGillvary opened the door and pulled her into the alley. "Elliot saw us leave! Run!"

Elizabeth had no choice but to do as she was told. Besides, she could not pull away–Mr Gill held her hand in a tenacious grip. The cobbled pavement in the alley was filthy; she tried not to think about how soiled her shoes were becoming. Mr Gill was humming again. "I do believe you're enjoying this!" she panted, running alongside. He grinned down at her. Though his face was in the shadow, she could see the shine in his eyes.

They rounded the corner and ran along another back lane. When they reached a larger street, he halted.

"Where *are* we?" she demanded.

"High Street," he said. "The river is over there."

"And my cousin?" She turned, but he stopped her. "Do not look back."

His voice held quiet authority; Elizabeth knew she must obey.

"Looking back draws attention," he said, "which is the last thing we want. Now then." He drew her hand through his arm. "We take a little stroll together, as a loving couple."

"But my cousin! What if he sees us together?"

"He will think he is mistaken about your identity. In a bit I'll hail a chair to take you home."

Elizabeth fell into step beside him. "Aren't you forgetting something, Mr Gill? Neither of us have any money. What I had was left behind in the tearoom. Which is too bad, for I was needing the change."

"Oh, lord!" he said, laughing. "We *are* in the suds, aren't we?"

"This is not at all funny! And another thing—"

But Mr Gill was no longer paying attention. "Save your lecture, sweet," he said cheerfully. "For unless I'm mistaken, your cousin has followed us. No, Elizabeth!" he ordered. "Don't look!"

"But—"

"Keep your eyes straight ahead and keep moving. I'll plot a new course."

"You'll do *what?*"

"Analyze the situation and plan our strategy." Without warning, Mr Gill stepped into the busy street, pulling Elizabeth directly into the path of an oncoming carriage. It shot past with inches to spare. It was followed by a fleet of clattering wagons.

"That's scotched him, at least for the moment"

Elizabeth wrenched her hand free. "Merciful heavens!" she cried. "I might as well stop and talk to my idiotic cousin!"

"What? And confirm his suspicions?"

"It is preferable to certain death, yes!"

He had her by the arm again. "Ah, but remember," he said, guiding her along, "at this point your cousin merely suspects. Capitulate and you'll spoil the game."

"Game?" she cried. Without warning, he pulled her into another side street.

"Mr Gill, where are we going?" Elizabeth was out of breath and her feet hurt. Somehow the fringe of her shawl had become tangled in the buttons on his sleeve. Moreover, she was forced to lean on his arm rather more than she liked. He did not seem to mind.

"Doubling back to Milsom," he said, guiding her around the corner, "although, we'll need to cross High Street fairly soon."

"Again?"

He looked down at her. "Lost your nerve?"

"I am not accustomed to hurling myself into the path of carriages and wagons, Mr Gill! Of course I have lost my nerve!"

"You're out of practice, that's all. I find escapes from death quite invigorating, myself."

She gave him a withering look. "You would."

~ ~ ~ ~ ~ ~ ~ & ~ ~ ~ ~ ~ ~ ~

William Elliot ran out of the alley. His breath came in sharp gasps; he was not accustomed to running pell-mell like a madman! "I know they came this way!" he muttered, shading his eyes against the sun. The street was choked with traffic—and his cousin and her companion were nowhere to be seen.

He made his way along High Street, dodging pedestrians. He did not know whether this direction was the right one, or even if the woman in question was Elizabeth. Whoever it was certainly resembled her—and by the look on her face, she recognized him! That she wished to avoid him was bad enough, but who was her companion? Mr Elliot strode along the pavement. He could not afford to let a bit of luck like this slip through his fingers, not after the afternoon he'd had!

An hour ago he'd called at Rivers Street, again, and this time Lady Russell was at home. He'd spoken to her—or rather, she had spoken to him. Even now, it made his blood boil to think on it. Such a reception! The woman was downright insolent and all but forbade him to call again.

What was worse, Lady Russell refused to give any information about Sir Walter. That the man was not dead he knew by her attire. However, his visit was not a complete waste; he managed to prise from her ladyship that Sir Walter would be taking up residence at Kellynch Hall by summer's end.

"If he lives," Mr Elliot muttered. To speak with Elizabeth was now his prime object. Nothing must deter him—not even Elizabeth herself. But where was she keeping herself? If she wasn't living with Lady Russell, she must be living with…Anne? But that could not be right. Anne hated Bath!

Mr Elliot looked doubtfully along the street. And then his head came up. A smile of recognition worked its way across his face, and he broke into a run. For there, at the corner, was Elizabeth.

~ ~ ~ ~ ~ ~ ~ & ~ ~ ~ ~ ~ ~ ~

Snubs were lost on Mr Gill. Ever cheerful, he sauntered along High Street in his easy way. "Tell me about this cousin of yours, Miss Elliot."

She flashed a look at him, and then at her gown. Her hem was splashed with muck—what sort of muck she did not care to speculate. Undeterred, Mr Gill repeated his question.

Goaded beyond endurance and struggling to keep up with his pace, Elizabeth gave up the fight. If he was so curious about William Elliot, she would tell him all. And so the history of her father's dealings with the man was poured out, minus her own disappointed expectations.

"And so, he left for London," she finished, speaking in short sentences to conserve breath. "That was over a month ago. And in all that time we've had no contact with him. Yesterday he called at my godmother's twice. Each time he asked for me."

Mr Gill looked down at her; his eyes were bright. "Is he in love with you?"

"Heavens, no! What a stupid idea! I doubt that William Elliot could love anyone!" She gave him a sidelong look. "I am coming to understand that the men of my family do not love others, Mr Gill. They love only themselves."

"I see."

"Don't laugh, it isn't funny!" She readjusted her hold on his arm. "You cannot imagine how dreary it is to live with people who are so self-absorbed!"

"And what about you?" he said, stepping into the street and guiding her across.

"Isn't it obvious? Unless I am able to find the fare for a carriage or for one of those disgusting sedan chairs, I am destined to *walk* all that way! Which is absolutely insupportable!"

He burst out laughing. "That's not what I asked, and you know it," he retorted. "We were speaking about love, Miss Elliot. I repeat: What about you?"

Elizabeth kept her eyes focused on the street.

"What's the matter?" he taunted. "Cat's got your tongue?"

"Mr Gill," she said, "I have no interest whatsoever in speaking about love. I am, in fact, engaged in doing something infinitely more useful; I am looking for dropped coins. Since both of us are reduced to the depths of poverty, I suggest you do the same!"

The tramp back to Milsom Street had done Elizabeth in; McGillvary could see that. The strain was evident in her face, and she leaned more heavily on his arm than before. Yet, she did not hurl abuse at him—abuse that he rightly deserved. It was painful to see her toil on, knowing that he could hire a carriage. Yet he must maintain his ruse—and he was coming to see that the cost to his pride was very high.

She glanced back. "My cousin is the most tiresome beast in nature!" She hobbled on a few more steps. "Are we nearly there?"

McGillvary no longer chided her for looking; there was no need. This Mr Elliot had long ago abandoned the chase. A few more steps would bring them to the offices of Madderly, Kinclaven, and Planque where he supposedly kept a few coins in his desk. It was the best he could come up with under the circumstances, but he was heartily ashamed of such an excuse.

"You are a trooper," he said, giving her hand a friendly squeeze. "And yes, we are almost there."

"I'm a what?"

"A trooper. You know, a stalwart soldier. A seasoned campaigner."

That brought her head up. "I most certainly am nothing of the kind! I'll have you know that mine is a delicate constitution! And if you dare to say otherwise, I shall hate you forever!"

He laughed. "I'm surprised if you do not hate me now! But I'm sorry just the same. We must have walked three or four miles. Your endurance is commendable."

"Endurance? And do you suppose an evening at a ball is any less exhausting?" Her voice sank a little. "The only difference is the shoes," she said, looking at hers. "Dancing slippers are far more comfortable."

"Will you be at the assembly Thursday night?" The words came out before McGillvary could stop them.

She gave a sharp sigh. "My father prefers to give his tickets to his physician, so no, I do not attend. In any case, it would not be the thing, as it is known that my father is ill. Unfortunately." She gave him a wan smile. "I do enjoy dancing."

"You could do as my daughter's friends and threaten to climb out the window."

A frown came into Elizabeth's eyes. "Is your daughter so much trouble, Mr Gill? Is she…wild?"

"Cleora? By no means!"

"But I thought you said—"

"I spoke in jest. Her rambunctious cousins I cannot vouch for, but Cleora? Never." McGillvary sighed in spite of himself. "My darling daughter is not fond of…society, Miss Elliot. She is terrified in the presence of strangers. She scarcely says a word."

"But you must help her!" Elizabeth's tone was earnest.

McGillvary spread his hands. "What do I know about raising a girl? I haven't a mother's touch, unfortunately."

"She needs a mother, yes. But she needs you even more! You are conversant with strangers. You must teach her to develop the skill."

"I'm no schoolmaster."

"It wouldn't be so difficult. Take her with you when next you go out. Explain ahead of time whom you'll meet and what their interests are. Give her an idea of what you might say. And then, do not leave her side, not even for a moment. You carry the conversation, while she is free to listen and learn." Elizabeth broke off speaking. At length she said, "Never shall I forget my first dinner party. There sat my father at the end of our long dining table, talking and laughing. He hadn't a care in the world." Her voice sank. "And I, in my stiff black silk, sat in my poor mother's chair. I was never so alone in my life, with the eyes of all those people upon me, expecting me to play hostess…"

Her head came up. "Bit by bit I learned. Oh yes, I learned. But it was not easy, Mr Gill. My father was no help at all. Our visits to London were the worst. In fact, I…" She hesitated. Her eyes searched his.

"Yes?" he prompted.

Elizabeth spoke slowly. "I developed a system—a sort of ledger—to aid me with the names and titles. I suppose I could—" Again came the searching gaze.

McGillvary waited. "Yes?" he said at last.

"I could bring my ledger, I suppose. To show you."

"I would be most grateful," he said solemnly. "And so will Cleora."

And then Elizabeth smiled at him, and that smile made all the difference. It was as if the sun had come out from behind a cloud.

"Do you know," she said lightly, "it is a very good thing that your Cleora is not—how did you say? Rambunctious? For slipping off to balls is over-rated, I'm afraid. I tried that once. It did not come off well."

"How can you say so?" he protested. "A clandestine escape is the very essence of romance! That is, for a young woman who is not my daughter."

"You sound like Caroline Bingley. No, romance is best left for fairy tales, Mr Gill. Balls are not at all romantic."

"And did you attend this disastrous ball with your friend Caroline? What happened?"

She gave a derisive snort. "It was definitely not a fairy tale event! Having given my fairy godmother the slip (and my godmother is more an ogre than a fairy!), I wore my own gown and went without the magical glass slippers. And the Handsome Princes I met that night were either too young or too old for my taste!"

"Or, much too fat and disguised as a toad. But I asked a question earlier which you haven't answered," he said. They were now at the doorway to Madderly, Kinclaven. He lifted her chin with a careless finger. "I am unused to having my questions ignored, so this time you must answer—"

McGillvary broke off speaking. There was a movement, just there to the right. He turned. His smile fled. "Do not turn around, Miss Elliot," he said, speaking low. "Your busy cousin has managed to follow us here."

She made a slight movement.

"I said, *don't!*" he repeated, pulling open the door. "Follow me. Say nothing."

He pushed her inside and ordered her into a chair in the reception area. Instead of shuffling quietly to a desk, Mr Gill strode into the inner chambers and, ignoring the men who greeted him, disappeared behind a door.

Elizabeth did not know what to make of this, but she was too tired to care. Every one of her limbs ached, and it was all she could do not to slump over in the chair. Years of training stood her in good stead; she sat erect. Her gloveless hands were concealed beneath the shawl.

That Mr Elliot had followed her here seemed incredible. He must be mad, she decided. Or else she was mad. Who else but a madwoman would go traipsing through the back streets of Bath with a stranger and then hide in his office? And not just any stranger, but a stranger who enjoyed the chase!

Within a very short time Mr Gill was back, and he ordered one of the clerks to hail a cab. Soon she was being handed into a very nice carriage. Mr Gill climbed in after her.

"Is my cousin still there?" Elizabeth said, leaning her head against the squabs. Doing so would crush her bonnet, but she was past caring.

"Aye," he said.

Elizabeth opened her eyes very slightly. "What is he doing?"

"Hiring a carriage of his own, I imagine. Look."

She groaned. "Stupid man!"

Mr Gill's attention remained fixed on what was going on across the street. "You said he was anxious to see you, my dear. Apparently you were right. And so, what direction do I give the driver?"

Elizabeth fell silent, considering. "I ought to visit my father and deliver his letters, but…" She hesitated, remembering Lady Russell's reluctance. "I daresay you'll think I'm foolish, but I don't wish Mr Elliot to follow me home. And I oughtn't to visit my father, either. I have a notion Mr Elliot shouldn't be seeing him just now."

"A wise precaution."

Elizabeth frowned as she thought. "If I remember correctly, Mr Elliot does not know where my sister lives. He left Bath before she was married."

"Is there a side street we could take? A back entrance?"

"Even if there was, I've had my fill of alleys for today, thank you! Unless–"

"Aha! I knew you'd think of something!"

Elizabeth flushed at the admiration in his voice. "If I could get into the park, there is a path through the mews that leads to our garden. Miss Owen told me about it. But the gate is probably locked, and the park is walled in, most likely."

Mr Gill was grinning. "Scale a wall, shall we? No trouble at all. Where is it?"

Elizabeth thought of something else. "Why do you suppose my cousin has not approached us?"

"Odd, isn't it? Either he's lacking the courage, or he's waiting to see you when I'm not around. Probably the latter." He paused and looked at her in a way that was hard to read. "Are you ready to face that?"

"Not yet."

"Good girl! Force him to confront you on your terms, not his!" He took the seat facing hers. "So, tell me more about this back gate."

"My sister's house is on St. Peter Square. Apparently there is a path that cuts behind the mews," Elizabeth explained. "Are you familiar with Belsom Park, Mr Gill?"

McGillvary kept his features well schooled. "I am," he said promptly. "Perhaps better than you realize. In point of fact, we are neighbours, Miss Elliot. I live a half-mile or so from St. Peter Square. I have a set of rooms in an old house."

He could barely keep a straight face as he said this, but it was the perfect truth. The Belsom mansion was extremely large and very old. "It's a bit expensive to live there," he added, "but it's well worth the trouble. It's a good address for business."

"Oh," she said. "Business."

"And now, if you'll excuse me, I'll just have a word with the driver." He opened the carriage door. "Keep an eye on your cousin while I'm gone. We don't want him to get away."

"But I thought..."

The rest of Elizabeth's words were lost. McGillvary stepped up to the driver. "Might I have a word?" he said. At the sight of McGillvary's wallet, the look of determined apathy vanished from the driver's face. And once McGillvary flashed the five-pound note and explained what was required of him, the man looked downright cheerful.

Mr Gill came sprinting back and climbed in. "We're set," he said, slamming the door. The carriage lurched forward. "There's a little-known way onto the grounds of the estate, and our driver knows exactly what to do." He glanced out the window and turned to her with a grin. "Now, let's shake off your cousin, shall we?"

No sooner had the vehicle picked up speed but it turned sharply down a side street, sending Elizabeth flying. Mr Gill caught her in his arms.

"I'm so sorry!" he said. "You'll need to hold on tight, my dear! For the chase has only just begun, and we'll be cracking on!"

"At this rate," said Elizabeth tartly, "what we'll be 'cracking' is every bone in my body!"

~ ~ ~ ~ ~ ~ ~ & ~ ~ ~ ~ ~ ~ ~

Meanwhile, in the Wentworth's sitting room, Miss Owen was bearing her part in an uncomfortable conversation. She sat bolt upright and held a small plate that contained a piece of cake. The cake had been made by Mrs Yee, and Winnie knew it was delicious, but she dared not risk eating a single bite. Any number of things might go wrong, and then where would she be? She could picture it: a dropped fork, or the cake sliding onto the carpet, or spilt tea, or a choking fit. No, it was better to remain still and keep her dignity intact.

Mrs Stevenson-Bragg, of course, had no such qualms. She balanced her own plate with perfect ease and even managed to sip her tea and blot her lips with the napkin. Winnie wondered how she did this. Indeed, Mrs Stevenson-Bragg achieved many things that were wonderful to Winnie. Her golden hair hung in perfect ringlets, and her white muslin dress hadn't a single wrinkle. Winnie didn't want to think about her own appearance. She hadn't given it a thought before she came—and it obviously showed.

She had not meant to stay to tea at all! But Mr Yee came in with refreshments, and here she was, trapped.

Miss Owen took herself to task for using such a word, but she couldn't help it. Mr Yee *would* thrust her into these situations! In fact, he had probably persuaded Mrs Stevenson-Bragg to come into the sitting room in the first place, although she had no idea how he had managed such a thing. But then, Mr Yee was so clever; he managed everyone and everything. The worst of it was, he was such a dear that one must do his bidding. And so Winnie sat, looking longingly at her cake as Estella Stevenson-Bragg chatted on.

"But then you have never been to London, have you?"

"No, indeed." Winnie was thankful to have something to say. She could hardly respond to Mrs Stevenson-Bragg's complaints about Mrs Wentworth or Miss Elliot, but London seemed safe enough.

"Poor girl. At this time of year, London is simply delightful."

"If one is rich," said Winnie, without thinking.

Mrs Stevenson-Bragg gasped.

"I mean," said Winnie quickly, "that any place is delightful when one is comfortably situated and known to one's neighbours. Bath is such a large place; I cannot imagine London. So many people!"

"The brightest and the best!" Mrs Stevenson-Bragg gave a heart-felt sigh. "And so much to do and see! The Opera, the Theatre..." Mrs Stevenson-Bragg set down her cup and saucer. "But alas, I fear you are right, Miss Owen. London is frightfully expensive. Bath is very nice in its own way. In fact, I have quite decided the matter. We shall settle in Bath."

"I...er," Winnie adjusted her grip on the plate. "Wouldn't your husband...that is..."

Estella Stevenson-Bragg dismissed this objection with a wave of her hand. "Mr Bragg? Mr Bragg likes what I like. Yes, we shall settle in Bath." She smiled confidingly. "And eventually, I hope, in this very neighbourhood."

"B-but what about Brookfield?" Miss Owen swallowed; did she have the name right? She searched Mrs Stevenson-Bragg's face for clues. "I mean," she said, "wouldn't your husband wish to stay at his school, as it is so grand? It isn't anybody who gets to be Headmaster..." Winnie could feel heat rising to her cheeks. She hadn't put that last bit quite right, but she couldn't help it. The thought of this woman as a neighbour was dreadful. Why, she was almost as bad as disagreeable Great Aunt Owen!

"My dear Miss Owen, you know too little of the world. My husband is a gentleman. He oughtn't to have a profession at all."

"But he is a scholar, and a gentleman can certainly be that! My cousin Bertram is." Winnie's face grew warmer. "I should say, my second cousin Bertram, who is once removed. But he is a gentleman just the same...and a scholar."

Mrs Stevenson-Bragg lifted her chin. "Ah, but my husband and I mean to be independent, Miss Owen."

"I...see."

"You are not independent, are you? You live with your family?"

"Yes. With my cousin—my second cousin—Mr Minthorne," she said. "He is Bertram's brother. He is a physician. I manage his household for him, as well as the surgery."

Mrs Stevenson-Bragg sat up. "Good gracious, do you mean you are his housekeeper?"

With all her heart, Winnie Owen wished she could escape. But she must be honest, and besides she knew Mr Yee was listening to everything she said. He would scold her for saying anything but the exact truth. "Not precisely," she said. "Mr Minthorne is unmarried and must have someone to oversee the servants."

"A housekeeper," Mrs Stevenson-Bragg repeated. "Forgive me, but I was told that you are a family friend. What you are, actually, is a servant."

Winnie did her best to smile, but it was no use. Mrs Stevenson-Bragg excused herself and left the room, leaving Yee to show Winnie out.

"For yourself you must speak," Yee said, as he refilled her teacup. "You did not."

Winnie remained silent–how could she explain? "The truth is I am a …a coward, Mr Yee. The things I wish to say, I don't. And the things I don't wish to say–the horrid things–those things I do!"

"*O wretched man that I am,*" quoted Yee, with a lifted eyebrow.

Winnie had to smile. "Indeed, that is very true!"

"As well as a friend to this family." He took up Estella's empty cup and plate. "Eat your cake, Miss Owen," he said softly.

~ ~ ~ ~ ~ ~ ~ & ~ ~ ~ ~ ~ ~ ~

"I must once again beg your pardon, Miss Elliot." Mr Gill held back the branches of the overgrown boxwood bush. "These are larger since I last did this. There's not room enough to swing a cat in here."

Elizabeth took hold of his hand and eased her way past. "How is it that you know about this place?"

"Oh, I used it now and again, as a boy." He put his weight against another branch and pulled her through the opening. "I'm not unfamiliar with Belsom Park. My father represented the McGillvary properties over the course of a long career." He paused. "I now carry on the business in his stead."

As soon as she was free of the hedge, she immediately set to brushing leaves and twigs from her skirt. "Is that what you were doing at the counting house that day? Representing the McGillvary family?"

"The counting–? Oh," he said. "Yes."

An expression of dawning triumph crept into her eyes. "Then it's true," she said. "The McGillvarys *are* in trade."

"What's wrong with being in trade?"

"Why, surely you know! It's so vulgar!" She spoke as if this were the most obvious truth in the world.

"You mean it is prudent."

"I did not misspeak," she said, smiling. "I have met Admiral McGillvary on several occasions, Mr Gill. He is very vulg...ungentlemanlike."

"Because he invests his money prudently?" Mr Gill wagged his finger at her. "One of these days, Miss Elliot, the gentry will wake up and discover the wisdom of diversification." He could not resist adding: "If your father had done so, perhaps you'd not be in the fix you're in."

Elizabeth was about to reply in kind, but then thought better of it. "I apologize," she said stiffly. "Of course you are hoping to make a success of your business. I wish you good luck."

He lifted an eyebrow. "Even if I am vulgar?"

"I don't see how you can help being that," she said kindly, and laid her hand upon his sleeve.

Mr Gill returned the smile. "Do you know, Miss Elliot," he said, as they began to cross the wide lawn of the park, "I find it remarkable that in all these years no one has strangled you!"

"I could very well say the same about you!" she said, smiling. "But that's not right–I do know why no one has strangled you. I have had a demonstration of it today. You simply run away, Mr Gill!"

"I, run away?" he countered. "Never!"

She dimpled. "Isn't that what someone does when he 'gives chase'?"

McGillvary looked at her in astonishment. Such a question required a month's answer, or none, so he held his peace. Instead he asked, "Where shall we look for this gate of yours?"

The smile immediately left her face. "We'll need to risk going nearer to the house for that." There was worry in her voice. "Do you happen to know where the little lake is?"

"Is it the one due east of the house?"

Elizabeth gave him a look. "How should I know the direction? Honestly, you men expect everyone to be a walking compass!"

"I beg your pardon," he said meekly. "Since the sun comes up in the east, I assumed you'd know."

Elizabeth laughed. "Now that," she said, "illustrates my point perfectly! A true gentlewoman has no idea where the sun rises! She is never up that early!"

184

McGillvary had to smile. His late wife would have said the same thing.

"As for me," she continued, "I hate mornings! And most especially breakfast, during which time one is expected to be friendly and smiling to everyone for no reason!"

"Miss Elliot," he said appreciatively, "I share your pain. Under such conditions one must bear up."

Some time later, Elizabeth let herself in through the back gate. She turned to wave at Mr Gill and then walked to the house. By now it was late in the afternoon; the flowerbeds were in shadow. As quietly as she could, she slipped inside. She walked on the balls of her feet, scarcely daring to breathe. The door to the sitting room was open; there were voices. Someone was with Estella.

"Oh yes," she heard Estella say, "I saw it on the day Miss Elliot and I toured Great Pultney Street, though it was only from a distance." Estella gave a gusty sigh. "The Sydney Hotel, in the heart of the Sydney Pleasure Gardens. I must say, I was impressed."

And then, Estella's tone grew sharper. "Miss Elliot is the strangest creature, Mr Minthorne. She lives as a veritable hermit! I expected that a woman of her station would comport herself very differently!"

Elizabeth grasped the hall table for support. So, Mr Minthorne, the physician from next door, had come, and Estella was entertaining him with her usual charm. She waited to hear more.

"For instance," Estella continued, "there is to be a grand gala next month in the Sydney Gardens. And a concert with illuminations and fireworks, but does Miss Elliot care?"

"I understand that her father has been ill," said Mr Minthorne. "Perhaps she does not wish to be in company?"

"I rather doubt it," said Estella. "However, I did extract a promise that we shall attend the breakfast at the hotel one day this week, so that is something. I say, is the labyrinth a good one? If only Mr Bragg would have one planted out at Brookfield. The grounds there are very spacious. A labyrinth is so medieval and mystical. Don't you agree?"

Elizabeth had heard enough. As she passed the mirrors in hall, she glanced at her reflection. Her tangled hair was a sight, and her hat, adorned as it was with leaves and twigs and a bedraggled ribbon, was ruined past recognition.

She began to climb the stairs; it was an effort to lift her feet. What was it Mr Gill had said? Ah. *Bear up.*

Dinner that night was uneventful, though it was difficult to wait so long to eat. Elizabeth was so weary that she could scarcely lift her fork. As it was, her hands had been so scratched by the boxwood hedge that she kept them hidden on her lap. After a few cautious sips, she pushed away the wineglass, fearing that she might fall asleep.

The surprise of the evening came later. As she left the dining room, Yee brought out a package. "This was just delivered, Miss Elliot."

Elizabeth studied the name imprinted on the wrapping. "This must be a mistake," she told him. "I ordered nothing from Fischer & Rowe." There was no card, but she opened it anyway. Inside, nestled in silver paper, was a pair of kidskin gloves in a luscious shade of pearl. She lifted one to her cheek. It was wonderfully soft and supple. She searched the wrapping for a card, but there was none.

As quickly as she could, she escaped to her bedchamber. Once there, she again opened the box. She pressed the gloves to her breast. How in the world had he managed it? The goods at Fischer and Rowe were far beyond his means! But when she reached for the other glove, she saw something. Hidden in the glove was a card—no, two cards. She drew them out and hugged herself in pleased surprise. For there they were: two lovely tickets for Thursday's assembly.

~14~
The Coxcomb and the Coxswain

Elizabeth closed her eyes as Estella chatted on. She knew she should have the waiter adjust the umbrella to better shade their table, but the sunlight warmed her back deliciously. The rigors of yesterday's chase, felt mainly in her back and legs, had meant an uncomfortable night of tossing and turning and an even more uncomfortable morning. What was worse, she could not utter a single word of complaint! For no one must know what happened yesterday, especially Estella!

And so here she was taking breakfast on the green lawn of the Sydney Hotel beneath white awnings and umbrellas.

"I must say, this is quite the place to be!" said Estella. "So many ladies and gentlemen! Everyone who is anyone must be here! And this coffee! It is simply divine!"

Elizabeth opened an eye; was her cousin serious? Yee's coffee was far superior to the bitter brew the waiter was forever pressing on them. But then, it was hardly worth the effort to point this out to Estella. Elizabeth shut her eyes again; the white linens and bright silver service were blinding.

"And these little cakes," Estella continued, "are simply heavenly! Divine coffee; heavenly cakes. Isn't that happiness itself?" She gave a gurgle at her own cleverness.

Happiness itself, thought Elizabeth. She opened her eyes. The first thing she saw was her own half-empty cup of coffee.

"Such a delightful breakfast!" said Estella. "I cannot think why we haven't partaken of it before today!"

Elizabeth could think of several reasons. Foremost were the numbers on the gilt-edged bill of fare. Elizabeth had never paid attention to such things until recently. The prices were incredible! However, she could hardly say so to Estella.

Estella returned her cup to its saucer. "This is a fine day for rowing."

"I wouldn't know," said Elizabeth. She winced as the black-coated waiter expertly refilled her cup from his shiny silver pot.

"You seem out of sorts today. Have you the headache?"

Elizabeth pressed a hand to her temple. "I did not sleep well last night."

"A little trip around the canals will put you to rights in no time! I understand the Pleasure Gardens have some delightful follies–the bridges are said to be very picturesque."

"I wouldn't know."

Estella lowered her cup. "Elizabeth, do you know the gentleman over there? He is smiling at us in a most singular way."

Elizabeth's heart turned over in her chest, but she did not move. "I know a great many gentlemen in Bath." Holding her breath, she added, "What does this one look like?"

Estella's response was to sit up straight in her chair. "You'll soon see for yourself," she said, "for he's coming this way."

Elizabeth turned quickly. She saw not a russet-haired fellow in tweed, but a slender gentleman in a bright blue frock coat and hat. She narrowed her eyes against the sun. It was her cousin. He wore pale yellow pantaloons and a cherry striped waistcoat. What was it Mr Gill had said? Force him to meet you on your own terms? Well, she would see.

"Mr Elliot!" she said doubtfully. "Is that you?"

"Now, Elizabeth, for shame!" He made his bow. "Do you pretend not to know me? After the pretty chase you led me on yesterday?"

Aware of Estella's curious gaze, Elizabeth pulled herself to her full height. "I beg your pardon?"

Mr Elliot's smile became teasing. "Not a word of greeting for your poor cousin. Not even to know me on the street." He shook his head in disbelief. "Never did I think my dear Elizabeth would be so rude!"

Elizabeth met his look evenly. "Aren't you a little mixed-up, cousin? You might ask me to overlook your rude behaviour!"

"Mine?"

"You left Bath without a word to anyone. Not even to me."

"But, my dear, I thought I told you. I had pressing business in London!"

"You might have written a note of explanation."

Estella gestured to the empty place at the table. "Perhaps your cousin would you like to join us?"

Elizabeth forced a smile. Estella *would* introduce herself. "This is William Elliot, my cousin. Mr Elliot, Mrs Stevenson-Bragg." She blinked. "Who is also my cousin."

He tipped his hat to her and slid into the vacant chair. At once the waiter was at his elbow, filling his cup with coffee.

Elizabeth studied Mr Elliot with narrowed eyes. "You are no longer wearing mourning, I see. Perhaps that is why I did not recognize you."

He lifted the coffee cup. "How like you to rebuke me. June is just around the corner; should I have waited until the very day?"

"It is nothing to me what you do, Mr Elliot."

Estella looked from one to the other. "We were about to take a boat around the canal," she squeaked. "Isn't that jolly?" Avoiding Elizabeth's eyes, she added, "Would you care to join us, Mr Elliot?"

~ ~ ~ ~ ~ ~ ~ & ~ ~ ~ ~ ~ ~ ~

That same morning found Patrick McGillvary out for his usual ride. As the day was fine, he allowed himself to range farther than his usual track. Without realizing it, he found he was heading for the lower lake, covering the same territory he had walked with Elizabeth Elliot the day before.

A smile pulled at McGillvary's lips. What was she up to today? Ah, yes. The Breakfast Promenade and the trip around the canal. "Boating," he said aloud. His smile widened into a grin. Elizabeth was so obviously repulsed by the idea.

The ride to Sydney Gardens did not take long. Miss Elliot and her cousin, Estella, were not strolling on the hotel's lawn, so he headed for the dock. When he did not see them there, he took the circuit around the canal itself. Presently, he came to a spot where the banks were overgrown with rushes. He could, however, hear voices and the sound of oars. There was a boat out on the canal, although he could not see it. From the sounds of it, the occupants were in some distress.

"Have a little patience, pray!" a woman shrilled. "Of course he knows how to row! All gentlemen know how to row!"

McGillvary edged his horse nearer to the bank and listened. In his experience, few men, gentle or otherwise, possessed this skill. More splashing proved him right.

"Mr Elliot, really!" another woman cried out. "Have a care! We're about to capsize!"

At the sound of her voice, McGillvary's eyebrows shot up. He urged his horse forward until he was abreast of the boat. He dismounted with a gloved hand on the horse's bridle to keep it from jingling.

A man's voice answered her. "To do *what?*"

"Capsize," the woman repeated. "Don't you know anything about boats, Mr Elliot? To capsize means to overturn! Which you are jolly well about to do to us!"

From the sound of things, the speaker was Elizabeth—and she had every reason to worry. There followed more splashing and muttering. Obviously, Elliot was making another attempt to move the oars in concert.

"You have nothing to worry about, my dear," he replied.

"Nothing?" cried Elizabeth. "I do not call colliding with other boats nothing! I call that humiliating!"

McGillvary bit his lip. His shoulders began to shake.

"Confound it!" the man shouted. "There are no other boats anywhere near us now! Must you always be bringing that up? I've been working since Monday to find you, and now that I have, I am treated like a common lackey!"

"You were the one who turned away the oarsman!" she shot back. "How was I to know you meant to drown us?"

At the word "drown," the other woman began to whimper.

"Move aside, Mr Elliot!" said Elizabeth. "I have had enough! Give the oars to me!"

Oh, lord, thought McGillvary. It was a good thing I happened by. He dismounted and tied his horse to a scraggly willow.

As Elizabeth and her cousin argued about who was more qualified to row the boat, McGillvary slipped out of his riding coat, rolled it, and tossed it under the tree. He threw his hat, gloves, and riding crop alongside and made his way to the bank. Quietly, he parted the reeds.

Sure enough, floating in the middle of the canal was a skiff. Elizabeth Elliot was perched in the aft seat alongside a woman in pink, whom he assumed to be Estella. Elizabeth was clad in white—in any other setting, a vision of loveliness. As it was, her hat was askew, and she looked particularly angry.

McGillvary took it all in, a smile playing about his lips. Mr Elliot, whom she had obviously entrapped into escorting them, knew nothing about boats and even less about rowing! Was this Elizabeth's way of punishing him for yesterday's chase?

"Oh, for heaven's sake," said Mr Elliot. "Stop screeching!" He gave a mighty pull with the oars. Unfortunately, the blade of one oar missed the water entirely. Mr Elliot fell backward, sending the boat rocking. Both women screamed.

McGillvary clicked his tongue. Only the most dull-witted oarsman would catch a crab like this! But the women were not in immediate danger, so he remained where he was.

With surprising quickness, Mr Elliot righted himself. He removed one of the oars from its lock and began jabbing at the bottom of the canal with it.

"What are you doing now?" demanded Elizabeth.

"Steering! It works for those damned Venetian fellows, it should work for me!"

Elizabeth put her hands on her hips. "What damned Venetian fellows?"

"The boatmen of Venice." Mr Elliot climbed unsteadily to his feet. He held the oar aloft. "They use poles to manoeuvre their boats in the canals. I shall do the same."

Elizabeth looked at him with open scorn. "This isn't Venice, Mr Elliot!" she said wrathfully. "And I see only one 'fellow' here! Although, your choice of adjective to describe him is perfect!"

Mr Elliot glared at her and shifted the oar to the other side of the boat. It was too short to reach the bottom.

Mrs Stevenson-Bragg's voice rose to a wail. "I'm going to drown," she cried. "I just know it!"

"Estella, be quiet! Here." Elizabeth passed something to her that McGillvary couldn't see. "Make yourself useful," she said. The woman ignored this and continued to wail.

"Here now!" cried Mr Elliot, slewing around. "That's my hat! What are you doing with my hat?"

"Removing the water you so obligingly have brought into the boat." Elizabeth poured a hatful of water over the side. "Do the damned Venetian fellows do this too?"

"But that's my new hat! You're ruining it!"

"And this," she countered, "is my new gown! Which is likewise ruined! By you!"

With a cry, Mr Elliot made a lunge with his oar. This time it struck bottom. The skiff went careening into the reeds on the opposite side of the canal. Unfortunately, Mr Elliot forgot to let go of the oar. The boat went out from under him. He hit the water with a splash.

McGillvary gave a crack of laughter. Elliot had done quite enough, it seemed. He waded into the canal; the water came up to his elbows. "So much for my new boots," he remarked to no one in particular.

"Miss Elliot," he called, sloshing over to the skiff. "Good morning!" He took hold of the gunwale and grinned up at her.

"Mister Gill!" Elizabeth stared at him in disbelief. "What are you–"

"Mrs Stevenson-Bragg, I presume." McGillvary nodded politely to the woman in pink. "Patrick Gill, at your service. And now, ladies, if you will allow me..." Grasping the gunwale with both hands, McGillvary hoisted himself into the bow of the boat. It was a difficult business, and the boat rocked precariously. But this time neither woman screamed.

"Now," he said, a little out of breath, "if you will kindly hand me your cousin's hat, Miss Elliot, I'll bail out all this water."

Wide-eyed, Elizabeth did as she was told.

McGillvary took hold of the dripping hat and grimaced. "Good lord." He turned the hat this way and that. "What a shade of blue!"

"It's rather like a peacock, isn't it?" agreed Elizabeth, smiling for the first time. "And look." She pointed. "He has the frockcoat to match!"

McGillvary glanced over his shoulder at Mr Elliot, who by now had hauled himself out of the water on the far side of the canal. He stood there, dripping and glaring.

"How came your cousin to join you this afternoon?" McGillvary reached overboard to retrieve Mr Elliot's floating oar. "You told me he is the greatest beast in nature, and that you loathed the very sight of him."

"He is, and I do! But I'm afraid it's rather a long story." She leaned nearer. "You see," she whispered, "he *would* join us for breakfast. I couldn't turn him away without causing a scene." She hesitated. "To be honest, I allowed it because–" Elizabeth shot him a look that was both guilty and ingenious, "because I knew that if he joined us, he would offer to pay for our breakfast! Which he did! And then, when Estella invited him to come boating with us, I–"

McGillvary finished her sentence. "You allowed him to foot the bill for that, too. Good girl."

"It was very poor economy on my part," she admitted. "My dress is ruined, I'm afraid."

Mr Elliot, meanwhile, was becoming increasingly alarmed. "Elizabeth!" he shouted. "Who the devil is that in the boat with you?"

"He's a friend of mine!" she yelled back. "Don't worry! He's been in the Navy! He knows how to row!" Elizabeth turned, conscience-stricken. "You do know how to row, don't you?"

McGillvary grinned and fitted the oar expertly into the oarlock. "Certainly." he said. "Anyone knows that all gentlemen know how to row!"

Elizabeth burst out laughing. "But shouldn't we offer to help Mr Elliot?"

McGillvary met her gaze evenly. "No," he said, and took his first stroke with the oars.

"But we can't just leave him there, Mr Gill." she said. "It's awfully rude. And what about his horrible hat and coat?"

He gave her a look of weary endurance and manoeuvred the boat to the opposite bank. Mr Elliot's things were tossed unceremoniously onto the shore.

McGillvary then brought the boat to the middle of the canal. "So," he said, "what happened to the boatman?" He paid no attention to Mr Elliot's shouts for help.

"Oh!" Mrs Stevenson-Bragg spoke up. "Mr Elliot sent him away! But I think you are being most unfair to Miss Elliot's gallant cousin. Before we were mired in the rushes, he entertained us very well."

"He very nearly capsized this boat," said McGillvary, "putting both your lives in peril! I do not call that gallant!"

Again Elizabeth laughed. "My poor, idiotic cousin! He so prides himself on honour and gallantry! I think it must run in my family."

"Very likely." McGillvary took another stroke with the oars. "Would you ladies like to see the rest of the canal?"

Mrs Stevenson-Bragg bounced up in her seat. "Oh, surely!" she cried.

What else could Elizabeth do but agree? It was a fine, warm day—a rarity for so early in the spring. The water sparkled in the sun and reflected the blue of the sky and the green of the budding trees. Under Mr Gill's competent command, the skiff skimmed leisurely over the smooth surface of the canal. Elizabeth spread out her skirt to dry. Mr Gill loosened his neck cloth and rolled his shirtsleeves to his elbows. He looked exactly like one of the oarsmen on the dock–but Elizabeth did not mind.

It was wonderful to see how well Patrick Gill kept the boat under control. With only an occasional dip of the oars, he manoeuvred it wherever he chose!

"You handle the boat very nicely, Mr Gill," said Estella. "What a stroke of luck for us that you happened along when you did!"

"Indeed, rowing does not seem so hard. At least, not the way you do it," said Elizabeth, watching his hands work the oars. They were strong hands, capable hands–the hands of a rescuer.

"It isn't," he said. "Not if one knows the way."

Elizabeth looked him full in the eyes. "Teach me," she said, impulsively.

Patrick Gill raised an eyebrow; his dimple deepened. "Very well." He slid forward in his seat to show her. "The main thing is, one must keep the blade of the oar perpendicular to the water, like this." He demonstrated. "It takes some doing because it wants to roll around."

"Why couldn't my cousin manage it?"

"Because one must do two things at once. Come here, and I'll show you." He made room for her beside him.

Estella looked sceptical and clicked her tongue, but Elizabeth did not care. Crouching, she haltingly made her way the short distance to Mr Gill and eased onto his bench.

"Very good," he said. "No sudden movements. Now." He moved the oar into position. "You hold this with both hands, here. Keep the blade at odds with the water. Pull when I do. Ready?"

"Ready." Elizabeth bit her lip in concentration and gave a mighty tug. The boat slewed to one side. Estella gasped. Mr Gill burst out laughing.

"Gently, Miss Elliot, gently!"

She looked at him in wonder. True, he'd chided her, but his voice was kind.

"We must work together," he said. "Let's try this a different way." This time he put his arm behind her back and took hold of her oar just below her hands. "Ready?"

"Yes...er, no! Just a minute!" Elizabeth let go of the oar and tugged at the ribbons of her hat. Its wide brim kept her from seeing him properly. She tossed it to Estella.

"Now I am." She looked expectantly at him. Her heart was pounding in the oddest way, but she was determined to overlook it. His arm was warm across her back; she could feel the muscles of his shoulder tense when it was time to take their stroke together. She was determined to overlook this, too. And this time she pulled on her oar at exactly the right moment.

"Very good, Elizabeth," he murmured into her ear. "You are a quick learner, my dear."

Elizabeth averted her eyes. But for some reason, this slight, delightful compliment sang in her ears for the remainder of the day.

～15～
A Tangled Web

Patrick McGillvary turned over in his bed, unwilling to begin the new day. Not yet. Just one minute more. At last the clock struck eight. Reluctantly he opened his eyes.

How long had it been since he had a dream like this? Too long. Too blasted long. She'd been here only moments before, a dream woman with silken hair spread over his pillow. And then dawn had come, sending shafts of rosy light to caress her bare shoulders. This time the woman had a face and a name: *Elizabeth.*

McGillvary's lips curved into a smile. Yes, she was Elizabeth. And he'd no objection to make, none at all. His gaze wandered to the fringed curtains of the imposing four-poster bed. He now used the master's bedchamber, his father's until last year. He'd never slept with a woman here, but Elizabeth had been with him, of that he was certain. She had teased him and called him by name. Just by closing his eyes he could hear her say it: *Patrick.* And he had not had to search his memory for hers, as was so often the case with women. *Elizabeth,* he had said. He said it now, under his breath: *Elizabeth.*

And there was more. In the dream she called him darling. Coming from her, this was delicious. Scores of women had called him darling, of course. But somehow when Elizabeth Elliot said it, it was a gift. He'd never heard her say his Christian name, though he'd used hers freely enough. But last night she murmured endearments with passionate abandon.

Again he smiled. Passionate abandon? He'd see that!

But to which Patrick had she given herself? He winced, for he knew the answer. To Gill, of course. Elizabeth had given herself to Patrick Gill. This clerk was becoming more trouble than he was worth! McGillvary tossed back the bedclothes and sat up.

All things considered however, it had been a most amusing game. The oh-so-disdainful Miss Elliot had condescended to meet with a lowly clerk not once, but several times. At tonight's assembly, his victory would be complete; the lowly Mr Gill would collect his kiss and disappear forever.

Except that Miss Elliot was a darling.

McGillvary frowned. A snarl in the rigging, this was.

Pym came in with coffee and a freshly pressed shirt. McGillvary could hear him in the dressing room, laying out the shaving gear. He cradled the steaming cup, still thinking about Elizabeth.

She admitted that the ball at Chalfort House was a disappointment. That, at least, was something. And who could blame her? That awkward scene on the terrace—how well he recalled her revulsion. The fair Elizabeth might have all the earmarks of a fortune hunter, but now that he'd come to know her, was she? Clearly she had no stomach for Rushworth!

McGillvary knotted the sash of his robe. She deserved a real kiss. Not a clumsy, slobbering smack from Rushworth, but the sensual kiss of a lover.

He yawned and stretched a leg. What a sorry bit of black irony. For here she was, fretting over someone like Rushworth or even her spineless cousin, when a plumper plum—one ripe for the plucking— was right at hand.

A plum for plucking. Was that what he was? A willing victim for a fortune hunter like Elizabeth Elliot? And why did this not bother him? He knew the reason: the lowly clerk, Gill. Gill, who had nothing to offer her, had somehow managed to win her trust and confidence. She liked him solely for himself. She told Elliot that he was her friend. This was altogether extraordinary.

Starkweather came in with a list of appointments. McGillvary gave it a glance and put it aside. What would Elizabeth Elliot make of such a morning, filled with meetings and capped by a luncheon? She would take it in stride, of course. She would carry it off with a high hand. There would be none of his late wife's fear-filled tremblings and protestations, no. Elizabeth would relish the challenge, charming every one of his prickly subordinates into smiling submission. Yes, Elizabeth would carry the day beautifully. Hers was the gift of command.

Sometime later, McGillvary wandered into the yellow drawing room still thinking of Elizabeth. He paused before the tall windows that overlooked the city. This morning Bath was swathed in fog, rather like a mystical fortress from a fairy tale. This comparison brought a smile. His Elizabeth had a head on her shoulders; she did not believe in fairy tales. Whatever else had happened at Chalfort House, she had not discovered her handsome prince.

Which brought him back to the heart of the challenge and to-night's assembly. Would she leave disappointed? Not if he had his way, for he would also attend, this time as himself, Patrick McGill-vary, not Patrick Gill. They would dance together, and they would talk. And she would end the evening in his arms, not Rushworth's or Elliot's.

And then he remembered. He had danced with Elizabeth at Chalfort House—as himself. And he had conversed with her—also as himself...and she despised him.

~ ~ ~ ~ ~ ~ ~ & ~ ~ ~ ~ ~ ~ ~

Sir Walter Elliot gave an unhappy sniff as he took the stack of letters from his daughter. "How long have you kept me waiting this time? Confound it, Elizabeth, it's Thursday!"

"As I told you, Father, I was detained." She watched as he sorted them. "There's one from Madderly, Kinclaven, and Planque which looks to be important."

He looked up. "And what concern is it of yours?"

"I think it has to do with the extension the manager offered when I—" She broke off. What was she saying? He knew nothing of her visit to Mr Lonk!

Fortunately he was not paying attention to her words. He tore open Mr Gill's letter and squinted at the page. "Confound it," he said, patting the pockets of his robe. "Whenever I need them they are never to be found. Elizabeth," he said, "do you see my spectacles anywhere about? Amanda Russell put them in what she calls a safe place...which means they are utterly lost!"

"In your breast pocket, Father."

He grimaced and applied himself to the letter. "By Jupiter," he said, looking up, "this is rather unexpected. An extension. We have thirty additional days."

The pronoun did not escape Elizabeth. "Are *we* late in making our payments, Father?" She was careful to maintain an innocent face.

He removed his spectacles and scowled. "I don't know what things are coming to when a young woman must poke and pry into her father's business affairs," he said. He cast Mr Gill's letter aside and went searching for his handkerchief. He found it and blotted at the perspiration on his brow.

While he was thus occupied, Elizabeth made a grab for Mr Gill's letter. She did not bother with the text but went straight for the signature—and felt a stab of disappointment. He hadn't signed it at all. *Herbert Lonk* was written there. But beneath this name was scrawled another. Elizabeth glanced at her father before examining it more closely. Two letters in the name stood out from the rest: an *M* and a *G*. Elizabeth's eyes narrowed. Thanks to Mr Gill, she knew exactly whose signature this was: *McGillvary*.

She dropped the letter as if it were a snake. Vividly, she recalled the darkened terrace and the Admiral's mocking laugh as she was hauled away by Lady Russell. Wouldn't it figure that he was witness to her father's humiliation!

~ ~ ~ ~ ~ ~ ~ & ~ ~ ~ ~ ~ ~ ~

All that long morning Patrick McGillvary was kept busy with the Stewards' Symposium. This event was the brainchild of his father, who understood the value of treating subordinates well. And so once a year he collected his property managers from the various estates, along with several prominent financiers who managed his family's fortune, and entertained them at Belsom. Patrick now carried on the event, and although the principals might have had qualms about presenting their reports, this was a red-letter day on their calendars.

At the conclusion of the meetings, the men sat down to a sumptuous midday meal, followed by a leisurely afternoon in the yellow drawing room amid cigar smoke and conversation. The spectacular view of Bath, today obscured by mist, was remarked upon, as always. In similar fashion, the quality of the cognac was admired. The latter, well-aged and served in crystal snifters tenderly cradled in the palm, was considered a special treat, calling for comments about the liquor's bouquet and aroma.

McGillvary saw to the comfort of his guests with practiced efficiency. Cigars were brought and passed, a job he undertook himself. He was just congratulating himself on how well the afternoon was progressing when his secretary appeared.

"Pardon the intrusion, Admiral," he said, in a low voice, "but Henry has the chaise out front. Will you be needing it as usual?"

McGillvary lowered his glass. "Of course not, Starkweather. What is Henry thinking?"

Mr Starkweather looked uncomfortable. "Begging your pardon, sir, but it's Thursday afternoon."

"It's Friday, Starkweather."

Mr Starkweather cleared his throat. "Actually, sir–"

McGillvary's smile stiffened. "It is Friday," he repeated. Receiving no answer, he swung round to look at the clock. It showed five minutes before two. "I know it is Friday," he muttered, frowning. "Only yesterday I saw her, and–"

"Shall I tell Henry to take the carriage back, sir?"

McGillvary studied Starkweather's face. "No," he said. "Tell Henry I'll be out directly. And send Jamison to me. Immediately."

McGillvary tapped his foot as he waited. He filled his pipe but did not light it; he took up his glass, but did not drink. How could he have made such a mistake? In his mind's eye he could see Elizabeth waiting in that shabby tearoom, alone–her posture erect, her gloved hands clasped. He had always taken pains to be early for their appointments, but today–!

Jamison understood what he required. Soon, McGillvary's steward came in with a tray of fresh glasses and a bottle.

McGillvary turned to face his guests. "Gentlemen," he announced. "I have, unfortunately, been called away." He held up a hand to silence the exclamations that followed. "However, I do not leave you comfortless."

He lifted the bottle from his steward's tray. "Do me the honour to give me your opinion of this. A little something from my private collection: Slivovitz. Otherwise known as plum brandy."

As he left the room, McGillvary shook his head. These men would be here when he returned, sleeping it off. For all its heavenly taste, plum brandy was wickedly potent stuff. He disliked wasting it on these fellows, but was else could be done?

However, when he saw the vehicle Henry had readied, McGillvary's smile vanished. "Of all things, Henry," he said, striding forward. "What possessed you to bring out the phaeton?"

Henry bowed. "To the Abbey Churchyard, sir?"

"On the double." McGillvary climbed up and took the reins. Henry climbed up behind. So much for an inconspicuous arrival! But in the end it did not matter. He pulled up several blocks from the Abbey, tossed the reins to Henry, and jumped down. "Never mind waiting," he flung over his shoulder. Henry's reply was lost in the rumble of traffic.

As he strode toward Cheap Street, McGillvary pulled out his wallet. This time he had plenty of small bills and a pocket full of coins. So far, so good. As Bailey's tearoom came into view, McGillvary strained to see in. Sure enough, there was Elizabeth at their table, waiting. She looked up and smiled.

McGillvary's pulse began to race; she had smiled like this last night. But it was not until he pulled the door to the tearoom that he realized his blunder. He had forgotten to change his clothes.

He could feel himself blushing all the way to the roots of his hair. What was worse, Elizabeth had left the table and was coming toward him. Quickly, he removed his hat and ran his fingers through his neatly combed hair.

"Mr Gill," she said, playfully. "You are late!"

"And you," said he, making his bow, "are lovely." He paused to smile. "Isn't that the same dress—"

"From yesterday? Yes, it is!" She spread her skirt and turned. "See? No more dirt! So my dress wasn't ruined after all!"

He led her to her chair, but Elizabeth did not sit down right away. An expression of wonder was in her eyes. "Why, Mr Gill," she said. "Look at you!"

McGillvary suppressed a grimace, laid his hat on the table, and took up a menu. He occupied himself with reading through it, although he knew exactly what they were to have. He could feel her curious gaze taking in every detail of his appearance. It was not as though he was wearing anything impressive: a pair of bisque trousers with a matching waistcoat and a close-fitting navy blue frockcoat. This, however, represented a substantial departure for the tweedy Gill.

Elizabeth's voice was hushed with admiration. "I must say, I am impressed." She tilted her head, the better to examine him. "Indeed, you look wonderful, Mr Gill."

The sincerity in her voice caused him to flush. He peeked at her over the top of the menu. Her eyes were shining. "I-I had an important meeting this morning," he said, "with one of my...er, significant clients."

"I can see that," she said. The girl came with a pot of tea, and McGillvary gave the order.

"So," said Elizabeth, as soon as they were alone again, "where was this meeting? Buckingham House?"

"Nearly." He took the cup she offered. The last thing he wished for was tea, but he took a sip anyway. It scalded his lips.

"And, my goodness. Is that a *diamond* I see?"

He put a hand to his neck cloth. Sure enough, Pym had inserted a diamond stickpin into its folds. From the feel of it, this was one of the larger stones. McGillvary drew it out. He was about to put it into his pocket but Elizabeth stopped him. She held out her hand. "May I see?"

Feeling trapped, he opened his hand.

"This is amazing," she said, holding it to the light. "My father had my diamonds replaced with *paste*, although I'm not supposed to know it. But the quality is nothing to this! You are to be congratulated."

He muttered something about a younger brother in London with good connections and put the stickpin into his waistcoat pocket.

Elizabeth looked at him expectantly. "So," she said. "Tell me all about your important meeting. Did you see anyone I know?"

McGillvary cudgelled his brain but to no avail. Where could Gill have gone? And then it occurred to him. What could be simpler? He had been called to Belsom Park. To the Stewards' Symposium to meet with...himself! Half-laughing, half-ashamed, McGillvary began to describe his morning.

"A luncheon? Famous! What was on the menu? That is to say, what were you served?"

The question was innocent enough, but for the life of him, McGillvary could not remember the meal. "Beef?" he said. "Lobster-something-or-other? Some sort of soup?" The truth was, he'd barely tasted the food. "I was so intent on the conversation," he confessed, "that I don't exactly recall."

"Indeed?" A frown appeared in Elizabeth's eyes. "Describe the table," she said.

This took him completely off guard. "The what?"

"The table," she said, with exaggerated patience. "Tell me about the china." She raised her eyebrows at his silence. "The design on the plates—what did it look like?"

"I don't precisely..." Plates? Why should he notice plates? "I don't recall a pattern."

Elizabeth tried again. "Think," she said. "Was there something painted on the plates? Or were they plain, with a gilt band?"

"Honestly," he said, beginning to laugh, "I have no idea."

She sighed. "Very well. What sort of sound did the cups make when you stirred your coffee?"

He grinned. "Does that matter?"

"Of course it matters. When bone china is struck with a spoon, it makes a chiming sound, rather like a bell. What is more, the most expensive bone china is thin and translucent." Elizabeth lifted her saucer to the light. "You see? This is cheap earthenware."

"You cannot be serious!"

"Very well, tell me about the table linens. Were they plain white, like this, or was there a brocade pattern woven into the fabric?"

"Why the devil should I care? What difference does it make?"

"It makes a great deal of difference, Mr Gill," she said. "I am attempting to discern the degree of importance Admiral McGillvary placed on your visit! Were you ushered in with fanfare and a red carpet? Or were you let in the service entrance with the dogs?"

Patrick McGillvary gave a crack of laughter. "Oh, with the dogs, certainly!"

"Well, it sounds like a Public Day to me," she said. "Second-best silver, everyday linens, barely-passable china, and an unremarkable meal. In which case, you were being patronized, my dear."

This was dead-on; McGillvary could barely contain his mirth. "Do you think so? The Admiral seemed pleased to entertain us."

"I rather doubt that." She lifted her teacup. "I daresay he is skilled at disguising his displeasure when the need arises."

"I daresay he is." He leaned forward, and said, impulsively. "Are you acquainted with Admiral McGillvary, Miss Elliot?"

She flinched. "We have met on several occasions," she said stiffly. "He is generally thought to be an agreeable man."

"But what do you think of him?" he said. She did not answer, but he refused to let it go. "I know you have an opinion. Do you think him to be agreeable?"

Elizabeth looked at him for a long moment. "I think," she said lightly, "that Admiral McGillvary is much too full of his own importance. However," She hesitated.

"Yes?" he urged. "Go on."

"However," she repeated, giving him a look, "as he is one of your most important clients, I shall keep the remainder of my opinion to myself." She bent and pulled a large basket from beneath her chair. "I have brought my ledger, as I promised. Let me show you how it is set up so that you can help your daughter do the same."

McGillvary knew better than to press the issue. He brought his chair to her side of the table and helped to clear a space.

"Now then," she said, opening the book, "what your daughter must do is to learn the names of everyone in your set. You will be a great help to her in this. And then, she must write down what she learns. Mind you, she must do this after every event. If she does not keep current, the ledger will be of little value."

McGillvary inched closer to see the page. "*Leighton*," he read aloud, then bit his lips to keep from laughing. He pointed at the page. "And these are the things you've learned about the Leightons?" He continued to read. "Well of course Hugo Leighton is a poor sport at cards!" He pointed to her entry. "That's no surprise! If you ask me, the man is a weasel-faced cheat! But I see you have written *Capitulate!* beside the entry." He looked up. "I cannot believe you mean it, Miss Elliot."

Elizabeth lifted her chin. "Of course I mean it. What else is a lady to do? Call him out?"

"I can teach you a trick or two with the sword, if you like."

"I imagine you could," she said, returning his smile. "But capitulation, though dishonest, is more dignified."

McGillvary returned his attention to her book. "You have a remarkable system here, Miss Elliot. Are these entries arranged alphabetically?"

"More or less. It is the most tiresome chore to keep everything up-to-date! But, it is imperative to keep abreast of the latest news, especially before every Significant Event"

"Such as the assembly tonight?"

"Why, yes," she said. "Especially before an event like that."

McGillvary continued to turn pages. His fingers itched to find his own page, for it would be quite near to *Leighton*. Then he had another idea. He moved to the back of the book, until he found the page he wanted.

"*Rushworth*," he read, and looked up at her. "I think I know him— that is, I know who he is. A pursy, potbellied fellow. Overflows his chair."

A shadow crossed Elizabeth's face. "Would you call him...fat?" she said.

"You certainly do! What you wrote here, I think, says it all." He kept his finger high up on the page, but as she bent over the book to see what she had written, he searched for the newest entries at the bottom—those made at Chalfort House.

Received tonight a token of our promise.

Long years of practice had taught McGillvary to keep his features schooled, but his mind was racing. What the devil did *our promise* mean? The final entry, which was at the bottom of the page and was dated only yesterday, confirmed his fears.

Have had a letter. Coming to Bath any day now. Has good news about the…

The sentence went off the paper.

McGillvary fingered the edge of the page. Aloud he said, "I recall hearing about Rushworth. His wife ran off with another man."

"I think she must have hurt him very deeply."

"Er, yes." He had difficulty gauging her expression. "But never mind. He likely has his divorce now." He looked at her, hoping to be able to turn the page.

"I'm not so sure. I think that requires an Act of Parliament, or some such thing."

"That would be for the remarriage. Expensive business."

"Mr Rushworth is rich. I doubt he'll even notice."

"Then he is a fool," said McGillvary. "Even a rich man notices an expenditure of that sort."

"I suppose." Elizabeth turned the pages on her side of the ledger, working her way back to the beginning of the book. "At any rate, you now know how to make a book like this for your daughter. That is the main thing."

McGillvary watched the names on the pages as she flipped them. There was no chance to see Rushworth's second page, but perhaps he could see another. At the right moment, he put out his hand.

"Aha! What have we here?" He grinned at her and spread the page flat with his hand. "Well now, Miss Elliot. What have you written about McGillvary? He, too, is quite plump in the pocket. Rather more so than Rushworth, in point of fact. What dirt do you have with which to blacken his name?"

Her face reddened. "Nothing that is not common knowledge."

McGillvary could not help himself; his eyes devoured the page. "Just a minute!" He read aloud:

Connected briefly with Miss Augusta Hawkins of Maple Grove, near Bristol, last spring.

"That is a lie! Who the devil is Augusta Hawkins?"

"It says here," Elizabeth pointed, "that she is related to the Suck-lings, whoever they are."

"Good lord!" he marvelled. "That gawky, tittering relation of Captain Suckling's?"

"Do you know them, Mr Gill?" She looked surprised.

"I know of a Captain Suckling," said McGillvary grimly, "who is probably a younger brother. He had some female relative in tow at Portsmouth—someone he was forever trying to fob off on...on the officers."

"While you were in the Navy? Oh." She continued reading. "It says here that she was worth ten thousand pounds when she married a clergyman. I wonder that you thought her so gruesome, Mr Gill, if she had a fortune like that." She shrugged. "At any rate, Admiral McGillvary certainly thought her gruesome. But then, he is not one to care about damaging a woman's reputation."

"And just where did you hear that?"

"From Lady Russell. According to her, the man is a thoroughgoing rake." Elizabeth closed the book. "I am sorry to say it, as he seems to be a friend of yours, but it is common knowledge that the man is a skirt-chaser, Mr Gill."

"It is common knowledge that his marriage was unhappy!"

"Aren't most marriages?" she countered. "But that does not excuse disloyalty."

"Disloyalty?"

"I find it amazing that these military officers, like Admiral McGillvary, can be so flippant about their vows! They will lay down their lives in service to the crown; they will keep their word of honour to their fellows at all cost. But to their wives?"

Patrick McGillvary was rendered speechless. Ranting about his high-handedness at Chalfort House, declaiming his opinions, scolding him for vulgar business practices—these he expected. But never this.

"Unless they are like my sister's husband. Constancy seems to be his only virtue." Elizabeth returned the ledger to her basket and reached for her gloves.

"You're leaving." His voice sounded oddly flat.

"I'm afraid so. I've much to do before tonight." She looked up at him and smiled—a wistful, unguarded smile.

She thinks I'm Gill. He had dropped countless clues today, yet she had followed none of them. He swallowed and looked down at his hands. What had he done?

They shared a hack for the trip home, but as they neared St. Peter Square, Elizabeth coughed. "Let me off at the corner, please," she said.

What else could he do but comply? For he was Gill, the clerk, her friend, but not one she could own. He opened the door and assisted her to alight.

"Elizabeth," he said. He kept hold of her gloved hand. "Will I see you tonight? At the assembly?" He could feel his lips pull into a smile–the sad, half-desperate smile he had seen on the faces of so many women. It was now his turn to plead.

Elizabeth dipped her head with adorable coyness. "Perhaps," she said, smiling. And then she removed her hand from his and was gone.

The trip to Belsom Park was accomplished in silence, save for the voice of conscience. It was a voice to which Patrick McGillvary had not listened for a very long time. Today, it shouted.

Liar!

He repeated it aloud as the carriage turned into Belsom's gates and passed the guardhouse. *Liar.* The word had a raw, unsavoury bite. And it was the exact truth: he was a liar. And an adulterer.

As the clerk Gill, he had won her trust and confidence. How had he repaid her? "I have lied," he said aloud. "I have lied and lied and lied. Even today..."

So great was his self-loathing that he did not react to the sight of a marine's horse being led to the stables.

~16~
Nothing Ventured, Nothing Gained

The door to the salon opened; William Elliot looked up. A slender woman in a lilac gown drifted into the room and closed the door behind her. Both Mr Elliot and her husband stood.

"There now," she said, untying the ribbons of her bonnet and casting it aside. "Didn't I tell you I would fix things?" She smiled at Mr Elliot and laid her shawl on the arm of a sofa. Her husband came forward to plant a kiss on her cheek.

"Dear Wallis," she said, sinking onto the sofa, "might I have a glass of sherry? And one for Elliot as well. Indeed, this calls for a celebration!"

William Elliot resumed his seat; his eyes never left her face. "I take it you were successful?"

"But of course. I told you I would be." She took the glass.

"That's my Annette," Colonel Wallis said, beaming. He handed the other glass to Mr Elliot. "Clever little moppet, isn't she?"

Mrs Wallis took a sip of the sherry and then leaned forward. "My dear Elliot, it was simplicity itself. Once you described Mrs Stevenson-Bragg, the rest was child's play! I had the *nicest* conversation with the Master of Ceremonies–surely you remember him? The man who officiates at the Pump Room? Yes, I thought you did. And he knew exactly who she was. Sure enough, before long she came in. Without your Elizabeth."

Mr Elliot pursed his lips. Would she never come to the point?

"Oh, don't scowl so!" Mrs Wallis cried, putting out a hand. "Miss Elliot would've been very much in the way! For of course, we were introduced first thing. And let me tell you, I learned *ever* so much. For instance," she said, "do you know where Miss Elliot will be this evening? Guess."

Mr Elliot met her look evenly. "I have no idea."

"At the assembly, of course! And what is more, she will be going *alone*! That is to say, without her father. Don't you see, Elliot, it is simply *perfect*! Wallis will dance with Mrs Stevenson-Bragg, and you may have your Elizabeth all to yourself."

"She isn't my Elizabeth."

Mrs Wallis shrugged. "That will soon be remedied, won't it?"

"I must speak to her about her father."

Mrs Wallis laughed. "Among *other* things. Wallis tells me she is just the one for you. The perfect Lady Elliot. Didn't you, dearest?"

Colonel Wallis cleared his throat. "Did this lady mention the other fellow, Annette? You remember, Elliot. The Navy chap who is married to the sister?"

William examined the contents of his glass. "I haven't forgotten, thank you."

"Oh, *him*!" cried Mrs Wallis. "That would be...let me see, what was his name? Frederick! Yes, dear Mrs Stevenson-Bragg had something to say about Frederick! Apparently he was the one who invited her to Bath. At any rate," continued Mrs Wallis, "Elizabeth's sister and this Frederick are away travelling somewhere, so you needn't worry about running into them. And what is more, I learned where they live!" She smiled in simple pride. "Haven't I done well?"

"Extremely well, Mrs Wallis. I am greatly in your debt."

She made a play with her lashes. "Well, you don't seem very pleased."

"Nonsense, my love." Colonel Wallis' voice boomed from across the room. "Of course he's pleased! The man is thinking, dearest. Strategizing. Already plotting his next move, as well he should."

She turned to her husband. "Wallis," she said, "you haven't said a word about my new gown! Isn't this the most delicious, flowery shade?" She spread the delicate muslin of her skirt. "Elliot says that I remind him of the sweet-scented kiss of spring. What do *you* say?"

~ ~ ~ ~ ~ ~ ~ & ~ ~ ~ ~ ~ ~ ~

Lady Russell lifted the calling card from the silver salver. "Elizabeth has certainly been in demand lately," she said, reading the name. "Very well, Longwell. Show him in." She set her book aside and straightened her cap. She did not know why he had come, but at least he was not William Elliot!

"Mr Rushworth," she said, rising. "How pleasant to see you again. Good afternoon."

He removed his hat and returned her greeting.

"I'm afraid Elizabeth is no longer here. She is staying with her sister for several weeks. Is there something I may do for you? Some message I may convey?" She waited while James Rushworth sorted through his thoughts.

He spoke slowly, twisting the brim of his hat. "I called at Sir Walter's house on Camden Place, and I was sent here. And now you say Miss Elliot is gone?"

She smiled at his distraction. Clearly, he was overwrought. "My dear Mr Rushworth, Elizabeth's sister lives here in Bath; you may call upon her this very afternoon. Let me give you the direction."

His lips formed into a round O, and his cheeks grew very pink. "*Thank* you, your ladyship!"

"Not at all, Mr Rushworth." Lady Russell moved to her writing desk. "The pleasure, indeed, is all mine."

~ ~ ~ ~ ~ ~ ~ & ~ ~ ~ ~ ~ ~ ~

Some little time later a soft knock sounded at the door to Elizabeth's bedchamber. Elise went to enquire and, after a whispered conversation, came back with a card. She presented this to her mistress.

Elizabeth put down the nail file. Who would call this late in the afternoon? Her question was answered as soon as she read the name on the card. Wordlessly, she replaced it. So, he had returned to Bath. Others might be sent away, but not him. She pressed a hand to her temple. What was it about that man? He had the talent for calling at the most awkward moments.

And then she remembered. There was one thing that must be done before she went down to the sitting room. Elizabeth rummaged through a drawer for his fob, a thing she'd not looked at in weeks. It had worked its way to the very back and was tangled with a frayed ribbon. Elizabeth held it with the tips of her fingers, not wanting to touch any more of it than necessary. She chose the longest of her gold chains. How thankful she was that Anne was not here to witness this meeting, for Anne would surely notice the fob and ask questions–and Elizabeth was not able to answer any of them.

Mr Rushworth's reaction to her entrance was everything a lover could hope for. The coy smile, the blush, the shining eyes–all the signs of love were there, displayed with such force that even a dimwit like Estella could not mistake. Fortunately, Estella was not in the sitting room. They were alone. Seeing the lively sparkle in his eyes made Elizabeth think better of this. The only thing to do was get rid of him. She remained standing and did not invite him to sit.

"My dear Mr Rushworth," she said, extending her hand cordially. "You have returned at last. How delightful."

He bowed over her hand, but when he spoke he sounded out of breath. "I came as soon as I arrived. Before anything, in fact."

It was then that Elizabeth noticed his clothing. He did not wear his wrinkles well, as Mr Gill was able to do. And there was something else. Was the cut of his waistcoat to blame, or had Mr Rushworth grown stouter while he was away?

"Thank you for calling." Elizabeth knew she was repeating herself, but she could think of nothing else to say.

He made a helpless gesture. "My pleasure." And then there was silence.

Elizabeth noticed another thing: Mr Rushworth did not have Mr Gill's ready address or polished manners. Why, if she did not know any better, she would say that Mr Gill was the gentleman and Mr Rushworth was the clerk, which, of course, was absurd.

It was left for her to carry the conversation. "How was your journey?" she said. But while he answered her mind kept repeating: *Twelve-thousand pounds a year. Twelve-thousand pounds a year.* She was coming to see that it would take plenty of gold to guild a man like James Rushworth!

The clock on the mantelpiece struck the hour, which was quite perfect. "You will not mind, dear Mr Rushworth, if I bid you farewell for the present? I have so very many things to do before this evening."

She saw hope leap in his eyes. "This evening?" he cried. "Will you be attending the assembly this evening, dear Elizabeth?"

She nodded—and swallowed her objection to his open use of her Christian name.

"What could be better!" he cried. "Of course, I must have my share of dances. Two, at the very least."

Elizabeth resolved to wear boots to the assembly.

Mr Rushworth's smile became ingenious. "Or perhaps, three dances? Mama won't be there. I can do as I like."

"But my very busy cousin will be," said Elizabeth lightly. "So we must behave with decorum." Too late she realized that *behave* was not the right word to use. Unlike Mr Gill, Mr Rushworth did not understand sarcasm. By the look in his eyes, he'd taken a very different meaning!

"But your busy cousin is not here *now*," he said. With surprising nimbleness, Mr Rushworth crossed the room and closed the door. He wheeled to face her and moistened his lips. "This time," he said, "we won't be interrupted."

Interrupted? Elizabeth's heart nearly stopped. She took a step back.

"Mr Rushworth," she cried. "Please!"

But this was wrong, too! Did he think she was *asking* to be kissed? Mr Rushworth came nearer, with a hungry look in his eyes.

And then the door opened. Yee put his head in. "You rang, Miss Elliot?" he said mildly.

Elizabeth almost fainted with relief.

"We most certainly did not!" said Mr Rushworth.

Yee did not go. He came fully into the room and stood with his arms folded across his chest. He kept his gaze on Elizabeth. "Miss Elliot?" he said.

She took a long breath. "Mr Rushworth is just leaving."

"I am?"

She put out her hand. "Until this evening, Mr Rushworth," she said.

He made an awkward bow—but not without a parting shot. "Until this evening, then," he said. "Dearest, loveliest Elizabeth."

~ ~ ~ ~ ~ ~ ~ & ~ ~ ~ ~ ~ ~ ~

Patrick McGillvary squared his shoulders as he studied his image in the tall mirror. The uniform, which was new, was flawless. So, too, were the hat and the gloves. Tonight he needed to look his best, for tonight he would tell Elizabeth.

It was a simple thing, really. He would say the words, and she would listen. And then she would become angry, which she had every right to be. He took a turn about the room, thinking. No, Elizabeth would not take the news well. Who knew what she would say to him? Nothing that he did not deserve.

A smile twisted his lips. Not for nothing would he be unmasking in public, for she would be constrained by propriety to treat him civilly! Not that he wish her to be contained…

His smile became wistful. Actually, Elizabeth was the most beautiful when she had fire in her eyes. But she would get over it, and they would dance together. On Tuesday they would have a good laugh.

Except that he wouldn't be in Bath on Tuesday.

McGillvary took another circuit around the room. So, he would tell her who he was. Then he would tell her that he was leaving for an undetermined period of time.

His frown deepened. When he sent her the tickets, this had seemed so easy. Of course, he couldn't have known about being called to London, and he couldn't foresee being forced to unmask in such a public way! His pacing brought him back to the mirror.

"I cannot tell her tonight," he decided, speaking to his reflection. "It wouldn't be fair." Their conversation would surely be observed, and then there would be talk. Gossip and speculation would dog Elizabeth for the remainder of the season—and he would not be present to support her.

He shrugged off his uniform coat. What a place, Bath! A man could not handle his personal business without remark from every quarter! To be himself tonight would ruin her. So, Patrick Gill he must be.

This would not be easy, for he was known to so many. Discovery was likely—no, it was inevitable. "I've done enough and maybe too much," he murmured, reaching into the wardrobe for an unadorned, Navy blue frock coat. "But lie to her again, I shall not!"

~ ~ ~ ~ ~ ~ ~ & ~ ~ ~ ~ ~ ~ ~

"I should have known she would linger over her toilette!" Elizabeth said, after Elise brought the message. Estella requested fifteen minutes more, but Elizabeth knew better. She did not mind, not really. She took her seat at the dressing table, mindful to arrange the skirt of her gown. Out came her ledger. It had been a while since she had written in it. Indeed, all of her outings had been with members of her family or with a clerk named Mr Gill.

This thought brought a smile. How interested he'd been in this book! While she hunted for her writing things, she hummed a tune. Mr Gill certainly was a funny one!

She decided to work on William Elliot's page and wrote:

Boating At Sydney Gardens.

Images filled her mind. Elizabeth sighed, she smiled, she dipped the pen in the inkpot–but she did not write anything more. For the outing at Sydney Gardens was all about Mr Gill, not Mr Elliot. Indeed, now that she thought about it, she could not recall her cousin's face clearly. What she did remember was a pair of mischievous eyes–sometimes blue, sometimes green. And the feel of his arm across her back.

Elizabeth laid down the pen. She hadn't the desire–or the strength–to write anything tonight. She closed the book and replaced it, thinking instead of sparkling water, green willows, and the warm presence of a person called Patrick Gill.

Sometime later, Estella came rustling in. "Dear cousin," she cried, "I do beg your pardon! Your maid is quite the slowest creature on the face of the earth! Shall we depart?"

Elizabeth merely smiled. Gathering the skirts of her sapphire gown–and her precious memories–she rose and drifted to the door.

~ ~ ~ ~ ~ ~ ~ & ~ ~ ~ ~ ~ ~ ~

In the end, McGillvary's decision to be truthful won out. He would not embarrass Elizabeth by appearing as himself, yet he would reveal his identity just the same. Privately. But at an assembly such as this, there would be no chance for privacy save the exchange of a letter.

His explanation was short and to the point, concluding with one of the most sincere apologies he had ever written. He sat back and read the message again, dissatisfied. His words lacked something, but what? The heft and weight of truth?

"Not the heft of words," he muttered, reaching for another sheet of paper, "but of the page." He began to copy out the message again, but this time he wrote on stationery bearing his personal seal: a bold 'PM' entwined with a harp and fouled anchor.

~ ~ ~ ~ ~ ~ ~ & ~ ~ ~ ~ ~ ~ ~

The trip to the Assembly Rooms did not take nearly as long as Elizabeth anticipated. But she was nervous. In Estella Stevenson-Bragg such excitement was to be expected, for she was unaccustomed to such events. But Elizabeth could only be ashamed of her school girl's apprehension. She simply could not rid her mind of Mr Gill!

Estella was unhappy with her instructions to the driver. "You cannot mean to depart at midnight, Miss Elliot!" she complained. "Won't you please tell the man one o'clock? Or, perhaps two? I cannot bear to be taken away at such an early hour!"

"I'm afraid you'll have to bear it," Elizabeth said. "For we do not have a carriage at our disposal. And I am not about to pay extra to reserve one during the busiest hour." She did not wait to hear her cousin's response. As soon as she came down from the carriage, her attention was focused on the ladies and gentlemen entering the building. She looked and looked, but could not find the one she most wished to see.

"Miss Elliot!" A man called her name, and Estella gave a cry of recognition. Elizabeth turned. It was only her cousin. As always, he was smiling. After the escapade with the rowboat, she expected a snub. She pulled herself to full height. "Good evening, Mr Elliot."

He bowed, and motioned to a gentleman in uniform who came forward. This man smiled, too. "Of course you remember Colonel Wallis, cousin," Mr Elliot said. And then, with a flourish, he offered his arm to her.

Elizabeth gave him a long look before placing her hand on his sleeve. There was no one she wished to be seen with less than Mr Elliot. However, she did not wish to enter the Assembly Rooms without an escort, either. As they moved through the crowd together, Elizabeth became less at ease. She decided to address the situation directly. "I see you have recovered from your unfortunate accident." She gave Mr Elliot a long look. "If I may say, your attire this evening is much more becoming. Whatever became of that dreadful blue hat?"

Mr Elliot blinked but made a quick recovery. "I banished it from my wardrobe straightway. I would rather do anything than risk your disapproval, cousin." His smile appeared again. "I take it you do not care for blue?"

Elizabeth raised an eyebrow. "Not peacock blue. However, I am rather fond of sapphire." She indicated her gown.

Mr Elliot bowed. "I beg your pardon."

When they reached the ballroom he spoke again. "If you must know, I was guided in my choice by another. I allowed myself to be persuaded by that person's enthusiasm for fashion. I ought never to have done so, of course. Your taste is unerring."

"You ought never to have paired that peacock coat with yellow trousers. And unless you wish to be taken for a Dandy, you should discard the striped waistcoat, as well. Those large buttons were quite ridiculous."

"Allow me to say how much I appreciate your candour."

"I rather doubt that."

"But it is true! None but the very best of friends would dare to be so direct! And now that I think on it, you are so right! That coat was awful!" He lowered his voice. "But then, has it not always been so between us? From the first, you and I have been especial friends."

This, unfortunately, was the wrong thing to say. Elizabeth did not bother to disguise her scorn. "From the first, do you say?" She lifted her hand from his arm. "Before your marriage, yes, there was a time when we were friends. Briefly. Before you gave me the Cut Direct."

Mr Elliot did not take her meaning, or else his memory was faulty. His impossible smile appeared again. "But you will not be so unkind. Please, will you honour me with a dance, dear Elizabeth?"

Elizabeth compressed her lips. She could hardly ignore his outstretched hand without causing a stir. She cast a fleeting look about the room, but the person she sought was nowhere to be seen. Stifling a sigh, she turned to her cousin. It was only a dance, after all.

Still, as they entered the ballroom and took their place in the set, her gaze strayed now and again to the crowd. At least Mr Elliot was a polished dancer. And as the dance progressed, she caught several admiring looks from ladies. Elizabeth almost laughed. Who would admire William Elliot?

Penelope admired him. This shocking thought came from nowhere. Why, she hadn't thought about Penelope Clay for weeks! However, she must admit that Penelope was always willing to discuss William Elliot's merits. She was a bit too willing, perhaps?

As the dance came to an end, Elizabeth spied a face in the crowd she recognized: James Rushworth. She quickly averted her eyes. After today's scene in the sitting room, she would rather have anyone else for a partner. When her cousin enquired, she readily consented to a second dance.

She watched Estella accept Colonel Wallis as a partner and came to a decision. After this dance, she would dance with Colonel Wallis. This was distasteful, for she had never taken to Colonel Wallis; but he was certainly better than Mr Rushworth. Then, after Colonel Wallis, why, she would simply have to find someone else.

~ ~ ~ ~ ~ ~ ~ & ~ ~ ~ ~ ~ ~ ~

Patrick McGillvary entered the Assembly Rooms with more un-ease than he had felt in years. He had come late on purpose, hoping that he would be lost in the crush. True, he wore his hair in Mr Gill's rumpled style and was dressed with extreme simplicity, but he knew such tricks could not hide his identity for long. He moved through the ballroom, keeping his eyes averted. Presently, he found a group of matrons sporting elaborate turbans. He positioned himself behind them. From such a vantage point he would be able to observe without being noticed.

Sure enough, Elizabeth was dancing. She was not difficult to spot: a blaze of sapphire among washed-out pastels. McGillvary had to smile. Even with Rushworth as a partner, Elizabeth was a graceful, accomplished dancer.

And he might lose her. If only the stakes were not so high! One outcry, one mention of his name—! And yet, in spite of the risk, he continued to watch the dancers. Indeed, he could not tear his gaze from Elizabeth, even though she was dancing with another man.

Sir Cameron Greene was also on the dance floor, mincing through the patterns with a young lady in white muslin. McGillvary rehearsed his plan. He would give Cam the letter for Elizabeth and watch as he delivered it. Once she learned the truth, he'd come forward to speak with her.

It was a simple plan, and for a moment it looked as though he would be able to pull it off. The dance came to an end, and Eliza-beth made her parting curtsey to Rushworth. McGillvary brought the letter from his pocket. But Sir Cameron was nowhere to be seen. There was no sign of the lady in white, either. Had the man vanished into thin air? McGillvary set his teeth and went to search for him.

And then he saw it: Elizabeth, being led onto the dance floor by a smiling Sir Henry Farley.

McGillvary's head came up. Caution was cast aside. His Eliza-beth, dance with that pox-ridden lecher? He'd rather be keel-hauled. He stuffed the letter into his pocket. The beginning notes of the dance began to play, but McGillvary did not care. He strode onto the dance floor.

"Your pardon, Farley." McGillvary took hold of Elizabeth's gloved hand. "The lady has promised this dance to me!"

It was hard to say who looked more shocked, Elizabeth or Sir Henry, as McGillvary guided her through the figure of the dance.

217

McGillvary knew he was in too deep, but he no longer cared. He saw only Elizabeth's enchanting smile and shining eyes. "You promised me a dance, did you not?" he said.

"I did no such thing!" she whispered. "And you oughtn't speak to Sir Henry in such a way!"

"I dislike the way he looked at you," he said. They were parted by the figure of the dance. When they came together again, he said: "Do you mind?"

Elizabeth lifted her chin. "Let the matrons talk! You are a beautiful dancer!"

They went on in this happy way until the closing measures of the dance. "Elizabeth," he said. "I must speak with you. Alone."

She caught the seriousness of his tone. "Mr Gill, I..." Her face grew still. "No," she said softly, "I do not mind."

He led her from the dance floor. "I've not much time left. I've been called away to London on business."

He could see the disappointment in her eyes. That, at least, was something. "My dear," he said. "If there was any way to keep from leaving, I would take it."

"When...when shall I see you again?"

"Soon," he said. "I promise. I'll drive back for our tea on Tuesday if I can."

"Don't be ridiculous. You must go to London. Of course you must. All gentlemen go running off to London."

"Elizabeth..." He took hold of her hand and lifted her fingers to kiss them. "My dear," he said, "I–" A flash of gold at her wrist caught his eye. When he saw what it was, he stiffened. "What the devil is this?" He spoke more harshly than he'd intended. Elizabeth drew back.

"That?" she faltered. "Why, my pearl bracelet, of course."

"Not the bracelet. This." He took hold of a man's watch fob, which dangled among the pearls. "Why are you wearing this?"

"It is nothing! Truly! A foolish piece of jewellery, that is all."

"Is it?" He turned the seal to the light. The script R was clearly visible. He looked intently at her face; she was blushing hotly. "It appears to me to be a token. Is that what it is? A love token?"

She looked at him in obvious dismay, but said nothing.

The seal was certainly Rushworth's, and she was not proud to wear it. But why the secrecy? Had he been mistaken in her?

"When will you return to Bath?" she said.

"I am not certain." His fingers closed on her wrist. "And while I am away, you must promise me not to dance with the likes of Farley. Or go boating with your cousin, or kiss Rushworth in the garden–or anywhere else! Is that clear? For I shall not be here to rescue you."

"Yes, Mr Gill," she whispered.

"I'll send you a message when I return." He let go of her hand. "So that we may meet at Bailey's as usual."

"My sister could be home by that time," she stammered. "And our butler is very protective. How shall I explain your letter?"

He thought for a moment. "You once told me that you visit the pond. The one on the estate."

"But only once or twice. I-I go there to read. But it is rather awkward, as there is no place to sit."

An idea occurred to him. "Did you never see the bench?" he said, committing Burns to a long night of work. "When I return, I'll leave the note there."

"But Miss Owen! And the children! They often visit the park. Won't they see it?"

He raised an eyebrow. "I am not such a flat as I appear. I know the rules." He lowered his voice. "Look under the seat and you will find it."

"I say! Paddy!" A voice boomed behind him. McGillvary winced. He had been recognized.

"Look for the bench, my dear," he said, giving Elizabeth's hand a parting squeeze. "Farewell!" He turned and disappeared into the crowd.

"Bench?" cried Elizabeth. "But there is no bench in the park. Is there?"

—&—

End of Book 1

—&—